An Imitation

by Simon McCleave
A DC Ruth Hunter Murder Case
Book 3

No part of this publication may be reproduced, stored, or transmitted in any form or by any means, electronic, mechanical, photocopying, recording, scanning, or otherwise without written permission from the publisher. It is illegal to copy this book, post it to a website, or distribute it by any other means without permission.

Names, characters, businesses, places, events and incidents are either the products of the author's imagination or used in a purely fictitious manner. Any resemblance to actual persons, living or dead, or actual
events is purely coincidental.

First published by Stamford Publishing in 2021
Copyright © Simon McCleave, 2021
All rights reserved

For Sophie Pemberton, a beautiful, generous and brave woman, whose joy and positivity are a lesson to us all. We love you and we are thinking of you xx

PROLOGUE
Peckham, London SE15
Monday 26th January 1998

AS TASH SLOWLY REGAINED consciousness, she felt the soft cotton sheet beneath her fingertips and realised she was lying on her bed, naked. She wasn't quite sure how she had got there. A mad party, pub or club? She couldn't remember a bloody thing. It wouldn't have been the first time though. *Must have been a hell of night!* She tried to focus her eyes as she blinked and looked around. The clock on her bedside table showed 11pm, and the bedroom was bathed in the soft light of candles.

What the hell is going on? I don't remember doing that. I don't remember anything. I thought it was morning.

She glanced down at her bare chest, and saw that her necklace was missing. The silver necklace with a tiny four-leafed clover that her friend Jane had given her for good luck. She never took it off.

I really hope I haven't lost it. I'm such a drunken idiot, I must have blacked out!

As she attempted to adjust her naked body on the cold sheets, she realised she couldn't move. However hard she tried, she just couldn't make any of her limbs work.

Oh my God, I'm paralysed. What happened? Oh my God ...

Her heart began to race, and she felt sick with fear.

'Hello?' she cried, her voice hoarse.

Listening intently, she could hear nothing except from her heart's rhythmic beat against her chest.

Am I alone in here? Who did this to me?

With a dark and growing dread, she gazed up at the intricate Victorian corniced ceiling and tried to piece together the evening. She remembered drinking champagne in Soho House, a fashionable private members' club on Greek Street, Soho, frequented by the great and the good of the film and television industry.

Having turned twenty-four yesterday, Tash had been stringing out her birthday for as long as she could. She had plenty to celebrate. Since leaving the London Academy of Music and Dramatic Art, LAMDA, she'd been fully employed as an actor. Most of her contemporaries were still waiting tables, tending bars, or had given up their dreams of trying to make it. Those who had managed to gain some acting work seemed to spend their time performing in gritty plays above small pubs in North London, or in walk-on roles in television soap operas.

Tash's success had been steady rather than spectacular. Decent parts in critically acclaimed plays at The Royal Court Theatre and then the National Theatre Studio, and a supporting role in a psychological drama on the BBC. More recently, auditions for several Hollywood films had brought her directly into contact with the seedier side of the movie business. She had naively thought that the days of *the casting couch* were long gone.

'How are you feeling?' asked a voice she recognised.

She was startled as her eyes roamed nervously around the room.

'What the fuck are you doing?' she shrieked, the words sticking in her throat as if her vocal chords had been weakened.

Her heart was pounding incessantly. She realised that she had been drugged and was now at this person's mercy.

'It's going to be all right, I promise you,' the voice said.

'What do you want?' she gasped. Whatever the drug was, it had seemed to affect her breathing.

As the person climbed onto the bed, she saw the face she recognised begin to kiss her calves and slowly work their way up her inner thighs. She couldn't feel anything except the hint of pressure against her skin. The sight of that face made her feel physically sick.

'Get off me!'

'I've bought us a present,' the voice said in a virtual whisper.

They lifted a man's tie that lay crumpled on the floor. It was black with light blue stripes.

The muscles in her throat began to tighten. 'What ... are you ... doing?'

Her captor smiled and pulled the tie out straight between their hands.

'I'm going to have to roll you over,' they said gently.

'Please don't hurt me,' she sobbed as she was turned onto her front and felt the folds of the sheet under her.

The sense of complete and utter vulnerability was terrifying.

She felt a heaviness on her lower back as the person straddled her, and she began to imagine what they were about to do.

Please don't let me die like this!

They shifted their weight forward so they were now sitting on the middle of her back. Her chest was compressed and it was becoming impossible to breathe.

'Please don't do this ...,' she panted, desperately trying to suck in air. 'Please ...'

'Now just stay like that for a second,' they said quietly. 'Don't say another word. It's just a little game, that's all.'

There was something distinctly strange about their tone of voice. It sounded like they were talking to a very small child.

She felt the soft material of the tie rest on the back of her neck for a moment while one end was pushed under her throat and looped like a choker.

Please God, I don't want to die.

For a few seconds, they didn't move. Her pulse was racing as she tried to drag in air.

Suddenly, the tie was snapped tight around her throat and neck as it was jerked upwards with great force.

She wanted to thrash out with her legs and arms but it was no use. She just couldn't move or breathe.

I'm not going to die like this!

If she could just twist her hips enough to throw them off balance, then ...

Her head started to swim.

I refuse to die ...

She felt the energy drain from her body, as if she was slipping into a dream.

Just keep fighting ... Just keep fighting ...

And then everything went black.

CHAPTER 1

AS SHE SIPPED THE LAST mouthful of wine from her glass, Detective Constable Ruth Hunter resolved that two glasses were enough on a 'school night'. Sitting back on the sofa, she glanced over at her partner of the past six months, Shiori, who was working at the table. Shiori was American, with Japanese heritage. Even though her paternal grandparents had moved to San Francisco in the 1920s, they were forcibly removed from their home in 1942 and imprisoned in one of the internment camps the US government had established for Japanese immigrants. The conditions in the camps were terrible, and both of Shiori's parents had been born in them. Ruth knew that Shiori's work as a journalist was fuelled by her family's history.

Ruth watched as Shiori peered over her glasses at the papers in front of her. *She really is quite beautiful,* Ruth thought.

Sensing Ruth's gaze, Shiori raised her eyes. 'You okay?' she asked.

Ruth nodded. 'Yeah, fine.'

Shiori gestured to the television which Ruth had muted ten minutes earlier. 'Hey, the news is on. I'm dying to see what Clinton has to say for himself.'

She had been absorbed by the shocking revelations about her country's Democratic President.

Ruth shook her head. 'Such a shame. I always thought he was one of the good guys.'

'None of them are. It's all just varying degrees of lying, manipulation and ego,' Shiori said in a withering tone as she got up from the table and came to sit next to Ruth. 'That's the irony', she continued. 'The kind of character traits required to propel you into the White House also make you completely unsuitable for the actual job of President.'

Turning up the volume, Ruth smiled at her. 'That's a depressing thought.'

The BBC newsreader looked at the camera. *'And we can now go over to our Chief Washington Correspondent, Martin Mitchell, for the latest developments in The White House today.'*

'Thank you, Nicholas,' Mitchell said, with the looming iconic shape of The White House behind him. *'It was a few hours ago that lawyers acting on behalf of Monica Lewinsky confirmed that she has given them a full account of her relationship with President Clinton. Prosecutors are still trying to decide if they will offer her immunity. This comes on the same day that the President rallied to his own defence.'*

Footage on the screen showed President Clinton walking with Hilary Clinton into The White House. *'The President has been silent for three days. But the political damage is rising and Mr Clinton continues the battle to save his Presidency.'*

'He looks terrible,' Ruth said of Clinton.

'He looks guilty,' Shiori growled.

President Clinton gazed at the camera from behind a podium. *'I wanna say one thing to the American people. I want you to listen to me. I'm going to say this again. I did not have sexual relations with that woman, Miss Lewinsky. I never told anybody to lie, not a single time. These allegations are false. And I need to go back to work for the American people. Thank you.'*

As Clinton turned towards the door out of the press room, his wife could be seen clapping enthusiastically.

'Jesus! Why is she applauding him?' Shiori snapped angrily.

Ruth shook her head. 'He's a lying wanker. Monica Lewinsky is a 22-year-old intern and he's the most powerful man on the planet. If that's not an abuse of power, I don't know what is!'

Shiori looked at her watch. 'Speaking of which, where is my feckless ex-husband with my child?'

'It's gone 10pm,' Ruth muttered, rolling her eyes. Shiori's daughter, Koyuki, was only five, the same age as Ella.

Shiori's ex-husband, Jerry, had moved back to London last month and was trying to rebuild his relationship with Koyuki.

The front doorbell rang and Shiori sprung up. 'Right on cue.'

As she went to answer the door, Ruth moved up the sofa so she could see down the hallway. There was little love lost between her and Jerry. He did little to hide his homophobia or his concerns about Koyuki growing up in *that kind of environment*.

'Hello darling,' Shiori said as she took her sleepy-looking daughter in her arms. She glared at Jerry. 'And you're late.'

He shrugged to show that he didn't care. 'I was on a work call.' He then peered down the hallway at Ruth and gave her a sarcastic wave. 'Hi Ruth.'

He's such a prick, she thought.

DETECTIVE CONSTABLE Lucy Henry stirred the milk into her coffee and watched as the black liquid mellowed to a chestnut brown. She was lost in thought – but that was nothing new in recent weeks. She took a sip from her mug and gazed around her kitchen.

Detective Chief Inspector Harry Brooks came in and didn't even bother to make eye contact.

'You make me one?' he muttered, gesturing to her drink.

'No, I asked you five minutes ago and you didn't reply.'

'Didn't hear you.' He let out an audible huff and went to the cupboard to fetch a mug for himself.

Lucy was about to apologise but then thought *fuck him.*

The atmosphere inside the house had become increasingly tense. For the past eight months Harry, her guvnor at Peckham CID, had been living with her. Such a relationship wasn't permitted within the London Met, but they had managed to successfully keep it secret. Lucy's work partner, Ruth, was the only person in CID who knew what was going on.

It had started as a blossoming relationship but things were now difficult and uncomfortable. Lucy and Harry had been trying for a baby for six months with no success. He was in his late 40s and a test had revealed he had oligospermia, which in layman's terms meant he had a low sperm count and was firing a lot of blanks. Added to this was the fact that Lucy had been diagnosed as having an inhospitable uterus for an embryo to implant, so their chances of conceiving were dismally low.

Lucy had enthusiastically suggested IVF or even adoption but Harry's interest in having a child seemed to have waned in recent months. It was now a major bone of contention as Lucy was desperate to have children. They both knew that the writing was on the wall for their relationship but, as with so many things, they just hadn't had a full and frank conversation.

'This is fun,' Lucy said sardonically as Brooks stared at the boiling kettle.

There were a few seconds of tense silence.

Harry looked at her. His slightly sour expression had changed into one of sadness. 'Maybe we should talk?"

Lucy shrugged. 'Talk about what?' She knew she was being hostile but what were they going to talk about? She wanted children. He clearly didn't anymore.

'Us. This isn't good, is it?'

As Lucy lowered her emotional defences, she felt her eyes well up with tears. 'It's never going to be good, Harry. We want different things.'

He moved over to give her a hug but she recoiled. 'I can't do this.'

'What do you want me to do?' he asked quietly. 'Do you want me to move out?'

Wiping the tears from her eyes, Lucy headed out of the kitchen and made for the stairs. 'I'm going to have a bath.'

'Luce? You didn't answer my question,' he snapped abruptly. 'Do you want me to move out?'

'It sounds like you've already made that decision, Harry,' Lucy replied as she went up the stairs.

THE WIND HOWLED AS Detective Sergeant Tim Gaughran turned on the heater in his car. It was freezing. He glanced over at his parents' large, detached house that was on the border between Peckham and East Dulwich. The lights were on downstairs so he knew they were still up.

It had been over five months since his father, Arthur, had spoken to him. During a historic murder case that Gaughran had worked on, it had come to light that his father had taken bribes while working for the South London Murder Squad in the mid-1950s. Although Arthur had eventually not had to face historic charges, it had been Gaughran who had taken him in to Peckham police station for questioning. For some reason, Arthur had seen this as an act of betrayal, rather than the discreet and benevolent act of a son trying to protect his dignity. Gaughran didn't understand it. If it hadn't been him, then it would have been another copper that his father didn't know who would have slapped cuffs on him and taken him in.

After several conversations with his guvnor, DCI Brooks, Gaughran could only assume that his father's pride and ego had been so hurt that he was acting irrationally.

Taking a cigarette from the inside pocket of his jacket, Gaughran lit the Camel Light and took a long drag. He had actually given up nearly two years ago until he had cracked under the stress of the past few months. He was drinking too much as well and had even asked his work colleague, DC Syed Hassan, out for a pint after work, even though it was on a Tuesday. In the past, Gaughran didn't like to drink on work nights. He preferred a clear head in the mornings for what was a challenging and, sometimes, dangerous job. However, he was starting to use alcohol as a way of making sure that he could sleep at night.

Reaching for the cold metal of the handle, Gaughran opened the car door and felt the icy wind against his face. He got out and closed the door softly as he took another drag on his cigarette. As he walked across the road the silence of the night was broken by the deep throaty sound of a dog barking in the distance.

His suit jacket was doing little to keep out the cold and his overcoat was on the backseat. He shuddered as he moved slowly down the street, and came level with the ground floor window of the living room in his parent's home. They hadn't pulled the curtains. His father and mother were sitting in two adjacent armchairs watching the television. After a few seconds, they both erupted in laughter.

Gaughran dropped the cigarette on the pavement and stubbed it out with the heel of his shoe. He turned back and headed for his car.

CHAPTER 2

Tuesday 27th January

SIPPING FROM HER HOT coffee, Ruth sat at her desk in CID and cast her eyes over the tabloid newspaper that she had picked up from the canteen. It was 8.30am. She contemplated the mountain of paperwork on her desk. The day before, they had raided a marijuana factory that had been set up in a top floor flat on the notorious Willowbrook Estate. It was a professional set-up with lights and irrigation systems on timers. Every single square inch of the flat had been utilised for growing marijuana plants. Ruth could smell it as soon as she got out of the lift. The thick pungent scent of flowering cannabis. She had no idea how the neighbours hadn't smelled it. At a guess, they were either being paid off or intimidated into keeping quiet.

There were twelve statements to type up, plus the forensic photographs of the flat to number and log. Just as she had decided to read more about President Clinton's bizarre use of a cigar during sex, she spotted Lucy arriving at her desk. She looked awful. Tired and drained and, by the puffiness around her eyes, she had been crying. Ruth knew that things between her and DCI Brooks weren't going well but they hadn't had a chance to catch up in recent days.

Lucy saw her and forced a weak smile.

Ruth got up from her desk and went over to her. She was concerned.

'Morning,' Lucy mumbled, pretending to be shuffling through her paperwork.

'You all right?' Ruth asked quietly.

Lucy shrugged. 'Not really.'

'You and Harry?'

Lucy gave an almost imperceptible nod. 'I'll tell you about it later, eh?'

The door to the CID office swung open and Brooks strode in purposefully. He was holding a notepad. 'Right, guys. I'm going to put the briefing on hold. Uniformed officers have just called in a suspicious death. A Natasha Weston. Flat in Banfield Road?'

'I know it, Guv. Right by the Common,' Gaughran announced.

'Any more details about why it's a suspicious death?' Ruth asked.

'Yeah,' Brooks nodded grimly. 'They're pretty sure she's been asphyxiated.'

BY THE TIME RUTH AND Lucy arrived at Natasha Weston's address, the road had been taped off and there were three patrol cars parked sideways to close the road off to traffic. The pavement was already alive with neighbours talking, pointing, and trying to see what was going on.

At least the press aren't here yet, Ruth thought.

Lucy gestured to the white forensics van that was parked directly outside the premises. 'SOCOs got here quickly.' The back doors were open wide and a SOCO was stacking away evidence inside.

'Makes our job easier,' Ruth said as they headed towards a young female police constable who was manning the cordon.

Once SOCOs were on the scene, detectives could get an approximate time and cause of death for starters. Plus, there was nothing like getting the initial instincts of a forensic officer about what might have happened.

They flashed their warrant cards. 'DC Henry and DC Hunter, Peckham CID,' Lucy said.

The WPC gave them a self-conscious smile. 'I know.'

Peckham nick was relatively small, and an ambitious WPC would have already clocked female detectives in CID and asked around. *Smart girl.*

Ruth noticed that her face was distinctly pale. 'You okay?'

The officer gave them an unconvincing nod. 'Yeah.'

Lucy indicated the premises. 'First dead body?'

She shook her head. 'No, but it's my first murder ... and she's so young. She's my age.'

Ruth gave a sympathetic smile. 'Don't worry. I felt like that a few years ago. But you do get used to it.'

'Were you first on the scene, Constable?' Lucy asked.

She nodded and took a deep breath. 'Yes.'

'What can you tell us?'

'Victim is Natasha Weston, age twenty-four. She's an actress,' the officer began, looking down at her notepad which she was trying to hold still. 'Her friend, Jane Sinclair, came to pick her up for an audition at eight this morning but there was no response. She was worried and called us. We borrowed the spare key from the neighbour downstairs, went in, and found her dead.'

'Who called in the SOCOs?'

'My Sarge got here just after us. As soon as he saw the victim, he called it in.'

'Thank you, Constable,' Ruth said reassuringly. 'Are you running the scene log?'

'Yes,' she answered. She indicated to her left. 'My Sarge is talking to the victim's friend over there, if you need to speak to her.'

'Okay ... will you be all right?' Ruth asked.

The WPC nodded. 'Yeah, of course.'

Ruth and Lucy ducked under the tape and headed for the two-storey house that had been converted into two flats.

'First murder scene,' Lucy said. 'That's a horrible feeling.'

Ruth grimaced. 'I remember mine. Husband had nearly decapitated his wife in the bedroom. There was blood everywhere.'

They reached the iron gate and the stone path that led to the open front door.

'Go into the flat first?'

Lucy nodded as she and Ruth signalled to the SOCOs that they were coming inside. They were each handed a forensic mask and shoe coverings before entering the property.

There was an open door on the right-hand side of the entrance hall and a carpeted staircase up to the first floor. The paint in the hallway was flaky and brown and an aged bicycle leant against an old radiator.

The air was thick with the strong smell of coffee and cigarette smoke which Ruth assumed was coming from the ground floor flat. She and Lucy went up the stairs that were covered in threadbare, red-patterned carpet. They entered the first-floor flat which was neat and tidy. Black and white photographs of a young woman hung in frames on the wall. She assumed they were shots of the victim as they were stills from a play and a film set.

A figure approached them as they crossed the threshold. Ruth recognised him as Chief Forensic Officer Martin Hill. They had worked with him before and they knew him to be very thorough. He was in his late 50s, blonde and thin, with a faint Cornish accent.

'Morning ladies,' he beamed in his usual cheerful manner. 'Victim is through here.'

They followed him along the landing and into a large double bedroom at the front of the house. The dark blue curtains were drawn.

Ruth's eyes were immediately drawn to the naked body of a young woman, face down with her head turned to one side, and sprawled out slightly on the bed. Her eyes were still wide open, but opaque. For a second, Ruth was unnerved by what she could see. The woman was so young. And she was lying naked and exposed while mostly male SOCOs took photographs and searched around her for forensic evidence. They were only doing their job, but it made her feel uncomfortable. It was so different to seeing a young man shot dead over a drug gang turf war on one of the Peckham estates.

'What can you tell us, Martin?' Lucy asked as there was a blinding flash from the forensic photographer who was taking close-ups of the victim.

'She was asphyxiated.'

'Manually strangled?' Ruth asked.

'No, I don't think so. From the marks around her neck I suspect a ligature of some sort.'

'Time of death?'

'I'm guessing between ten last night and the early hours of this morning.'

On the bedside table Ruth spotted a mirror with lines of white powder on it. 'I think we've got cocaine here.'

'Looks like it.' Lucy pointed to an empty bottle of Veuve Clicquot on the floor. 'Seems as if she might have been celebrating something.'

Hill nodded in agreement. 'There are some birthday cards in the living room. She was only twenty-four.'

'Anything else that might help us?' Ruth asked.

He shook his head. 'No signs of forced entry. No obvious signs of a fight or a struggle.'

'Maybe it was some kind of sex game that went wrong?' Ruth suggested. It had only been a few months since rock star Michael Hutchence had been found dead in a hotel room with a belt around his neck after his autoerotic asphyxiation went tragically wrong.

'I doubt that,' Hill said. 'The marks on her neck suggest a lot of force was used to kill her. I won't know conclusively until the post-mortem but my guess is that this was deliberate.'

Ruth glanced at Lucy. 'So, she knew her killer?'

'And she was murdered while, or just after, having sex with him,' Lucy concluded.

'Or *her*,' Ruth corrected.

'Yes, or her,' Lucy said with a knowing look.

A SOCO stood up from where they had been searching under the bed. 'Boss?'

Hill turned to look at him. 'Found something?'

The SOCO held up a man's tie that was black with thin blue stripes on it.

Lucy raised an eyebrow. 'Could be our ligature?'

IT WAS 10AM BY THE time Ruth and Lucy went into the ground floor flat. The resident, Mrs Weeks, a woman in her early 70s, had allowed officers to use the flat. Natasha Weston's friend Jane was sitting in the kitchen looking shocked and upset.

Ruth looked over at her. 'I know this is very hard for you, but there are a few questions we'd like to ask you if you're up to it?'

Jane put her shaky hands around a mug of tea. 'Yes, of course.'

Lucy took out her notepad and pen. 'You arrived here at 8am to pick Natasha up for an audition. Is that right?'

'Yes.' Jane nodded.

'What was the audition for?' Ruth asked.

'A television drama.'

Lucy glanced up from her notepad. 'Can I ask why you were giving her a lift?'

'Tash doesn't drive,' Jane said, then paused when she realised she'd used the present tense. She blinked as tears came into her eyes. 'I'm sorry ...'

'Don't apologise,' Ruth said kindly.

Lucy handed her a tissue. 'Here you go.'

'Thank you.' Jane dabbed her face and took a long breath to steady herself. 'Tash ... didn't drive. The audition was up in Elstree which is a bit of nightmare on the trains. So, I told her I'd drive her.'

'Can I ask you what you do, Jane?' Lucy enquired.

'I'm a runner on film and tv sets. I'm freelance and I'm not working this week so I said I'd drive her up there.'

'And how did you know Tash?'

Jane sipped her tea but her hands were still a little shaky. 'We went to LAMDA together.'

'LAMDA?' Ruth asked.

'It's a London drama school. Tash was the one to watch from our year. She had done so well ...'

For a few seconds, Jane stared into space and shook her head. 'It just doesn't feel real.' She reached up and touched her silver necklace – it had a small four-leafed clover on it. 'She has a necklace.'

'A necklace?' Lucy asked.

Jane gestured to the necklace she was wearing. 'It's identical to this one. I got it for her on the day we graduated from

LAMDA. She always wore it because she said that's why she had been so successful ... Do you think I could have it back ... you know, when ...'

Ruth couldn't remember seeing any kind of necklace on Tash when she was upstairs. Maybe it was somewhere else in the flat? Or maybe whoever had killed her, had taken it with them?

Lucy nodded. 'Of course. We'll make sure it gets to you.'

Jane pursed her lips and blinked away more tears. 'Thank you.'

'Did Tash have a boyfriend?' Ruth asked.

'Not really,' Jane said with a furrowed brow. 'There was this guy she was seeing sort of on and off.'

'What's his name?'

'Marcus Jankel?' she said as if they might have heard of him. 'He's a TV and film scriptwriter.'

Lucy shook her head. 'Doesn't ring a bell.'

'Oh, I remember,' Ruth said as she thought back to a newspaper article that she'd read. 'Didn't he write the series called 'The Darkness' that was on the BBC last year?'

'That's right,' Jane said. 'I think it was a pretty casual relationship between him and Tash.'

'Do you know where Tash was last night?' Lucy asked.

'She was meeting some people in Soho House early.'

Ruth looked at her. 'And by early, you mean?'

'Six-ish, I guess,' Jane said with a shrug.

'Did she say who she was meeting?'

Jane frowned. 'I'm pretty sure she was meeting her agent, Josh.'

'Josh?'

'Josh Harriot. He's an agent at UCA Talent.'

Lucy finished writing her notes and asked, 'Is there anyone you can think of who might have wanted to harm Tash?'

'No, I just don't understand it ...'

'No ex-boyfriends. Nothing in recent weeks that was out of the ordinary or had scared her?' Ruth asked.

Jane shook her head briefly and then stopped suddenly. 'Actually, she said there was a bloke who she'd seen around here a few times. She'd watched him walk past the flat and up towards Coldharbour Lane. Then he got on the same train as her last week.'

'Did she feel threatened by him?' Ruth wondered.

'No, I don't think so. When she tried to make eye contact, he looked away and seemed embarrassed.'

'I don't suppose she described him, did she?'

'Yes, she said he was really good looking. Mediterranean with shoulder-length black hair and one of those goatee beards. She said if Antonio Banderas had a really fit son in his early 20s ...'

Ruth nodded. She knew what Jane meant. She could also see that Jane had thought of something else.

'She didn't say anything else about him?' Ruth asked, giving Jane the opportunity to say what she was thinking.

'Yes. This is going to sound really weird.' Jane's expression had changed, and she frowned. 'She thought he was following her home the other week, but then he went off down some road over there.' She pointed in the general direction of where she meant. 'Tash said that maybe she should have dragged him into her flat and had wild, dangerous sex with him all night.'

RUTH AND LUCY WERE sitting in the heavy South London traffic at the foot of Albert Bridge. As they edged forward about ten feet, Ruth stared up into the grey canopy above them. A courier cyclist whizzed down the side of the car in a blur and then began to weave in and out of the cars in front.

She got a flash in her mind's eye of one of the black and white publicity photographs that lined the hallway in Tash's flat. In it, she was singing on stage. The look of sheer joy on her face was such an unforgivingly hideous contrast to the face of the young woman they had discovered on the bed.

'It's really got to me what we saw this morning,' she admitted.

Lucy nodded. 'It's horrible when they're that young.'

'Young, beautiful and talented. And then someone does that to her.' Ruth imagined how terrifying Tash's last moments must have been. Even though the more experienced detectives told her that seeing dead bodies at a murder scene would become second nature, she wasn't sure that she ever wanted that to happen. She thought having some kind of emotional attachment to a case made her a better copper. It wasn't a widely held opinion in CID where detachment was seen as the objective.

'Do we think she actually invited this mysterious, handsome stalker into her flat?'

Ruth raised her shoulders. 'No signs of a break-in or a struggle. And my bet is that the post-mortem shows she was having consensual sex with whoever killed her.'

'He's our prime suspect then.'

'Any idea what the guv'nor thinks?'

Lucy pulled a face. 'No ... and I don't think I'm the right person to ask him at the moment.'

'You two had another tiff? What is it this time? Toenails in the bath, smelly trainers in the bedroom ...' Ruth laughed. When Lucy didn't respond, Ruth wondered if she had put her foot in it. 'Sorry, I didn't mean to make a joke out of it.'

'It's fine. You weren't to know,' she said, sounding a little choked.

'For what it's worth, if you need to talk about it ...'

'It's the baby thing again,' Lucy confessed.

Ruth knew that their inability to conceive had been a growing problem in recent months. She had seen Lucy go from all the hope and excitement that comes with trying for your first child, to all the despair and pain of tests and increasingly bad news.

'What does he think about IVF?' Ruth asked. Lucy had mentioned it a few weeks ago.

'Hit and miss, and too expensive.'

'Adoption?'

Lucy shook her head – she was getting upset. 'No. I think he's using it as an excuse now.'

'But he knows how important it is to you?'

'He knows it's a deal breaker ... but that doesn't seem to bother him.'

'So, now what happens?'

'We move on.'

'Together?'

Lucy shook her head sadly. 'No.'

THEY TURNED INTO RUSTON Mews in London's fashionable Notting Hill. Originally named Crayford Mews, it had been built in the 1860s. The two-storey mews houses were originally used to provide shelter for horses, carriages and drivers in Victorian London. The ground floor comprised of stabling for the horses and storage for the Hansom cabs, whilst the first floor was accommodation for the drivers. Over a hundred years later the houses, with the original cobbled road surface outside, were now very expensive and stylish homes to West London's creative and media types.

'This is nice,' Ruth commented as they pulled up outside No. 8 where Marcus Jankel lived. She turned to look at Lucy and smiled. 'You okay?'

'Yeah, I'll be fine. Thanks for listening.'

'Oh, actually I've been secretly listening to *The Verve* album at a very low volume, so I haven't heard a word you've said,' Ruth joked.

'Ha, ha.' Lucy gave her a sarcastic smile and tilted her head towards the stereo. She heard music playing very quietly. 'Oh my God, you have actually been listening to *The Verve*! You bitch!'

Ruth laughed as they both got out of the car. No. 8 Ruston Mews was narrow and had recently been painted. There was a small glass-fronted balcony on the first floor with a series of plant pots attached to its rim. Colourful winter foliage spilled over the edge.

They went to the door, and Ruth knocked. Glancing down the mews, she wondered what it might have looked like a hundred years earlier. She assumed it would have been very noisy and very smelly for starters.

The painted black door, with gold knocker and letterbox, opened. An extremely handsome man in his early 30s peered out at them. He was tall, with shoulder-length brown hair. With his slightly pre-Raphaelite look, he definitely had the appearance of a writer, Ruth thought.

'Hi there, we're looking for a Marcus Jankel,' she said, showing him her warrant card.

He nodded without a flicker of emotion. 'Yes. Can I help?'

'We understand that you're a friend of Natasha Weston?' Lucy asked.

'Yes. I heard the news this morning. It's terrible,' he replied in his public-school accent.

'We'd like to ask you a few questions, if that's all right?' Ruth said.

'Of course,' Marcus said as he nodded, but he didn't seem particularly pleased by the intrusion. 'Come in.'

The inside of the house was fashionably decorated, and old movie posters adorned the walls. Ruth spotted one of her favourites, 'The Night of the Hunter', with Robert Mitchum.

'Let's go upstairs.' Marcus led the way up a flight of wooden stairs to the first floor where there was a large open space which was clearly his office. The floorboards had been sanded and varnished and there were a few Moroccan-style rugs on the far side. He gestured to a huge, dark red sofa. 'Would you like to sit down?'

'Thank you.' Ruth gazed around the room and then out of the window from which she could see the north end of Portobello Market.

'Coffee or tea?' he asked, but Ruth could tell he was only being polite.

Lucy shook her head. 'We're fine thanks.'

He sat down in a large armchair opposite the sofa and waited for their questions.

'We understand that you and Tash were in some kind of relationship?' Ruth asked.

Marcus shifted in the chair and crossed his legs. He was wearing jeans and black Chelsea boots. 'Not really a relationship.'

Lucy's eyes locked on his. 'How would you describe it then?'

He smirked. 'I guess you would say we were very casual, if you get my drift?'

'How often would you and Tash meet up?' Ruth asked.

He ran his hands through his hair and then reached for a packet of Camel Light cigarettes on a nearby table. 'Two or three times a month.'

'Can you tell us the last time you saw her?'

'Last night. We had a drink at Soho House,' he explained as he put a cigarette in his mouth. He offered the packet to them both.

Ruth waved her hand. 'We're fine thanks.'

Marcus frowned at Ruth with some kind of amusement. 'Funny. I had you down as a smoker.'

His comment and look unsettled her. *There's something a little off with him.*

'And what time was that?' Lucy asked.

Marcus lit his cigarette, took a drag, sat back and blew out the smoke into a long plume up towards the ceiling. 'Around 7pm.'

'Did you leave there together?' Ruth enquired.

He shook his head. 'No. Tash said she was going home early. She had an audition this morning, so she wanted to get an early night.'

'Did you see her leave?'

'No. But I came through the bar again at about 9pm and she'd gone.'

Lucy glanced up from her notepad. 'And where had you been?'

'A friend of mine was having a screening at the cinema there.'

'Was Tash there with anyone else?'

'Yes. She was having a drink with her agent Josh Harriot when I left her.'

Ruth looked at him. 'Was Josh Harriot in the bar when you came past at 9pm?'

Marcus took a few seconds to think. 'You know, I don't think he was.'

'And you didn't see Tash again?'

'No,' Marcus said as he glanced down at a mobile phone that was buzzing on the arm of the chair.

'And where were you for the rest of evening?'

'I left Soho House at about 9.30pm and came home.'

'Can anyone verify that?' Lucy asked.

He shook his head. 'No. I live here on my own. I guess a neighbour might have seen me, but I've no idea.'

'Can you tell us how you got home?' Ruth asked. If he had taken the underground, then they could cross-refer CCTV footage to confirm his story.

'Black cab.'

Well, there's no way of verifying that, she thought.

Marcus leaned forward and asked, 'Is there anything else? I'm very busy today.'

Ruth was starting to take a dislike to his manner. Tash was a young woman he had known, slept with, and had a drink with the night before. She had been brutally murdered but it didn't seem to have registered in any way with him.

'What do you do, Marcus?' she asked, ignoring his question.

'I'm a writer. Mainly television and film scripts. A bit of theatre once in a while,' he said as his gaze moved up to a framed poster of a play called 'FUN' that he had written for The Bush Theatre.

'Is that how you met Tash?' Lucy asked.

He nodded. 'Yes. We met on the set of a film I wrote for Channel 4 last year.'

'Is there anyone you can think of who would want to harm Tash?' Ruth asked.

Marcus sat back and tapped the ash from his cigarette into a silver tray. Ruth noticed a couple of smoked spliffs in there. 'No. She was such a lovely, harmless creature. Ethereal. I don't understand it.'

Lucy frowned. 'And Tash hadn't mentioned anything out of the ordinary in recent weeks? Nothing that was bothering or worrying her?'

'No,' he replied, checking his watch with a preoccupied glance. 'I'm sorry but there really isn't anything else I can tell you.'

And with that, he stubbed out his cigarette and got up out of his armchair to signal that he wanted them to leave. Ruth knew they'd got all the information they had come for, but it was still a conceited act that did little to dispel her view that he was pompous and entitled.

'Thanks for your help,' Lucy said as they followed him towards the stairs.

He paused and turned to face her, asking, 'Have we met before?'

She shrugged. 'I don't think so.'

'Interesting.' He smiled and looked directly into her eyes. 'I'm sure I recognise you.'

Lucy laughed. 'I don't think so.'

'Must have been your twin then? Same blue eyes. I noticed them when you first came in.' He turned around, and led them down to the front door where they thanked him again for his help.

Bemused by their encounter, Ruth and Lucy exchanged a look – *What the hell was that about?*

As they walked to the car Ruth commented, 'He gave me the creeps.'

Lucy seemed to be deep in thought. After a few seconds, she raised an eyebrow and said 'Really? I actually thought he was incredibly sexy.'

'Oh God!' Ruth pulled a face. 'And what was all that about meeting you before?'

'No idea, but I would have definitely remembered him.'

CHAPTER 3

IT WAS MID-AFTERNOON by the time Brooks had assembled the CID officers for an interim briefing. Although murders weren't uncommon in Peckham, this type of killing was quite unusual. The CID team were used to fatal stabbings and the odd shooting. These were usually a result of the gang warfare that sometimes broke out on the Peckham estates when they were battling over areas from which they could sell drugs. Sometimes these murders were horribly senseless. A teenager who had given someone the wrong kind of look or had strayed a few hundred yards off their patch. Other times, gangs from different parts of London, such as the Ghetto Boys from New Cross, would attack and kill someone as a show of strength. In recent months, hostilities had escalated between the Peckham Boys and a Brixton-based gang from the Angell Town Estate called GAS, which stood for guns and shanks – shanks being the gang slang for knives. This ever-increasing battle between the SW9 and SE15 postcodes had seen two murders and five attempted murders in three months. Officers had been sickened when they had found a 9-year-old girl shot in the arm by a stray bullet while she was playing in her father's shop on Rye Lane.

Lucy strode across the room to a fax machine which whirred into action. For a brief second, she made eye contact with Brooks. It was uncomfortable and sad. She longed for the times he would give her a sexy wink and they would grab each other surreptitiously on the staircase or steal a quick kiss in the car park. She couldn't see how that was ever going to happen again. Not being with him was going to break her heart. On a practical level, it also meant that one of them would probably have to transfer to another South London police station.

A fax began to print from the machine. Her thoughts turned to Marcus Jankel. She couldn't stop thinking about him, but she had no idea why. Not only was he attractive, with charisma and presence, he also had an enigmatic quality that bordered on darkness. She found it intriguing.

'Right guys,' Brooks said as he headed for the scene boards at the far end of the office. 'Can we settle down, please. Thank you.' The murmurs stopped and the team of detectives focussed their attention to the front of the room and their guv'nor.

'As most of you know, we attended a murder this morning over in Banfield Road, up by the Common.' He pointed to a map of the area where a red pin marked the location of Tash's flat. 'Victim is Natasha Weston, just turned twenty-four. She was an actress. Family are based in Andover in Hampshire and we have a family liaison officer with her parents as of this morning. This was a brutal, unprovoked attack on a vulnerable young woman, so I want us to do our best work for her family and get them the justice they deserve.'

Brooks looked over at Lucy and for a moment their eyes met. 'Lucy?'

Lucy took a breath and got up to address the room. 'Yes, Guv. A friend of Tash Weston's, Jane Sinclair, arrived this morning to pick her up for an audition. When she didn't answer the door or her phone, she became suspicious. A neighbour downstairs, Mrs Weeks, had a spare set of keys to Tash's flat and let in two uniformed officers. They discovered her body on the bed.'

'Anything on forensics?' Brooks asked.

Lucy shook her head. 'Nothing yet.' She pointed to one of the photos on the scene boards. 'We think she was strangled with this tie that was found at the crime scene.'

'Any sign of her phone?'

Ruth shrugged. 'SOCOs didn't find it. Neither did they come across a silver necklace with a four-leafed clover that Jane had given her a few years ago. Apparently Tash always wore it so I'm wondering if it was taken.'

'Okay, that's worth noting,' Brooks said, nodding his head. 'Anything else useful from the friend?'

'She claims that Tash thought someone had been stalking her in recent weeks. We've got a description.' Lucy moved closer to the scene boards and pointed to an area of the map. 'Tash claimed she had seen the suspect in the vicinity of her flat, and up on Coldharbour Lane, and then at Loughborough Junction station here. We're waiting for CCTV footage to see if we can find him. We're also going to create an identity sketch based on the description that Tash gave Jane.'

'Okay, good.' Brooks rubbed his chin for a moment. 'We don't have any signs of a break-in or a struggle, and we think that the killer was the person she was having sex with in her flat. Doesn't sound like she was attacked by someone who'd been stalking her.'

Lucy continued, 'Thing is, Guv, Jane told us that Tash thought that this bloke stalking her was very attractive.'

Gaughran creased his eyebrows. 'What?'

'Yeah, it gets worse. Tash told her friend Jane that she thought this man had followed her home one night but then he disappeared. She joked to Jane that she should have dragged him into her flat and had mad, dangerous sex with him.'

'Bloody hell.' Brooks seemed surprised. 'Right. Well we need to find this person, whoever he is. I think the CCTV from Loughborough Junction is going to be our best bet.'

Gaughran took the biro from his mouth and frowned. 'If she walked from the station down Coldharbour Lane, and he followed her, there's a couple of CCTV cameras that might have picked him up, Guv.'

'Thanks, Tim.' Let's make identifying this person our number one priority. What did you get from your trip to Notting Hill, Ruth?'

Ruth got up from her desk and headed for the scene boards. She gestured to a photograph of Tash that they had sourced from a casting directory called 'Spotlight'. It was a moody photograph of her sitting forward, hand moving hair from her face. It was what Lucy would call *sultry*, but she wasn't sure anyone used that word anymore. 'Tash was last seen in Soho House on Greek Street last night at about 8pm.

It's a private members' club for the film and television industry. She had a drink with this man ...' Ruth pointed to a photo. 'Marcus Jankel. He's a scriptwriter. Seems they were having a very casual sexual relationship. Marcus told us he went off to a screening and by the time he came back to the first floor bar, Tash had left. She'd told him that she had an audition this morning and was going to have an early night. The last time that Marcus saw her, she was drinking at a table with her agent, Josh Harriot.'

The phone rang on a nearby desk and Hassan answered it quietly.

Gaughran waved his hand to speak. 'I've got the PNC checks on both Marcus Jankel and Josh Harriot. Not as much as a parking ticket between them, as far as I can see.'

Brooks nodded. 'Does this Marcus Jankel have an alibi?'

'No, Guv.' Ruth shook her head. 'He says he got a black cab home from Soho to Notting Hill around 9.30pm and then he was home on his own for the rest of the night.'

'He lives in Ruston Mews, you said?' Brooks asked.

'Yes, Guv.'

'Place rings a bell. Maybe I've been there before,' he said, thinking out loud. 'What about Josh Harriot?'

'We've arranged to see him first thing tomorrow at his office.'

Brooks rubbed his chin thoughtfully. 'Tim, Syed. This Soho House must have some kind of reception. Let's talk to them and see if they saw Tash leave.'

Gaughran nodded. 'Yes, Guv.'

Hassan put down the phone and glanced over. 'That was Forensics. It's going to take a couple of days to determine any DNA profiles from the samples taken from the crime scene.'

'That's a shame,' Brooks said.

'They're also going to need an elimination batch as soon as we can get one to them. However, the good news is that someone down in Forensics recognised the tie.'

'Recognised it?' Lucy questioned.

'Yeah, light blue stripes on a black background. It's an Old Etonian tie.'

Lucy raised her eyebrows. Eton College is the most prestigious public school in England where Royalty and future Prime Ministers are educated. 'Eton?' she asked rhetorically. 'Could be a coincidence. It could just be a black tie with light blue stripes from Tie Rack at Waterloo station.'

A couple of detectives laughed.

Hassan smiled at her. 'Yeah except, clever clogs, it was made by Benson & Clegg, which means it is an authentic Old Etonian tie.'

'We're assuming that it didn't belong to Tash,' Ruth said.

'Eton is all boys, isn't it?' Gaughran asked.

'Yes.' Brooks then paused in thought for a few seconds. 'If our killer was wearing or carrying an Old Etonian tie, it means that he wanted us to know he went to Eton, or he's smart enough to try to misdirect us.'

'I don't know for certain, but I'm pretty sure Marcus Jankel is a public schoolboy,' Ruth said.

Brooks nodded. 'Check him out and see where he went to school.'

IT WAS DARK BY THE time Gaughran and Hassan parked up in a *Delivery Only* spot on Greek Street in the middle of London's West End. As Gaughran got out of the car, he saw the faintest touch of drizzle illuminated in the air by the bold red lights of *CHICAGO*, a musical that was playing at a nearby theatre. The pavements were full of impatient commuters heading to the nearest underground station, Tottenham Court Road, and theatre goers and diners arriving for a night out.

'It's just up here.' Hassan pointed to Greek Street, where Soho House was situated.

'It was Cassie, wasn't it?' Gaughran asked. Hassan had phoned ahead and established that a Cassie Barnes had been on reception the night before.

'Yeah,' Hassan said with a smile. 'Sounds very posh.'

A black London taxi, with its loud and distinctive diesel engine, stopped close by and its pungent fumes filled the air.

Even though he was a Londoner, Gaughran didn't like the West End. He didn't class it as 'proper' London anyway. It was more like an overpriced shiny theme park for tourists. He remembered the last time he had been up to town was over a year ago. He had taken his mum to see the musical 'Sunset Boulevard' for her birthday. She had described it as '... a double whammy' as it starred Elaine Paige, whom she loved, and was based on Billy Wilder's 1950 film starring William Holden - who she always described as 'very hunky'.

As they weaved through the crowded pavement, Gaughran was lost in thought. He remembered the excited look of wonder on his mum's face when the curtain had gone up. For a moment, she'd looked like the girl she had once been. It was a beautiful image that would be etched in his memory forever. But it also made him sad. It had now been nearly six months since he had spoken to her properly. The damage that had been done to his dad's pride and ego, at the revelations that he'd taken bribes, had ruined everything. He wasn't angry at his mum for taking his side. In fact he didn't think she really understood why he and his father had fallen out so badly. All she knew was that they had been married for over forty years and he had been her world.

'Here we go,' said Hassan, breaking Gaughran's train of thought.

They went in through a set of doors and found themselves in the small but plush reception of Soho House.

Gaughran, now back in DS mode, pulled out his warrant card. 'DS Gaughran and DC Hassan, Peckham CID. We're looking for Cassie?'

The young woman behind the desk had a blonde ponytail and was dressed in a smart black trouser suit. 'Hi, that's me. Are you the police officer that rang before?' she asked in a plummy accent.

Blimey, she's pretty, Gaughran thought.

'Yeah. We wondered if you could answer a couple of questions for us?'

Cassie's face fell. 'Oh God, is it about Tash Weston?'

Hassan nodded. 'Did you know her?'

'Not really,' she said. 'Only from working here. I couldn't believe it when I saw it on the news today.'

Gaughran looked intently at Cassie's face. She had small features and a smattering of delicate freckles across the bridge of her nose. She couldn't have been more than early 20s. 'Do you remember seeing her last night?'

Cassie thought for a few seconds. 'Sorry, it's just working here, one night blurs into another, if you know what I mean?'

Gaughran smiled. 'Take your time.'

Cassie took the large ledger, flicked through it and nodded. 'Oh yes, last night. We had a screening in the evening.'

'Does that help?' Hassan asked.

'Yes. I don't remember Tash arriving but I do remember her leaving.'

'Do you know what time that was?'

'Early. Nine, maybe nine thirty.'

'Sure?'

Cassie nodded. 'Yes, pretty sure.'

'Was she on her own when she left?'

'No, she was with an older woman but I've forgotten her name.'

Gaughran smiled again, reassuringly. 'Okay.'

'Barbara York!' she blurted out. 'I'm sure she left with Barbara York.'

'Where are we going to find Barbara York?' Hassan asked.

'She's an executive at Goldstein Films,' she replied, as though they would know exactly what she meant.

'Goldstein Films? They made 'Pulp Fiction' didn't they?' asked Gaughran.

'Yes. They're a big American film company. They make a lot of films. In fact, Barbara York is American.'

'And you saw them leave together?'

'Yes. In fact, I saw them getting into a cab together outside. Is that helpful?'

Gaughran gave his best smile. 'Yes, very.'

CHAPTER 4

LUCY POURED HERSELF another glass of wine and went from the kitchen towards the living room. Harry had disappeared upstairs about an hour earlier. At first, she thought he must be having a bath or a shower, but she hadn't heard the water running. Maybe he was having a nap but, unlike her, he wasn't really a napping kind of person.

'Harry?' she called upstairs from the hallway. She was aware that she sounded irritated, but she couldn't help it.

There were a few seconds of silence followed by a faint 'Yes?'

'You okay?'

There was no response.

Even though they were in a strange emotional limbo, she still loved him. She put her glass of wine down on a table and climbed the stairs.

'What are you doing?' she called as she strode along the landing towards the bedroom.

She reached the doorway and stood in shock as she saw his suitcase in the middle of the bed, open and full of clothes.

'What the bloody hell's going on, Harry?' she snapped.

He avoided her glare sheepishly as he put a handful of black socks into the case. 'Sorry. I just think that we need some time apart.'

'Are you fucking kidding me?' Lucy yelled. 'You thought we needed some time apart, so without a bloody word to me, you walked upstairs and started to pack your suitcase. What the fuck are you talking about?'

'I'm sorry,' he said quietly. 'I came upstairs for a shower. And then it hit me that some time apart might be good for us. So, I got my suitcase down and started to pack.'

'Great!'

'I was going to come down and talk to you about it.'

'Oh well, that's very fucking decent of you, Harry. Don't I get any kind of say in us having some time apart?'

He sat down on the bed with his shoulders hunched, and looked at her with sadness in his eyes. 'I don't know. I don't know what you're supposed to do in a situation like this. All I do know is that we're making each other miserable.'

'Couples work through their problems,' Lucy said, her voice now calm and steady. 'They don't pack their bags and run for the hills.'

Harry sighed deeply and rubbed his face. 'But we can't work through our problems, can we? I can't give you what you want.'

'Why not?' she asked as her eyes welled with tears. 'Why can't you do that for me? We have options but you're just not interested.'

'I don't know. I need some time to think,' he said softly.

'No, you don't.' Lucy wiped a tear from her cheek with the back of her hand. 'You've made your mind up. Having children with me, however that happens, is no longer an option for you. You're not moving out for a bit to have a think. You're just moving out, Harry. I just wish you'd not made a lot of false promises six months ago.'

She took a deep breath as she turned away, and walked across the landing and down the stairs.

As she grabbed her wine from the table, she could see that her hand was shaking. She went into the kitchen, grabbed a tissue, and wiped the tears from her eyes.

What the hell am I meant to do? she thought as the gravity of what was happening hit her and she began to sob.

RUTH REACHED OVER FOR another handful of crisps and sat back on her sofa. Ella was asleep in bed, and Shiori and Koyuki were at their house in Clapham. On the way home, Ruth had nipped into Blockbuster Video in Balham and rented the 'The Darkness', the BAFTA winning BBC crime thriller that Marcus Jankel had written nearly two years earlier.

So far, she had scoffed at the terrible inaccuracies in the portrayal of a police investigation. For starters, the central character was a male DCI with a gambling addiction who seemed to charge around breaking laws in his quest to find the truth. Ruth had never met a DCI who had ever left a police station. It was their job to oversee investigations from the comfort of an office. The DCI also seemed to have a habit of discussing the case at every stage with a glamorous blonde pathologist who appeared to have Sherlock Holmes-like instincts when it came to evidence. It was nonsense, but she was used to seeing such portrayals of police work on the screen.

She did, however, remember an ITV police series from the early 1980s that had had a profound effect on her ambitions to become a police officer. 'The Gentle Touch' had starred Jill Gascoine as Detective Inspector Maggie Forbes. Ruth just loved her. Not only was DI Forbes her first-ever role model, but she was also her first *girl crush*. The series was gritty and realistic and, with a female DI as its lead character, ground-breaking and way ahead of its time. As the title suggested, DI Forbes relied on her feminine attributes to solve crimes in a calm, considered and empathetic way. This was in stark contrast to the uber-masculine tough guy characters in The Sweeney or The Professionals, which she didn't like at all. She remembered that DI Forbes' husband, a PC, had been murdered in the first episode, leaving her to bring up their teenage son on her own. Aged only eleven, Ruth had found the episode incredibly shocking, but it did mean that from then onwards 9pm on a Friday night was always the highlight of the week. It also meant that when she was twelve, and her form teacher asked pupils what they wanted to be when they grew up, she was more than happy to put her hand up and say that she wanted to be a police officer. It often made her an object of derision, as joining *The Fuzz, Plod, The Old Bill* or *The Filth* wasn't a popular choice in an area of Battersea where many families had criminal connections. They said it made her *a rat, a snitch* or *a grass,* but Ruth didn't care.

She grabbed another handful of crisps and watched with a growing sense of unease and déjà vu as a young woman had sex with a man. They had just snorted cocaine and the room was lit by various candles. And now the man had rolled the young woman onto her front before straddling her back.

That's weird, she thought. *That's exactly how we found Tash Weston this morning.*

To her horror, Ruth saw the man reach for his jacket and pull out a tie from the pocket. He let it unfurl as the woman giggled and stretched up her hands to allow him to tie her up.

Except the man looped the tie under her throat and neck.

Ruth sat forward on the sofa. *This can't be happening! What the hell is going on?*

Suddenly, the man wrenched up the tie hard and began to strangle her. She made choking sounds and put her hands to her throat as her legs thrashed around. The man pulled the tie tighter.

Jesus Christ!

The woman stopped moving. She was dead.

A close up of the man's hands showed the tie he was holding. It was black with narrow light blue stripes.

Oh my God!

She paused the video and took a few seconds to try to absorb what she had just seen.

Grabbing the phone, she dialled Lucy's number. She could feel that her pulse had quickened by what she had just seen on the screen.

'Hello?' Lucy said very quietly.

She sounds like she's been crying.

'Lucy, it's Ruth. Are you okay?'

'Harry's left.'

'Left? What do you mean?'

'He's packed a suitcase tonight and left.'

'Oh God, I'm so sorry. Poor you. Do you want to come over here?'

'No, it's fine. There's a small part of me that's relieved,' Lucy said. 'And, no offence, I don't really want to talk about it. So, how's your evening?'

'Erm, very, very weird.' Ruth wasn't quite sure how to describe what she had seen.

'Weird? What are you doing? You're not watching 'I Know What You Did Last Summer' on your own again are you? The last time you did that, you couldn't sleep,' Lucy joked.

'No, it's actually weirder than that. I'm watching 'The Darkness.' You know, that BBC drama that Marcus Jankel wrote?'

'Okay. Is it crap or something?'

'It's not that, it's …' Ruth searched for the right words.

'Spit it out, girl,' Lucy said with a half laugh.

'I've just seen a man and woman snort coke and have sex, and then he sat on her back and strangled her to death with an Old Etonian tie.'

'What the fuck!' Lucy exclaimed.

'I know.'

'That's beyond weird,' Lucy said. 'What do we do?'

'We need to have another chat with Marcus Jankel.'

CHAPTER 5

Wednesday 28th January

GLANCING AT A COPY of the Daily Mail on a nearby desk, Ruth could see that the affair between President Clinton and Monica Lewinsky was still front page news. It was a shame with all the advances in feminism in the 1970s and 1980s, that such a blatant abuse of male power had been allowed to happen. Some female journalists had taken a dislike to Lewinsky, and Ruth was angry about some of the articles they had written about her. It seemed that because Clinton was a liberal democrat, he had to be defended. He was pro-choice, fought for women's rights and equality. He was *their guy*. He was married to Hilary after all, and she was a formidable woman. What some of the journalists seemed to forget was that Monica Lewinsky was a vulnerable 22-year-old intern earning $6 an hour who had been seduced by the most powerful man on the planet. That was never going to be okay, whatever that man's political persuasion was. It would be naïve to think that just because your politics were liberal, you couldn't be a sexual predator.

Ruth looked up as Brooks marched into the CID office. It was time for the morning briefing. Half an hour earlier, Ruth had set up the television and VHS player to show detectives what she had spotted last night on the TV drama 'The Darkness'. She couldn't help but then glance over at Lucy who was working across from her. Lucy deliberately ignored Brooks' entrance and carried on looking at the documents in front of her. There was no way that they could both stay in Peckham CID for a prolonged period of time if their relationship was now over. Not only was it unprofessional, but it could also get in the way of an investigation.

'Right guys,' Brooks said. His face appeared drawn and his eyes tired. After her conversation with Lucy last night, she knew why. She turned her chair around to face the front of the office, as she always did.

Brooks went over to the scene boards that were now full of photos, maps, and other pieces of evidence that had been gathered so far. 'What have we got?'

'Guv, we went to Soho House last night,' Gaughran began. 'The receptionist remembers Tash Weston leaving there with a woman called Barbara York. They got into a cab together.'

'What do we know about Barbara York?' Brooks asked.

'She's some big American film executive for a company called Goldstein Films,' Gaughran explained. 'The receptionist saw them getting into a black cab together.'

'Did Soho House order the cab for them?' Ruth asked.

Gaughran shook his head. 'Unfortunately not. They hailed it in the street. She might have been the last person to see Tash alive so we need to speak to her.'

Hassan nodded in agreement. 'I've put a call in and we're seeing her this morning, Guv.'

'I don't suppose Tash's phone has turned up anywhere?' Brooks asked.

Ruth shook her head. 'Nothing. I think her killer must have taken it with them.'

'What about her landline records?'

Gaughran looked up. 'They're being faxed over today.'

'Doctor's records, bank statements?'

'Same,' he added.

'Anything else?' Brooks asked.

Hassan picked up a file. 'Guv, background research on Marcus Jankel. He comes from a very wealthy banking family in Germany. At the age of ten, he was sent here to board at Eton College.'

There were murmurs between the other detectives. This news meant there was a direct link between Marcus Jankel and the probable murder weapon. Ruth knew it also linked to the BBC drama she had seen and was about to show to the team.

'Right,' Brooks said. 'That's far too much of a coincidence for my liking. Did you dig up anything else on him?'

'He moved back to Germany after getting an English degree from Oxford. He then married but his wife was killed in an accident in Hamburg only a few months after the marriage. He moved to London in 1988 and worked as a script editor at the BBC, Carlton, and Granada. Then he started to write scripts for television and films. He's very successful.'

'Okay. Any details on what actually happened to his wife?'

'I'm waiting for Hamburg police to fax something over,' Hassan explained.

'Ruth, you've got something for us, haven't you?' Brooks asked.

'Yes, Guv.' Ruth went over to the VHS machine where she had lined up the episode of 'The Darkness' at the relevant scene. 'I watched Marcus Jankel's BBC drama called 'The Darkness' last night ... and I saw this scene.' She pressed play and the detectives sat forward and peered at the screen.

The scene on the television played out. The couple snorted cocaine, and got onto the bed. The man rolled the woman over, and straddled her back before reaching for a tie and strangling her. The final close up showed the tie's design – black with narrow light blue stripes.

There were more murmurs from the watching detectives. It was an almost identical depiction of the murder they were investigating.

Brooks gave Ruth a dark look. 'That's effectively how we think Tash Weston was murdered isn't it?'

'Yeah, even down to the tie.'

'That doesn't make any sense,' Gaughran announced. 'Are we looking for a copycat killer here?'

Brooks frowned. 'Whatever we think, Marcus Jankel is right in the middle of this. His school, his script, his girlfriend.'

Lucy shook her head. There was no way that Marcus was guilty of Tash's murder. 'He would have to be an idiot to kill someone in exactly the same way as he described in his own script. And he's definitely not an idiot.'

Ruth pulled a face. 'Why? It would be the best alibi in the world. *There is no way I would murder someone in exactly the same way as in a script I wrote.*'

Gaughran snorted. 'Christ, it would take some balls to do that. And it would mean that he knew when he wrote the script two or three years ago that he wanted to commit an actual murder in the same way.'

'Not necessarily,' Ruth pointed out. 'The idea of copying it might have come to him much later. And there's definitely something strange about him.'

'I think we need to speak again to Marcus Jankel and see if he'll come in for a voluntary interview.' Brooks leant against a table. 'I've been in CID for over twenty years, and never come across anything like this before.' He looked at Ruth and Lucy. 'You've met him. What do you think? Think he's capable of doing this?'

Lucy shrugged. 'Charming, intelligent, and definitely arrogant - but not psychopath arrogant.'

'I think he was,' Ruth responded. 'He had that slightly cold, pompous, narcissistic way about him, like he was toying with us. Classic psychopath.'

Brooks raised his eyebrow. 'And you've met exactly how many psychopaths, Ruth?'

'Erm, one,' she said with a self-effacing smile. 'And he taught me PE so I'm not sure it counts because we just thought Mr Hobson looked like a psychopath.'

There was some laughter from the room.

Brooks shook his head.

'Bring Jankel in, and let's have a closer look at him,' Brooks said. He indicated the map on the board. 'Anything on the person who was stalking Tash yet?'

'Waiting for CCTV from the station and council,' Gaughran explained.

'Anything come up in the door-to-door witness statements?'

Ruth shook her head. 'Nothing, Guv. No one saw anything out of the ordinary that night or in recent weeks. And no one seems to have even seen Tash arrive home.'

Brooks cast his eyes around the team. 'Right guys, good work so far ...' He then reached for a tabloid paper which was open at page 5 and held it up to show them. The headline read *Police hunt for Tash's killer*. '... but we're under a lot of scrutiny on this case, so let's keep doing our best work out there.'

IT WAS 10AM BY THE time Ruth and Lucy were standing in the reception area of Josh Harriot's tenth floor office at UCA Talent Agency just to the north of Oxford Street in London's West End. His assistant had told them that he would only be five minutes – and that was ten minutes ago.

Ruth moved over to the window and gazed down at the Georgian square below. There were two figures in dark overcoats crossing the square diagonally, walking towards the office block. She saw they were nurses who must have just come off the nightshift. They weren't speaking but they walked close together, shoulders almost touching in a familiar way. Their breath rose as one single cloud of vapour before they disappeared from view.

'Sorry to have kept you,' a voice said. It was Josh Harriot. He was in his early 30s, and dressed in a casual DKNY navy suit. His blonde hair fell down over his forehead and he wore Preppy-style glasses. 'Do you want to follow me?'

He led Ruth and Lucy down a brightly lit corridor and into a small office.

He gestured to the long sofa. 'Please, sit down.'

'Thanks.' Ruth glanced around the room. There were several framed posters of films that she assumed Josh's clients had been involved in. Shelves were littered untidily with scripts and books.

He sat down in a large armchair, peered at them over his glasses, and leaned forward with a sombre face. 'I still can't believe it, you know.'

'How long had you been Tash's agent?' Lucy asked.

'Just over two years. I saw her in one of the final year productions at LAMDA and immediately realised she had something ... Do you have any idea who did this to her?'

Ruth shook her head. 'Not at the moment, I'm afraid. We're trying to build up a picture of Tash and her life.'

Josh ran his hands through his hair and let out a breath. He was still in shock.

'How well did you know Tash?' Lucy asked.

'Erm, pretty well.'

'Were you friends?'

'Yes, I like to think so. We'd meet for a drink after work sometimes or she would pop in here for a coffee and a catch up.'

Lucy looked up from her notepad where she had been taking notes. 'But nothing more than that?'

'God, no,' Josh snorted. 'She was my client and that would have been disastrous.'

Was his reaction a little too adamant?

'When was the last time you saw her?'

'Monday night,' he said. 'You know, when ...'

Ruth could tell it wasn't a sentence that Josh wanted to finish.

'And where was this?'

'At Soho House. It's on Greek Street.'

Ruth nodded. 'Yes, we know it.'

Lucy stopped writing for a second. 'Just the two of you?'

'To start with. A few people came over to say hello.'

'We're going to need a list of everyone who came over and spoke to her while you were there.'

'Of course.'

'What time did Tash leave, or did you leave together?' Ruth asked.

'She had an audition the following morning. I guess she left at around nine.'

'And you?'

'Probably half an hour later.'

'Where did you go?' Lucy asked.

'Oh, I went home. Straight home, I was there by ten.'

'Can anyone verify that?'

'Yes, my wife.'

'As far as you know, did Tash leave on her own?'

'I think so. I didn't see her with anyone else as she was leaving.'

'We have a witness who told us she left with a woman called Barbara York?' Ruth said, her eyebrows raised in question.

'Really?' he asked, a note of incredulity in his voice. 'Barbara York? Are you sure?'

'Why do you ask that?'

He hesitated, clearly not wanting to say more.

Lucy leaned forward. 'Josh? This is a murder investigation so anything, however sensitive, could be really important.'

He seemed anxious. 'I really don't think it's connected.'

He's hiding something from us.

Lucy fixed him with a glare. 'That's for us to decide,' she said stiffly. 'I'm sure you don't want us to think that you are withholding information that might help in a murder case?'

'No, no ... of course not,' he stammered as he ran his hands through his hair again. 'It really doesn't matter. Just forget I said anything.'

'We're police officers, Josh. I get the distinct impression that you're trying to hide something from us. That's not a good idea,' Ruth warned him.

He now had the look of a rabbit caught in headlights. 'This has to be off the record,' he insisted.

Something has really spooked him. He looks genuinely scared, Ruth thought.

Lucy nodded. 'Whatever you tell us is in confidence.'

'Tash was up for a part in a very big Hollywood movie. There was some kind of incident with one of the executive producers over at Goldstein Films.'

'Incident? What kind of incident?' Ruth asked, although she had a very good idea what Josh might be hinting at.

'I guess you might call it a misunderstanding.' He wasn't doing a very good job of getting to the point.

Lucy frowned at him. 'Are we talking about what was called in the old days, *the casting couch?*'

'I don't think it was that explicit. I think the executive producer got his wires crossed.'

'What's his name?' Lucy snapped.

'I can't tell you that or I'll never work again.'

'This man is a film producer, not a mafia boss, right?' asked Ruth.

'Yes, well sometimes it's hard to see a difference,' he replied.

'What's his name, Josh?' Lucy asked again.

He shook his head. 'Sorry, but I just can't tell you that.'

Lucy stood up. 'In that case, I'm taking you back to Peckham police station. And you'll probably need to get yourself a solicitor.'

Josh was clearly startled. 'You can't do that!'

'Oh, but I can. Obstruction in a murder case,' she said forcefully, 'and I'll have to put you in cuffs I'm afraid,' she added, as she gestured to her belt.

'What?' With his eyes darting around the room, Josh squirmed in his chair. 'Okay, okay, but this has to be anonymous,' he babbled anxiously.

Lucy nodded. 'Fine.'

'I'm serious ...' he said, inhaling deeply before adding '... Bob Goldstein.'

Goldstein Films, Ruth thought. *So, not just an executive producer.*

'And what happened?' Lucy pressed.

Josh cleared his throat and shifted in his chair. 'Goldstein took Tash to dinner at The Savoy. He told her he had a big part lined up for her in his next movie. At the end of dinner, he tried to get her to go to his hotel room with him.'

Ruth shook her head. 'Basically she had to sleep with him to get the part?'

'He didn't say that exactly, but that's about the size of it.'

'And she turned him down?' Lucy asked.

'Yes. She agreed to have a drink in his hotel suite but made it very clear that was all it would be. Tash was pretty ballsy when she had to be.'

'What happened?'

'Goldstein sexually assaulted her in the lift on the way up to his room, and Tash left.'

'Jesus!' Lucy exclaimed. 'Did she call the police?'

'No. She didn't know what to do. Goldstein is probably the most powerful film executive in the UK.'

'But she clearly told you what happened?' Ruth asked.

Josh nodded.

'And you didn't tell her to report it to the police?' Lucy asked with more than a hint of scorn.

'Before we had a chance to do anything, his lawyers were on the phone offering Tash money to sign an NDA.'

'A what?'

'A non-disclosure agreement. Goldstein would basically pay Tash money to keep her mouth shut and sign the NDA. If she did say anything, his lawyers would sue her for damages and effectively bankrupt her. Plus, she would probably never work again.'

Lucy and Ruth exchanged a look of disgust.

'Did she sign it?' Lucy asked.

'She was going to. The papers arrived at my office last week ... but then Tash changed her mind.'

'What did she say?'

'She asked me to ring Goldstein's lawyers and tell him to go and fuck himself. Then she said she was going to the tabloids.'

CHAPTER 6

GAUGHRAN AND HASSAN were in Soho at the London offices of the American company, Goldstein Films. They were there to interview Barbara York, but she had kept them waiting for fifteen minutes already. Gaughran wasn't impressed. He glanced down at the glossy magazines on the table in the reception area. There were two Vogue magazines - one with The Spice Girls on the cover, the other with Naomi Campbell - as well as trade magazines such as Variety and Screen International.

With an audible sigh, he got up and helped himself to a plastic cup of cold water from the water cooler which bubbled away noisily in the corner. The water was ice cold but tasted a little of plastic.

On the wall there was a framed photograph of two women with their arms around each other at an awards ceremony. They were holding a gold BAFTA award and smiling at the camera. A caption read, *Barbara York and her partner Lisa Forsythe, at last night's BAFTA awards at London's Albert Hall.*

Gaughran wandered across the reception area. On the walls on either side of a nearby window were framed film posters – *Trainspotting, The English Patient* and *Emma.*

Through the window, he could see across the nearby rooftops and the grey cloud cover that had sucked the colour out of the city skyline. He watched as an ambulance, with siren off and blue lights flashing, turned left from Charlotte Street and then accelerated hard northwards, heading for Oxford Street.

His mobile phone rang and he pulled it out of his jacket pocket. 'DS Gaughran.'

'Tim, it's Ruth. Where are you?'

It sounds urgent, he thought.

'Still waiting to speak to Barbara York. What's wrong?'

'We've just finished with Tash's agent, Josh Harriot. He's claiming that she was sexually assaulted by Bob Goldstein in a lift at The Savoy Hotel.'

Gaughran frowned and lowered his voice. 'Goldstein as in Goldstein Films?'

'Yes. He wanted Tash to have sex with him in exchange for a major role in their next film.'

'Nice,' Gaughran quipped sardonically as he cast his eyes over one of the film posters and saw *Executive Producer Bob Goldstein* at the bottom. 'Did she report it?'

'No. He offered her money to sign a non-disclosure agreement to keep quiet about what had happened. She agreed at first, but last week she told her agent to tell Goldstein to go and fuck himself and said that she was going to the tabloids with the story.'

'Christ!'

'By all accounts, Goldstein is a nasty piece of work.'

'What was Tash doing in a cab with Barbara York on the night she was killed then?' Gaughran asked, lowering his voice further and thinking out loud.

'Exactly,' Ruth agreed.

A woman in her 40s, blonde wavy hair, dressed in a flowing black and gold kimono with red trim appeared. Gaughran recognised her from the photograph on the wall. Barbara York.

'I'd better go,' he said, and ended the call.

The woman gave him a forced smile.

'Hi, hi, I'm so sorry. Having one of those mornings. Please come through.' She was a small, confident ball of energy and her accent was pure New York.

Definitely Jewish, Gaughran thought to himself. Not that he had any prejudice. He had met a lot of horrible and violent people in his job, and race and faith never seemed to be a defining factor in their character or behaviour.

'Thanks,' Hassan said as he got up. He exchanged a look with Gaughran who raised an eyebrow. It was all a long way from their usual interviews in the estates, houses, and flats of south east London.

'Come through, come through,' Barbara said as she ushered them into her office. 'Have you guys been offered coffee or tea or something?'

Gaughran sat down and shook his head. 'We're fine thanks.'

Barbara made herself comfortable in the chair behind her large desk, and before they'd had time to ask her anything she said, 'That poor, poor girl. I can't believe it.'

Hassan looked over at her. 'As I told your assistant, we're from Peckham CID and we're investigating Tash's murder.'

'Yes, of course,' she nodded. 'Anything I can do to help.'

Something about her riled Gaughran. Even though she had said very little, she seemed fake.

He took out his notebook. 'We understand that you saw Tash on Monday night?'

'Yes, that's right,' she said with a solemn expression. 'We shared a taxi south of the river.'

'How well did you know her?' Hassan asked.

'A little, mainly through work. But I've bumped into her a few times in Soho House and we've had a drink together.'

'So, you and Tash had worked together?' Gaughran asked.

'Sort of,' she replied. 'Tash had been on our radar as a bright young British actress. We wanted to find the right project for her. We'd been speaking to her and her agent, and she'd auditioned for a couple of things.'

'Why did you get a cab together?' Gaughran enquired.

'Tash was going to get the tube home. We have a company taxi account, so I told her to get into my cab. I arranged for the driver to take her home after he dropped me off. I thought it would be safer for her.'

'Can you tell us what happened on the journey home?' Hassan asked.

'We just chatted. About a couple of films we'd seen recently and ...' Barbara paused briefly. 'The driver took me home and I told him to take Tash on to where she lived. I just couldn't believe that she was killed that night. It's such a tragedy. I feel sick thinking about it.'

You're not behaving or sounding like a person who feels sick about it, Gaughran thought as he looked at her.

'And this was a black cab?' Hassan asked.

'Yes,' she confirmed.

Gaughran leaned forward. 'If you put the journey on your company account, then I'm guessing we should be able to track down the cab and the driver?'

Barbara shrugged. 'I guess so. If you ask Lara at reception, she can give you the taxi company's name. I'm sure they would have a record of the journey.'

'Thank you.' He spotted Barbara looking at her watch.

'I'm not sure there's anything else I can tell you,' she said.

Gaughran raised an eyebrow. 'I'm surprised that you offered Tash a lift after all that had happened in the last few weeks.'

Barbara considered his comment for a few seconds and then pulled a face. 'Sorry, I don't understand. All that had happened?'

Gaughran could sense Hassan looking at him. He hadn't had time to bring him up to speed with what Ruth had told him so Hassan was in the dark.

'We understand there was an incident between Bob Goldstein and Tash at The Savoy Hotel,' Gaughran clarified, studying Barbara to see how she would react.

'Sorry, but I don't have a clue what you're talking about,' she said, her tone becoming instantly cold and hard.

'Really? That's strange. Because we understand that he sexually assaulted her at The Savoy and wanted her to sign a legal document in exchange for her silence.'

Barbara's face hardened into a glare.

Wow, she didn't like that, he thought in amusement.

'I think that before I say anything else to you, I'm going to get my lawyers here.'

'Okay. I'm just pointing out that Tash had made a threat to go to the papers about what Bob Goldstein had allegedly done to her. And then you were seen in a cab taking her home on the night she was murdered. You can see how that might look?'

Barbara got up from her desk and walked purposefully towards the office door. 'As I said, I'm not prepared to discuss anything with you without my lawyers present. And I would like you to leave, right now.'

Gaughran and Hassan made their way out of the office and went into reception.

Hassan's eyes widened as he asked in a hush, 'What the hell was all that about, Tim?'

Gaughran grinned. 'Ruth tipped me off just before we went in. Do you think she was rattled?'

'Erm, just a little bit,' Hassan replied with a smile.

Gaughran gestured to the receptionist. 'Right, let's get this cab company's number. I'd like to see if the cabbie remembers what they were talking about, and what exactly happened when he dropped Tash home.'

RUTH AND LUCY DROVE slowly down Ruston Mews. The Victorian road was incredibly narrow and Ruth tried to pull the car into a small space front first. The space was marked *No Parking* as it was in front of a blue garage door, but they weren't intending to be very long. They just needed to clarify some of the coincidences that seemed to be surrounding Marcus Jankel and his possible involvement in Tash's murder. As far as Lucy was concerned, Marcus didn't seem like their man. The killer was clearly someone who had watched the television series and was now copying it. No one would be stupid enough to re-enact something they themselves had written, especially when it had then been viewed by nearly eight million people.

'I'll get out,' Lucy suggested, 'And you can reverse park it.'

There was a noise as a front door opened and a rather frosty-looking woman glared at them. 'You can't park there.'

Lucy got out of the car and held up her warrant card as she moved towards the woman. 'We're not going to be long.'

'My disabled husband is due back any time now. He can't walk, so how do you suggest he gets into our garage?'

Lucy turned back to Ruth who then gestured to a parking space at the far end of the mews.

'Sorry ... we'll park down there,' Lucy said with a forced a smile.

As Ruth began to reverse down the mews, Lucy noticed that Marcus was standing at his open front door watching what was going on.

'Parking is a nightmare around here,' he said, and then pointed behind him. 'Do you want to come in? I assume you've come to speak to me?'

'Yes. Thanks.'

'I'll leave the door ajar for your partner. DC Hunter, right?'

Good memory.

'Yes,' she said.

Following him up the stairs, Lucy 'checked out' his body. It was toned and slim, like that of a tennis player.

As they reached the first floor, Marcus smiled at her. 'I've got a pot of coffee on the go, if you'd like one?'

He's a lot friendlier than the last time we were here, she thought. She remembered his dark chestnut eyes that seemed to twinkle with his smile.

'Erm, yes,' she said. 'Why not?'

Going over to the coffee machine, Marcus glanced back at her. 'It's Lucy, isn't it?'

'How do you know that?'

He tapped the side of his nose as he poured a mug of coffee. 'I'm guessing white, no sugar?'

'Are you some kind of mind reader?'

He laughed as he brought the coffee over and handed it to her. 'Something like that.'

Their eyes met for a second as she took the mug from him.

'Thanks.'

He gave a smirk. 'I'm sure we've met somewhere before. I remember your beautiful blue eyes.'

Lucy sat down on the sofa, and he sat in the armchair opposite her. *Is he flirting with me?*

'I doubt it. You're more likely to find me in The Pig & Whistle in Peckham than Soho House.'

He smiled. 'I only go to Soho House for business stuff. I'm well aware it's full of self-seeking, vacuous wankers. The Pig & Whistle sounds nice.'

'Nice? It's really not,' Lucy laughed. 'I don't think it's your kind of pub.'

Marcus looked directly at her and sat forward. 'Sounds like you've judged me already, Lucy? Or is it Luce?'

She wasn't going to answer that. The tone of their conversation was getting way too friendly for someone who was meant to be a murder suspect.

'I'm pretty sure that no one who ever went to Eton has been to 'The Pig & Whistle'.'

'I've been to all sorts of places and met all sorts of people doing research for my scripts,' he explained. 'You'd be surprised at some of the places I've ended up in.'

'There are few things that we need you to clarify for our investigation,' Lucy said, changing the subject.

Marcus reached out and took a cigarette from a packet on the coffee table. He put it in his mouth and let it dangle there for a second before lighting it with his Zippo lighter.

He really is very sexy, Lucy thought.

'Are we back onto police matters now? That's a shame,' he said with a glint in his eye. 'I was enjoying getting to know you. I bet you're real fun when you're off duty, aren't you?'

She shrugged and glanced out of the window. 'It's not really for me to say, is it?' she said.

Ruth's taking her time...

Lucy knew that she was being unprofessional by allowing their conversation to continue in such a manner.

'Well, if you ever want a night out in west London, let me know,' he said as he got up, took a business card from his wallet, and handed it to her.

She took the card. She tried to convince herself that she had taken it so they could contact him about the case. But that's not why he had given her the card - and that's not why she had taken it. Her pulse had quickened when he had handed it to her.

They waited for a few awkward seconds and Lucy noticed a large original framed poster for the 1946 film, *The Postman Always Rings Twice*.

'Film noir classic,' Marcus stated, indicating the poster.

'Is it?' Lucy shrugged.

'You've never seen it?' he asked.

'Nope.'

'It's a film noir classic. A sex-starved wife and her lover plot to kill her husband. Morally very dark. And if you look in the right-hand corner, it's signed by Lana Turner.'

'I've heard of her. Wasn't she in *Peyton Place?*'

He laughed. 'Yes, I'm impressed. No one seems to be interested in old movie stars these days.'

'I used to watch black and white films with my dad on Saturday afternoons,' Lucy explained, and then regretted revealing something so personal.

He studied her for a moment. 'Lana Turner. That's who you remind me of. It's the blonde hair and blue eyes.'

'I don't think so ...' Lucy grimaced, '... but that's better than my old sergeant who used to say I bore an uncanny resemblance to a young Myra Hindley.'

Marcus smiled as he leant forward and flicked the ash off the end of his cigarette. 'Funny guy!'

'Hilarious,' Lucy said dryly. She felt a little uncomfortable at Marcus' comment, but she was also flattered. There was the sound of footsteps and Ruth appeared at the top of the stairs.

Marcus smiled over at her. 'Would you like a coffee? I managed to persuade Lucy to have one. We've just been chatting.'

Ruth shot her a look as if to say *Why the hell did he just call you Lucy?*

'I'm fine, thanks.' Ruth came over and sat next to her. 'Lucy?' she whispered under her breath.

'*I* didn't tell him,' Lucy whispered back.

Ruth took out her notepad. 'There are a few things in our investigation that we need to talk to you about.'

Marcus blew a plume of smoke into the air, sat back, and crossed his legs. He was wearing retro Adidas trainers. 'Okay. Fire away.'

'I watched your television series, 'The Darkness', last night,' Ruth said.

'I hope you enjoyed it,' he said casually as he leant forward and tapped more ash from his cigarette. A splinter of winter sunlight from a small, high window caught the smoke at an angle and made it look like dry ice.

'Not really,' Ruth admitted.

'Oh, that's a shame, although I guess you're surrounded by enough crime and murder in real life.'

She shook her head. 'That wasn't it.'

Marcus appeared confused. Lucy studied his reaction. He didn't seem to know what Ruth was getting at. If he was innocent, then he would have no reason to.

'You wrote about the murder of a young woman. She was strangled with a tie,' Ruth said.

He nodded casually. 'Yes, that's right. End of episode 2.'

'There are more than a few striking similarities between the murder you depicted in your script, and the murder of Tash Weston,' Ruth continued.

Marcus' face fell as he uncrossed his legs and looked at them both. 'What?'

Lucy nodded. 'In fact, it was virtually identical.'

'Oh my God!' he exclaimed as his eyes roamed nervously around the room. 'I don't understand ... I mean ...'

He was clearly lost for words and utterly shell-shocked.

'I'm sorry ... I don't understand why someone would do that? It's so ... weird.'

'We're convinced that these similarities are not coincidental,' Ruth added. 'There was even an Old Etonian tie.'

'What? Really?' Marcus muttered quietly. 'Oh God, you mean someone ... killed her with ... my tie?'

'Your tie?' Lucy asked.

'Yes,' he answered in a virtual whisper. 'I'd left it there the other day when I stayed over. It's the only tie I've got. Tash said she was going to bring it the next time we met.'

'But the tie also appears in your drama?' Ruth asked.

'It seems like a horrible coincidence, but yes,' he replied, sounding a little distraught.

'How do you explain that?'

'I can't, can I?' He leant forward and his brow was furrowed. 'You can't think that I had something to do with what happened to her?'

'Marcus, you don't have an alibi,' Ruth said sternly. 'And you were having a sexual relationship with Tash.'

'Oh my God.' Marcus shook his head in bewilderment. 'I didn't murder Tash. You can't seriously believe that.'

'Whoever killed Tash used every detail that was in your script,' Lucy reminded him.

He reached for another cigarette with shaking hands. 'Hold on. Think about it. I would have to be insane to murder someone in exactly the same way as I'd described in a script.'

Ruth raised an eyebrow. 'Or very arrogant.'

'Come on,' he spluttered. 'I'm not a bloody psychopath ... Someone's setting me up. Surely you can see that?'

Lucy glanced at Ruth – it was definitely another option.

'Do you have any idea who would want to do that?' Lucy asked. Having seen Marcus' reaction to the news, she was convinced that he wasn't involved in Tash's murder. However, she got the feeling from Ruth's demeanour that she wasn't satisfied yet.

He thought for a moment. 'I assume you've spoken to Josh Harriot?'

'Yes,' Ruth confirmed. 'Why?'

'You know he was completely obsessed with Tash?'

Lucy shook her head. 'No. Is that something Tash told you?'

'Yes. She said he was starting to give her the creeps. And of course, Josh went to Eton too.'

Ruth and Lucy exchanged a look – it was interesting news.

'Did you know him?' Lucy asked.

'Yes,' Marcus said with a knowing look. 'We were in the same year.'

Ruth looked at him. 'Were you friends?'

'To start with, but he became a ... I'm not sure how to put it ... a little obsessive.'

'Obsessive?' Lucy asked. 'How do you mean?'

'He seemed to hang on my every word. The other boys called him "The Little Worshipper". It was a bit creepy. If I changed my hairstyle, Josh would copy it within a few weeks. By the time we were in the sixth form, I was barely speaking to him.'

'And since then?'

Marcus shrugged. 'I went to Oxford. He went to Cambridge. And then a few years later we began to bump into each other at film premieres or industry places like Soho House.'

'So how would you describe your relationship with Josh Harriot?' Lucy asked.

'He's an agent and he's asked to represent me on numerous occasions, but I've always turned him down.'

'You said that Josh was obsessed with Tash. How did he feel about her having a relationship with you?'

'I don't think it went down very well,' Marcus admitted and pulled a face. 'He came up to me a few weeks ago in Soho House. He was very drunk and a little bit aggressive.'

'What did he say?'

'He said "For fuck's sake, Jankel. You've got everything in the world, but you don't appreciate any of it."'

CHAPTER 7

HALF AN HOUR LATER, Ruth and Lucy were on the sixth floor of BBC Television Centre. The iconic building was constructed in the 1960s and, due to its circular shape, was known as the doughnut by BBC staff.

'What the hell was all that *Lucy* business back there?' Ruth asked.

Lucy shrugged. 'No idea. I've never told him my name.'

'He acts like he knows you or something.' Even though their second interview with Marcus Jankel had seemed less strange, there was something about him that made Ruth feel uneasy.

'I've never met him before,' Lucy protested. 'We don't exactly move in the same social circles.'

'Well that's true,' Ruth laughed.

'Hey!' Lucy said with mock offence. 'What's that meant to mean?'

'Lucy, have you ever been out with a public schoolboy?'

'No, I don't think I've even been out with anyone with a degree actually. Have you?'

'Once. But then he told me he liked putting things up his bottom when he had sex so I dumped him.'

Lucy giggled. 'Oh my God!'

'There is still something decidedly strange about Marcus Jankel,' Ruth said thoughtfully. 'I've got a strong feeling that he's playing us.'

'Why? You saw his reaction when we told him about the murder in his script being so similar to Tash's murder. He was in total shock.'

'Maybe.' Ruth stared at Lucy for a second.

'What? Have I got a bogey hanging off my nose or something?' Lucy joked.

'You fancy him, don't you?'

'Not really,' Lucy lied.

'Bollocks!'

Lucy pushed a strand of hair away from her face and looked a little coy. 'I think he's sexy, that's all. There's something about him ...'

'For God's sake, Lucy! Just remember that he's a suspect in a murder case, not someone for you to have some silly teenage crush on.'

'Thanks for the lecture, Mum,' she laughed.

As they turned into yet another corridor at the heart of the BBC's documentary department, Ruth spotted a door marked *Film '98* and another that was marked *Barry Norman*. She loved Barry Norman's dry acerbic wit when it came to reviewing the cinema's latest releases, although she hadn't seen the programme in quite some time.

'I've always wanted to come to the BBC TV centre since I was a kid,' Lucy remarked.

Ruth gave a nod of understanding. 'It's one of those places you used to see on Saturday morning TV, isn't it?'

'What was it?' Lucy asked. 'Noel Edmond's 'Swap Shop' or 'Going Live'?

'I used to have a crush on Sarah Green,' Ruth laughed as they turned the corner into a long corridor.

They had managed to track down Janet Harriot, Josh's wife, who was working as a researcher and assistant producer for a BBC series called 'In the Footsteps of Alexander The Great.' During a quick phone call, Janet had told them she was in room 6043 and that she would be expecting them.

Ruth found the door and saw that it was open. A woman, early 30s, blonde and attractive, was sitting at a desk looking through a shooting script.

'Janet Harriot?' Ruth showed her warrant card. 'We spoke earlier?'

'Oh yes,' Janet said, getting up from her desk. 'Come in. Do you want to sit down?'

Home counties girl, Ruth thought.

There were a couple of dark green armchairs and a sofa.

'Thanks,' Lucy said.

'We won't trouble you for long,' Ruth began, 'but we're running a murder investigation, and we'd like to clarify a couple of things face to face.'

'Of course. Anything I can do to help,' Janet said as a dark expression came over her face and she shook her head. 'I couldn't believe it when I heard it on the radio.'

'We spoke to Josh this morning,' Lucy explained. 'Did you know Tash Weston?'

'Not really,' she replied. 'We'd chatted at a couple of parties. She seemed lovely.'

'We're trying to establish a timeline of Tash's movements on the night she was killed,' Ruth said. 'Josh told us he had a drink with Tash in Soho House but then he left and was home by ten.'

A baffled frown formed on Janet's brow. 'Ten?'

'That's what he told us,' Lucy confirmed.

Janet shook her head. 'No. He wasn't home by ten. I don't know why he would have told you that.'

Her whole demeanour began to change as she realised that in her haste to answer truthfully she had also failed to corroborate Josh's alibi.

Ruth fixed her with a gaze. 'Are you sure?'

Janet blinked rapidly as she shifted uncomfortably in her chair. 'Actually, come to think of it, I'm not sure.'

'Well you seemed very certain about it ten seconds ago,' Lucy said accusingly.

'I ... I don't really keep track of ... when he comes in,' she replied, stumbling over her words. 'I was probably watching the telly.'

Why is she lying to us?

Ruth waited a few seconds so that the tension in the office built and Janet felt more uncomfortable.

'Janet, you've just told us that he definitely wasn't home by ten o'clock. But now you've changed your story and you say you can't remember,' Ruth said gently. 'This is a murder investigation. Lying to us about what time Josh came home is a very serious offence.'

Janet bowed her head and fiddled with a ring on her finger. 'I'm sorry ...'

'There's no need to be sorry.' Ruth gave her a sympathetic smile. 'Josh is your husband, but you have to tell us the truth.'

There was a short silence as Janet considered her answer.

'He came home after midnight,' she said, almost under her breath.

'Did you see him?'

'Yes. He fell over downstairs, knocked over a lamp, and woke me up.'

Lucy frowned. 'He fell over?'

'Yes, he was really drunk. I got him off the floor and up onto the sofa but he wasn't making much sense. So I left him there to sleep it off.'

'Is this a regular occurrence?'

'In recent weeks it has been,' Janet said, her face stony. 'Before that, it was very rare.'

'When you say he wasn't making much sense ... what exactly do you mean?' Ruth asked.

She took her time before replying. 'He said he was a terrible husband, and he asked me to forgive him.'

Lucy frowned. 'Forgive him for what?'

'I've no idea.'

RUTH LEANT BACK IN her chair and tapped the biro against her lip. In front of her was a red-top tabloid newspaper from that morning. The papers were running with Tash's murder as a top story. It was obvious why, really. She had been a beautiful, innocent English rose of an actress, well-educated, and brought up in the Home Counties. The fact that she had been murdered in her own home also allowed a more sensational element to the story. Part of Ruth was dismayed by the coverage. It had only been six months since Dyana Robinson, a 21-year-old student from Peckham, had been stabbed in a case of mistaken identity as she walked home from college. Except no-one had ever heard of Dyana Robinson. She lived on an estate, her mother was addicted to crack, and one of her brother's was in prison. None of those were actual factors in her murder, but her lifestyle just didn't suit the newspapers' idea of a compelling, tragic story.

Ruth had already fed back to Brooks about what they'd learned from Marcus Jankel, and now needed to finish updating him on what Jane Harriot had told them. Lucy had made an excuse and had headed over to Forensics. Ruth sensed she was finding that being around Brooks made her feel really uncomfortable – which was understandable.

Brooks came back from the phone call he had taken and sat down next to Ruth's desk. 'Right, where were we?'

'Harriot's alibi,' Ruth reminded him.

'Why would you lie to the police about coming home drunk?' Brooks asked.

'You wouldn't,' Ruth said, 'unless you had something to hide.'

Brooks smoothed his chin with his hand. His face had a slight covering of stubble which was unusual as he was always clean shaven. 'Do you think there's anything in Jankel's claim that Josh Harriot was obsessed with Tash?'

'He painted a pretty dark picture of Harriot.'

Brooks looked at her with a quizzical expression. He had picked up on her uncertainty. 'What are you thinking?'

'I dunno.' She puffed her cheeks and then exhaled. 'I still think that there's something very unnerving about Jankel. Part of me wonders if he's toying with us. And maybe this whole backstory about Harriot is some kind of smokescreen?'

'You think Jankel murdered Tash in the same way as his script to prove how clever he is?'

'Maybe. Lucy doesn't see it like that, but he's definitely up to something. He was in a relationship with Tash, he has no alibi, and he described the exact details of her murder two years ago in a script.'

'What about his claim that he's being set up?'

'He would say that - it's part of his game. He wouldn't be the first killer to try and play games to outsmart the police.'

Ruth had read enough books on the subject, especially when she was a young officer and aspiring to be a detective. Just over a hundred years ago, someone purporting to be Jack the Ripper sent the Metropolitan Police a letter written in red ink, mocking their attempts to find him and enclosing part of a human kidney. In the US, serial killers such as The Zodiac and Son of Sam played out public games of cat and mouse by sending letters to the press taunting the police and providing cryptic clues to their crimes.

Hassan approached. 'Guv, I've done a full PNC check on Josh Harriot. Nothing came up.'

Brooks nodded. 'It doesn't mean he didn't do it, but in my experience murderers of this type have criminal records going back to when they were teenagers. Violence against women or sexual assault.'

'That would put Marcus Jankel out of the frame too then?' Hassan suggested.

Lucy came into the CID office and headed their way.

Brooks was visibly uncomfortable. 'What have you got, Lucy?' he asked, trying to sound breezy but failing miserably.

'Neighbour of Jankel's from Ruston Mews says that she saw him arriving home on Monday at around ten thirty in a black cab. He was alone.'

Ruth shot her a look. 'You sound relieved?'

'No,' Lucy snapped. 'I just said that, unlike you, my instinct is that Marcus Jankel didn't do this. That's all.'

Oops, seem to have touched a nerve.

There was something spiky about the way Lucy delivered this as if she had a point to prove.

'Okay,' Ruth said with a curious frown. 'There's still something a bit creepy about him. But if he really did come home at ten thirty, then he's not a suspect.'

CHAPTER 8

LUCY WAS SITTING ON the sofa staring at the wall. She finished her glass of wine but felt disappointed that she wasn't quite numb enough. She hadn't turned the lights on yet and the growing darkness had slowly erased the colours and contours of her living room. The song *Exit Music (For A Film)* by Radiohead from their album *Ok Computer* was playing with its suitably mournful tone. She wanted to just feel nothing. She closed her eyes and a tear came.

There was a noise from upstairs. Harry was packing away the last of his things, and the wait for him to leave was torture. *Just get your bloody things and go!*

Picking up the remote, Lucy hit the pause button. She needed music to change her mood, not allow her to wallow in pain and self-pity. She got up from the sofa and flicked through her CD collection. What could she play that would just lift her spirits?

Stevie Wonder's *Songs in the Key of Life*. Perfect.

The Latin-style dance rhythms of *Another Star* began and her feet started to move to the music. Dancing. That's what she needed. To go out, drink, and dance the night away. She couldn't remember the last time she'd danced. Unlike Ruth, the whole 90s dance music thing had passed her by.

The sounds of footsteps coming down the stairs drew her attention to the hallway. She turned to see Harry appear in the doorway.

'I think that's everything,' he said.

God, it was so sad to see him with his stuff packed. It only seemed like yesterday that she had helped him to unpack his boxes and suitcase. She had taken the piss out of his Pringle jumpers, which she'd said were the preserve of retired golfing businessmen.

'Okay.' She swallowed and tried to smile.

'I'll see you in the morning then?'

Lucy nodded and then asked, 'What are we going to do?'

'Do about what?'

'I don't think we can carry on working in the same CID office together, do you?'

'I've put in for a transfer,' he said, speaking softly.

He hadn't said anything about this before and it took the wind out of her sails.

Lucy's voice faltered. 'Oh right. You didn't say anything.'

'I spoke to the Super this afternoon. If I'm honest, I could do with a change. There's a DCI position coming up in Guildford.'

'Guildford?' she asked. Guildford was an affluent town in the heart of Surrey. It couldn't be more of a contrast to Peckham.

He gave a wry smile. 'I know. I won't know what to do with myself. But maybe that's okay for a while.'

There were a few seconds of poignant silence. Harry was going and in a few weeks he would be in Surrey and she would never see him again. This was the man she thought

THE IMITATION OF DARKNESS

she was going to build a life and family with. How had it all gone so wrong?

With tears streaming down her face, Lucy nodded. 'Yeah, well you've always been a bit of social climber, Harry.'

He laughed before reaching down to pick up his suitcase from the floor. 'Take care of yourself, Luce. Okay?'

She forced a smile as Harry turned away, headed for the front door, and left.

Looking at the bottle of red wine beside her, Lucy could see there was about a quarter left inside.

Fuck it!

She lifted the bottle, put it to her lips, and chugged it down. The warmth of the alcohol radiated in her stomach.

She grabbed her phone. Maybe she should ring Ruth? Or maybe her mum? There again, she wasn't in the mood for a supportive, tearful chat.

For a moment, her mind turned to Marcus Jankel. His dark brown eyes, high cheekbones and full lips. She would do anything to tumble into bed with him right now and forget everything.

She got up from the sofa, went over to her jacket and retrieved Jankel's business card. In her head, she rationalised why she was thinking about contacting him. Now that a neighbour had confirmed seeing him arrive home at 10pm, he had an alibi for the time of the murder. It was the right thing to do to let him know.

She composed a very short text – *Hi Marcus. I thought I should let you know that a neighbour has confirmed that you arrived home at around 10pm on Monday 26th January. If we* *have any more questions, or information we need for our investigation, we'll be in touch. Kind regards, DC Lucy Henry.*

As soon as the text was sent, she wondered if it was the right thing to have done. It wasn't the first time she had sent a text to someone during a case. It was more usual to phone them directly from work.

Her phone buzzed almost immediately.

It was a message from Marcus.

Hi Luce! I've got an alibi. That's good news. I've been terrified all day. You'll never guess where I am? I'm in the Pig & Whistle on Peckham High Street. I've just had a drink with a very dubious ex-con as research for a film I'm writing. Small world! Are you free for a drink? I'll be here for another hour if you want to meet up. Marcus

She read the message again and then put the phone down on the arm of the sofa.

RUTH SLUMPED DOWN AND began to watch the BBC news. She had left Ella and Koyuki playing noisily in the bath. There was a pizza in the oven for their tea so she had a few minutes to catch up on what was going on in the world.

The BBC newscaster, dressed in a navy jacket and tie, looked at the camera and said:

In Washington, Hilary Clinton defended her husband against allegations that he had an affair with White House intern, Monica Lewinsky, claiming that it was part of a 'vast right-wing conspiracy' against President Clinton ever since he first ran for office. She said that she and her husband had been accused of virtually everything during his political career.

The timer on the oven buzzed and, as she made her way to collect some plates, she wondered how Hilary Clinton could stay with her husband. Clinton had already been sued by Paula Jones in 1994. Ruth remembered that Jones was an employee of some kind of industrial commission. She alleged that Clinton had exposed himself and propositioned her at a political conference in Little Rock. They settled out of court. Ruth was 99% convinced that Lewinsky was telling the truth about her affair with the President and it was probably only the tip of the iceberg. Was Hilary Clinton so seduced by the power and glamour of being First Lady that she was happy to be publicly humiliated by her philandering husband?

A wave of heat hit her face as she opened the oven door and pulled out the baking tray with the large ham and pineapple pizza bubbling at its centre. It was the girls' favourite. Ruth thought that putting pineapple on a pizza was a crime. She cut the pizza into fingers and yelled, 'Right girls. Time to get out of the bath!'

Once she arrived in the bathroom, it was a chaotic whirl of towels, talc, clean pyjamas and dressing gowns.

Ella and Koyuki sat down excitedly at the table and began to grab slices of pizza.

Ruth laughed. 'Hey, you'd swear that you two hadn't been fed for a week.'

Something came onto the television that was making the girls giggle. Some Australian soap where two teenagers were snogging each other's faces off.

Moving swiftly for the remote, Ruth turned off the television with a smile. 'Well, we don't want to be seeing that when we're eating, do we girls?' she joked.

Ella grinned and said loudly, 'They were snogging!'

What did she say?

'Ella!' Ruth exclaimed, trying to sound serious but stifling laughter. 'Where did you hear that word?'

'Nicola Pritchard says it,' Ella replied, now with pizza on her face.

'She does. All the time,' Koyuki added with a serious expression.

'Well, let's try not to use that word, okay?'

'Why not? It's what my mummy and daddy do,' Koyuki said with a frown.

What?

'I don't think they do anymore,' Ruth said with a puzzled expression.

'No, they do.' Koyuki then nodded as she pulled the cheese off the pizza and ate it. 'They were doing snogging yesterday.'

Ella burst out laughing and Koyuki put her hands to her face and giggled.

How the hell could they have been snogging?

Ruth felt sick. 'Are you sure?'

Koyuki nodded. 'Yes. Yesterday. And last week when they were in bed.'

THE IMITATION OF DARKNESS

THE HEAT AND CIGARETTE smoke were intense as Lucy made her way across the main bar in The Pig & Whistle pub, which was about ten minutes' walk from her home. There had been live Premiership football on the television and the pub was crowded with groups of men nursing pints of lager. She scoured the seats and tables but there was no sign of Marcus. Maybe he had left? She realised that she felt disappointed.

She had changed her top, done her hair and applied some make-up, and put on Calvin Klein Obsession perfume. She had even opted to wear heels, even though she hated walking further than the end of the road in them.

God, what would Ruth say if she knew I was here? What would Harry say? They would both go mental.

Lucy didn't care. She was drunk and emotional and she wanted some male attention to distract herself and maybe even boost her self-esteem a bit. Marcus wasn't technically a suspect anymore now that he had been given an alibi by the neighbour who lived across the mews from him.

Looking into the far corner, she saw dark chestnut eyes twinkling at her.

Marcus.

He gave her a sexy grin and got up from the table as she approached. 'Evening officer. What do you want to drink?'

'Ha, ha … Vodka, lime and tonic,' Lucy said as she took off her coat and put it over the back of the wooden chair.

'Large one, I assume?' he asked, but he had disappeared into the sea of customers beside the bar before she had time to respond.

She sat down and pulled in her chair.

Where is the man he claimed he was meeting for a drink? It's strange that I've told him that my local is The Pig & Whistle and now he's here, miles from Notting Hill.

Even in her drunken haze, she wondered if Marcus had come to the pub just to meet her? However, he couldn't have known she was going to text him – so it had to be just coincidence. Didn't it?

'Here you go.' He put a drink down in front of her. 'Large VAT.'

'What was that from?' she asked, remembering the saying from some 1980s television series.

'Minder ... Arthur Daley.'

'I didn't have you down as someone who watched Minder,' Lucy commented as she sipped her drink.

Marcus raised an eyebrow. 'No? You think I'm some elitist public school boy who has never sullied himself with working class culture?'

'I guess you wouldn't be in here if that were true,' Lucy said. 'Where's your dubious ex-con?'

He laughed. 'I think the technical term is that he scarpered.'

'Why's that?'

'I told him you were coming and that you were a copper,' he said with a grin.

'What were you meeting him for?' She noticed Marcus' hands as he stubbed out his cigarette. He had long fingers and an old-fashioned signet ring on the pinkie of his left hand.

'I've been commissioned to write a film,' he replied. 'It's about a CID detective who goes to prison for a crime he didn't commit.'

'And your contact has been inside?'

Marcus nodded. 'Oh yeah. He knows everything there is to know about prisons.'

'What did he do?'

'He murdered his wife,' he said casually as he sipped an inch off what appeared to be a pint of bitter.

'You're kidding?'

He shook his head. 'No. Slit her throat and buried her under the patio at their house in Croydon in the early 80s.'

'Charming.'

'That's the funny thing. You would never know he was capable of that if you met him. But that's like most of the criminals that I meet.'

'We have that in common then,' Lucy declared raising her glass. 'Spending time with criminals.'

'Indeed we do.' He laughed and clinked his glass against hers. 'It was very kind of you to text me.'

Lucy shrugged. 'I didn't want you to sit worrying all night.'

'Which is what I've been doing. Even five pints of Old Speckled Hen wasn't really doing the trick.'

'I'm sorry about what happened to Tash. It must be very hard for you?'

Marcus paused briefly before he answered. 'I know this is going to sound very weird, but we weren't very close. We met for sex and not much more. I didn't know very much about her and she didn't want to know much about me. And that's the way it worked.'

Lucy raised her shoulders in acceptance. 'Hey, two consenting adults so I'm not judging.'

He looked at her with a glint in his eye and she felt a tingle of excitement. 'You know, you've inspired me to start developing another series.'

'What's it about?' she asked, clearly flattered by his comment.

He grinned. 'A female detective in South London.'

'Ha, ha.' Lucy rolled her eyes. 'Very funny.'

'I'm serious - she's the complete antithesis to Jane Tennison in Prime Suspect.'

He's not joking then.

'How do you mean?'

'She's warm, caring and empathetic. She really cares about the cases she works on,' he explained. 'The problem with DI Tennison as a character is that she had to essentially become a man to succeed as a detective. My character uses her strengths as a woman to be a better detective than the men she works with. She's not willing to compromise her emotional attachment to the cases she works on. *But* that gives her an edge over her male colleagues. She's a better copper *because* she's a woman.'

Oh wow. What a great pitch! Lucy thought as she felt a growing swell of attraction towards him.

'What happens to her?' Lucy asked as she finished her drink.

'She falls for the wrong man,' he said with a sexy grin.

'Why is he the wrong man?'

He looked her directly in the eyes. 'Because he ends up murdering her,' he answered, his face devoid of expression.

For a second, Lucy felt a chill run up her spine. *What the hell did he say that for? That was really weird.*

He burst into laughter. 'I'm joking! Oh my God, you should see your face.'

He reached over and put his hand on hers.

'You tosser!' she laughed.

Marcus kept his hand on hers, and Lucy basked in his admiring gaze. 'I really don't know what happens to her. I just think she's a really interesting character and I want to get to know her better.'

THE 3-WOOD SMACKED against the ball and it sailed away down the driving range. Gaughran squinted as it landed and then bounced down the fairway.

Two hundred yards. Nice one!

He had been at the GT Golf Driving Range in Camberwell for over half an hour. It was the perfect place to get rid of some stress by whacking golf balls. It was either that or head to the pub, and he'd been doing too much of that recently. His waistline had increased in recent months so he was trying to have lager-free weekdays.

In the old days, he would have been on the driving range at the Dulwich and Sydenham Golf Course, but that's where his father spent half his life. After their falling out, he wasn't going to chance bumping into him by accident. However, he couldn't help but feel a pang of sadness when remembering the laughs he, his Uncle Les, and his dad used to have when playing a quick round of golf before heading to the club house bar to tell war stories of their time on the force.

As the wind picked up, Gaughran glanced around. His navy Nike windbreaker was zipped up and kept out the cold. Nights like these were a good time to come to the driving range. It was virtually empty and much better than when the weather was good and you had to book a half hour slot.

With the Dunlop golf ball held carefully between his thumb and forefinger, he leant down and placed it on the rubber tee mat. He was about to exchange his 3-wood for a 3-iron.

'Bloody hell!' exclaimed a voice. 'I came down here so I wouldn't see anyone I know.'

It was his Uncle Les.

Gaughran had hardly seen his uncle in recent months, although there was no implication that he blamed his nephew for what had happened.

'Me too,' he said with a grin, but in reality he was glad to see him.

'I was watching you drive with that wood,' Les chortled. 'Bloody hell, Tim, you must have been practising a bit 'cos I've never seen you hit a golf ball that straight before.'

'Oh, well that's very bloody encouraging. Ta,' he said with a laugh. The fact that his uncle had bothered to stand and watch him for a while had cheered him up.

Les gave him a meaningful look. 'You okay? Keeping all right?'

'Yeah, you know.'

Les lowered his voice and asked, 'What do you know about this actress that was murdered?'

'Not a lot yet, but it wasn't some lover's tiff that went wrong. He sat on her back and strangled her with a tie.'

'Bloody hell, I'm guessing you're getting pressure from the top brass to find someone?'

'Our guv'nor is pretty good at shielding us from all that. But it's very weird to see the case we're working every time I go past a news stand.'

There were a few awkward seconds – he wanted to ask Les about his dad.

'You seen Dad?'

Les nodded. 'Played golf yesterday. Took a monkey off him but serves him right.'

'What am I meant to do, Les? Is he just not gonna speak to me for the rest of his fucking life?'

'Give him time, eh?'

'Give him time? He's the one in the wrong. He's acting like I fitted him up or something. He was the one on the fiddle.'

'You know what he's like, Tim. He's a proud man, and deep down he's embarrassed.'

'Can't you tell him he's acting like a twat?'

'I have. On numerous occasions. He's like a little boy who got told off and is having a sulk.'

'Yeah, well it's not doing Mum any good is it? He needs to fucking grow up a bit and think of someone other than himself and his great big ego.'

'Let me have a word with him, eh?'

'Yeah, that would be good, thanks.'

Les walked over and took the club from him. 'I noticed something when I was watching you swing. I think your grip is about an inch too high when you're driving. If you dropped it a bit, the ball wouldn't go so high, and it would go further.'

Gaughran nodded as he took back the club. 'Cheers.'

'Give it a go and I'll have a watch.' Les took a couple of steps back.

Gaughran addressed the ball and readjusted his grip.

CHAPTER 9

LUCY AND MARCUS TURNED into her road. He had insisted on walking her home as it was dark, although she had pointed out she was a police officer. Overhead were the twinkling red and white lights of a distant 747 descending towards Heathrow further west.

Lucy gestured to a boarded-up house that had been graffitied. 'Bit different to Notting Hill.'

'I guess,' he said with a shrug. 'Ladbroke Grove can be pretty moody at night though.'

They passed a small Catholic church, the light from the entrance bathing the pavement. The church was squeezed between a small office block and a car park. There was little to show that it was a place of worship. The building became narrower towards the roof where there was an apology of a spire.

Marcus stopped. 'This your local then?' he joked.

'I am Catholic,' Lucy explained, 'but very lapsed. You?'

'Jewish,' Marcus said as they continued walking down the road. 'Not practising though. Jankel is a Jewish name. It comes from the Hebrew name, Jacob.'

'You grew up in Germany, didn't you?'

Marcus raised an eyebrow. 'Someone's been doing their research. Yes, I grew up just outside Frankfurt.'

'But you don't have an accent?'

'I was sent over here to boarding school when I was ten. I stayed until I graduated from university, so I lost my accent.'

'Ten? What was that like?'

'Fine. I mean it left me insecure, emotionally unavailable with abandonment issues, but apart from that, I'm relatively unscarred.'

Lucy laughed as they stopped outside her house. 'Hey, at least you can laugh about it.'

He grinned. 'That's when I'm not drinking and crying on my own at night.'

Briefly, they stared into each other's eyes.

'Right, I'd better go.' Lucy gestured to her front door. 'And I'm not inviting you in, just in case you were wondering.'

'Don't worry, I already knew you were going to say that.'

'How?'

'I'm a writer. And I'm basing my latest character on you, so now I'm tuned in, I know what you're thinking.'

'Oh yeah?' Lucy said flirtily. 'What am I thinking right now?'

'You're wondering what you're going to do if I try and kiss you goodnight. It's a bit weird because up until today I was a suspect in a murder case. But now I have a watertight alibi and you've spent some time with me, you can see that I'm not actually a psychopath.'

How did he know that? He is so attractive.

'Oh really?' She rolled her eyes. 'You've got it all worked out, haven't you?'

'I'm normally pretty good at this,' he said with a conceited smile.

His arrogant confidence was making him sexier by the minute.

'Okay, well I'm not going to kiss you.' Lucy took her keys out of her pocket. 'And I'm going to say goodnight.'

'You think we could do some more research for my series?'

'Maybe,' Lucy said raising an eyebrow. 'That depends.'

'Depends on what?'

She studied his face which was lit by a nearby streetlamp.

Moving closer, she put her hand to his cheek and kissed him softly on the lips. He responded as their kiss became more passionate and urgent.

With a beaming smile, she moved away and smiled at him. 'It depends on whether you're a good kisser. And you are, so I guess the answer is yes.'

CHAPTER 10

Thursday 29th January

RUTH SIGNED HER NAME at the bottom of a witness statement and put it back in the relevant folder. She had come in early, not only to break the back of mounting paperwork, but also because she hadn't slept well. Koyuki's comment about her mum and dad snogging had played over and over in her mind. Was Shiori really getting back with her husband? She had always been adamant that she hated his guts for the affair he'd had with his assistant, and had described him as a selfish dickhead. Maybe she shouldn't read too much into what Koyuki had said. She was only five after all. That was both the beauty and the problem with small children. They told the truth with no filter and no thought of the repercussions. The world was black and white. Truth and lies. And if something was true, what was the harm in saying it?

She had recently taken Ella shopping to the supermarket in Balham. As Ruth had wheeled the shopping trolley past the security guard on the door, Ella had pointed at him from where she was sitting in the trolley and said, 'He's a black man, Mummy. He's a black man.' Ruth had wanted the earth to swallow her up as she told Ella to be quiet. The security guard had roared with laughter and said, 'Hey, it's true. I am a black man.' Kids, God love them!

Watching Lucy return from the photocopier, Ruth wondered what was going on. She was acting very strangely this morning and seemed to be avoiding her. She didn't know if it was something to do with her failing relationship with Brooks. Ruth knew that he had moved the last of his things out of the house last night but she had expected Lucy to come and talk to her about it rather than avoid her.

Just before 9am, the doors to the CID were pushed open by Brooks as he strode in carrying an armful of files. 'Okay everyone, if we can settle down. We've got lots to get through this morning.'

He walked over to the scene boards. 'I'm just going to run through what we know about Tash's final movements on the evening she was killed. At around six o'clock she had a drink with her agent, Josh Harriot, at Soho House. They were joined by her on-off boyfriend Marcus Jankel at around seven, but he left them together at about eight. During the evening, various other people came over to say hello but we're still waiting for a list of them from Josh Harriot. Tash was seen leaving Soho House at around nine with Barbara York. They got into a taxi together. The taxi dropped York in Battersea and continued onto Peckham, where we assume Tash was dropped home at around ten. No one saw her arrive home. She then had sex with someone who strangled her, probably before midnight. Her body was discovered when her friend Jane Sinclair came to pick her up the following morning for an audition.' Brooks nodded to himself and looked at his team. 'I assume that her mobile phone is still missing?'

'Yes,' Gaughran said, 'but we've tracked down the account and she was with Orange.'

'Can they check if anyone has used the phone since Monday night?'

'No one's used it, Guv.'

'I'd like a call log for the last few weeks to see any numbers she was calling regularly and whether she called anyone on the night she was murdered.'

'I've got her bank and credit card statements,' Hassan said. 'Nothing unusual. The last transaction was a round of drinks at Soho House on Monday evening at eight thirty, which fits our timeline.'

'Right, what's the latest with Josh Harriot?' Brooks asked.

Ruth glanced at her notebook. 'Harriot lied to us about the time he arrived home from Soho House. He told us that he was home by ten. His wife, Janet, told us that he came home after midnight, that he was very drunk and upset, ranting and apologising.'

'Any reason why he might have lied to us?'

'I can't see one.'

Lucy signalled to speak. 'Marcus Jankel told us that Harriot was obsessed with Tash and wasn't very pleased that she and Marcus were in some kind of relationship.'

'Yeah, in fact he made some veiled drunken insult to Jankel recently,' Ruth added.

Brooks moved closer to the boards and pointed at the scene of crime photos. 'It strikes me that whoever murdered Tash was either a psychopath who had seen the television drama and copied it, or someone who wanted to put Jankel in the frame for the murder.'

'Are we ruling Jankel out as a suspect at the moment?' Hassan asked.

Brooks glanced at Gaughran. 'How viable was the neighbour who saw him arriving home at ten o'clock?'

'She seemed reliable, Guv. She's young, and works as a chiropractor from home. From what I can tell, there's no reason for her to lie about seeing Jankel arriving home at that time.'

As Ruth looked at the photo of Josh Harriot on one of the scene boards, something occurred to her. 'Guv, aren't we missing something here?'

'What's that?'

'We're 99% certain that Tash was having sex with whoever murdered her, aren't we?'

'Yes.'

'If we're looking at Josh Harriot as a suspect, then Tash must have decided to have sex with him the night she was killed. But Jankel told us that she was finding Harriot's behaviour around her increasingly creepy. That doesn't add up, does it?'

'Fair point,' Brooks said.

Gaughran shrugged. 'Pity shag?'

Ruth shook her head. 'I don't buy it.'

'Neither do I,' Lucy agreed. 'He's her agent, and she knows that he's got some crazy crush on her. If she shags him, she makes the whole thing a hundred times worse.'

'She's an actress,' Gaughran said. 'In the old days, actress was another word for prostitute.'

Ruth rolled her eyes. Gaughran was reverting back to type again. 'That's very enlightened of you, Tim.'

'It's my view that actors and actresses have super-sized egos but they're also incredibly needy with low self-esteem,' he explained. 'That's why they're so promiscuous.'

'Bloody hell, Tim!' Ruth laughed. 'Since when were you Dr Freud?'

Brooks was deep in thought as he studied the scene boards again. 'What if Josh Harriot rang Tash. He told her that he needed to speak to her urgently. Maybe it's something to do with this whole Bob Goldstein thing. Harriot turned up on her doorstep and he was drunk. He confessed that he had feelings for her. One thing led to another. They took drugs and had sex.'

Ruth added, 'And what if Tash said something demeaning. She told Harriot that it was a pity shag, or it was a one-time thing. Maybe she mentioned Marcus Jankel. Harriot flipped. If he couldn't have her, no one could, and he killed her.'

'It fits as a hypothesis,' Brooks said, 'but at the moment we have no evidence to even put Harriot in her flat.'

Hassan glanced over. 'And if Harriot had been to her flat before, then that screws forensics unless we get something totally incriminating.'

'Okay,' Brooks agreed. 'Ruth, Lucy, pull Harriot in for a voluntary interview. How are we doing with forensics from the crime scene Hassan?'

'Still waiting, Guv.'

'We need Harriot's mobile phone and phone records.'

Gaughran gestured to some papers. 'Guv, we've just got the records for Tash Weston's landline. It's itemised.'

'Anything stand out?'

'Last phone call received was ten thirty the night she was killed. A three-minute call from a mobile phone.'

'Right Tim, cross-check that with any phones Josh Harriot might own. Ruth, did you guys get anywhere with this dispute with Bob Goldstein?'

'Harriot told us that Tash had agreed to sign a non-disclosure agreement with Bob Goldstein and his lawyers. They were going to pay her cash for keeping her mouth shut about him sexually assaulting her. There was also a suggestion that she would get a lead part in one of his films.'

'So why did she change her mind?'

'We don't know. But she told Harriot to tell Goldstein's lawyers that she had changed her mind about signing the NDA and would be going to the tabloids with her story.'

'Any idea what his response was?'

'No, it was left that the lawyers were going to pass her response onto him.'

'And then she was killed. That seems very convenient for Goldstein.'

'Except that Tash would not have been having consensual sex with Bob Goldstein,' Lucy pointed out.

'Why not?' Gaughran asked. 'He's a powerful film producer. I thought that's how the industry works?'

'She'd already had the chance to go to his hotel room and sleep with him at The Savoy, the night he assaulted her. Having just threatened to go to the tabloids with the story, why would she decide to have sex with him? Plus, have you seen Bob Goldstein?'

Gaughran shook his head. 'Do I take it that he is no oil painting?'

'Put it this way, I've seen more attractive gargoyles on St Stephen's Church roof round the corner,' Lucy quipped.

There was laughter from some of the detectives.

Ruth nodded. 'Goldstein is a very large, slightly sweaty, very unattractive middle-aged man. And Tash was about to expose him as a sexual predator. In fact there's a chance that there might have been criminal charges brought against him.'

Brooks rubbed his chin thoughtfully. 'You're right, it doesn't add up. But Tash's death is incredibly fortunate timing for Goldstein – and that doesn't sit comfortably with me. Tim, what did Barbara York have to say for herself?'

'Not a lot. As soon as I revealed what I knew about Goldstein, the NDA and Tash's threats, she refused to talk to us without a lawyer present.'

'Anyone speak to the cabbie who took Tash home from Soho?' Brooks asked.

'Still trying to track him down,' Hassan said. 'The cab was on the Goldstein Films' account so we should be able to find him.'

'Okay. I think that even though Bob Goldstein had a lot to gain from Tash's death, it's unlikely she was attacked by him. The sex she had was consensual so that effectively rules him out.' Brooks gestured to the boards again. 'And we still have our mystery stalker man that Tash had reported seeing. Anyone got anything on him yet?'

Gaughran shook his head. 'Still waiting for the station and council CCTV to come through, Guv. I'll chase it.'

The phone rang and Hassan answered it quietly.

'Thanks, Tim. Normally we could have ruled out a total stranger, but the comment Tash made to Jane about dragging in some handsome stalker concerns me. I think we need to find him, even if it is just to eliminate him from our enquiries.'

'Guv,' Hassan said. 'That was the results of Tash Weston's preliminary PM and the tox report.'

Brooks frowned. 'Anything come up?'

'There were no traces of vaginal penetration.'

'So, she didn't have sex with the person who killed her, or anyone else that night?'

'No, Guv. However, she did have high traces of Flunitrazepam in her bloodstream.'

'And do we know what that is?'

'It's essentially medical grade Rohypnol.'

Brooks eyes widened. 'So, she was drugged?'

It was a very significant development.

'Yes, Guv.' The pathologist told me the percentage concentration in her blood indicates that she was probably unable to move when she died.'

'She was paralysed?' Lucy asked to clarify.

Hassan nodded.

'Jesus,' Brooks said, shaking his head.

Ruth looked over. 'Do we have any idea how long it takes from being taken to reaching its full effect?'

'She would have started to feel the effects twenty to thirty minutes after she had taken it,' Hassan explained, 'but apparently it doesn't reach its peak until two hours after ingestion.'

'Which means that if someone spiked her drink just before she left Soho House,' Ruth said, thinking out loud, 'she might not have felt the full effect of it until ten thirty or eleven that night.'

Brooks nodded. 'Unfortunately, that does mean that anyone in Soho House on Monday evening could have put something in her drink.'

'And if they knew that two hours later she would be nearly incapacitated, they could have gone to her flat, forced their way in, and killed her,' Lucy suggested.

Brooks took a few seconds and then said, 'Okay. That really does change the focus of our investigation.'

CHAPTER 11

LUCY AND RUTH WENT out of the CID office and headed for the back staircase. They were still trying to get their heads around the fact that Tash had been drugged and that she hadn't had sex with anyone. They now had to question many of the conclusions they had drawn about the case.

'That means that Josh could have spiked Tash's drink, waited for an hour, and then gone round there,' Lucy said thinking out loud.

'Maybe he thought if she'd had some kind of disinhibiting drug, she would be more open to his advances,' Ruth suggested.

'And if he arrived and she rejected him, he killed her and then decided to try to frame Marcus - which suggests pre-meditation,' Lucy said. It was strange mentioning Marcus' name in the context of the investigation. Ever since she had woken that morning, she hadn't stopped thinking about him and their kiss. She felt an exciting tingle every time she thought about it.

They reached the bottom of the stairs and turned right into a long corridor.

'You all right this morning?' Ruth asked. 'You seem a bit quiet.'

'Yeah, of course.' She knew full well that she was avoiding Ruth. They had the kind of relationship where they told each other everything, and Ruth could read her like a book. There was no way she could tell her that she had met Marcus for a drink, let alone about the flirting and the kiss. Ruth would be furious. Marcus had been a suspect in a murder case and she knew that Ruth thought there was something creepy or even dangerous about him. She couldn't see it. In fact, if anything, she thought he had a little-boy-lost feeling about him. Despite his dry humour, she had seen it in his eyes when he'd talked about his time at boarding school.

'Sure?' Ruth asked. 'I know that Harry moved his last bits out last night. That must have been horrible?'

'Yeah, it was. I drank a bottle of wine and went to bed early.'

'Oh right. I was half expecting a phone call.'

'To be honest, I'm done talking about mine and Harry's problems. No offence, but I just don't want to think about it.'

Ruth gave her a sympathetic smile as they headed for Interview Room 1. 'No, of course. I can understand that.'

'I'm just going to keep myself busy with this case.' Lucy hoped that she hadn't come across as brusque. They walked in silence for a few seconds and then she asked, 'Do we think Josh Harriot is our prime suspect?'

Ruth nodded. 'If we believe what Marcus Jankel told us, then he has motive. He lied about where he was at the time of the murder.'

Brooks appeared coming down the corridor – he was heading their way.

'Something wrong, Guv?'

'Phone call from Soho House. They've checked their records. Josh Harriot got them to call a cab at nine o'clock on Monday evening.'

'Do they have details of where it was going?'

'Just noted as South London.'

'If he left Soho at nine but didn't arrive home until gone midnight, where was he for those three hours?'

Lucy avoided eye contact with Brooks as she gestured to the interview room. 'Let's go and find out.'

'Thanks, Guv,' Ruth said.

They arrived at Interview Room 1, opened the door and went in. An hour earlier, they had picked up Josh Harriot and explained that they would like to take him to Peckham police station for a voluntary interview. He had seemed terrified and offered virtually no resistance to their request. Lucy wondered if he was struggling with a guilty conscience.

Lucy and Ruth sat down opposite Josh. Next to him was his solicitor, a middle-aged man, balding, and wearing glasses. They had explained to Josh that he didn't need a solicitor for a voluntary interview but it seemed he had decided to get one anyway.

'Hi Josh,' Ruth said as she pulled in her chair and put the case files down in front her.

He nodded, his eyes flitting nervously around the room.

'You understand that although you have not been arrested or charged with any offence, you are under caution. And that means anything you say in this interview can be used as evidence in a court of law?'

Josh glanced quickly at his solicitor. 'Yes.'

Lucy leaned over and pressed the record button on the tape machine. 'Interview at Peckham police station. Interview Room 1, 29th January, 11.50am. Present are Joshua Harriot, his legal counsel Mr Edward Barnes, Detective Constable Ruth Hunter, and myself, Detective Constable Lucy Henry.'

There was silence for the next few seconds while Lucy and Ruth flicked through the case files in front of them. It allowed the tension to build and for Josh's already frayed nerves to get the better of him so that, hopefully, he would tell them the truth.

'Josh,' Ruth said gently. 'Can you tell us about your exact movements on the evening of Monday 26th January?'

Josh ran his hand through his blond hair and stifled a sigh. 'I went to Soho House for a drink at about six.'

'Were you meeting anyone in particular there?' Lucy asked.

'Yes, I was meeting Tash Weston, who was a client of mine.'

'Why were you meeting her?'

'As I've ... explained in great ... depth to you already ...' he stuttered, '... Tash had been asked to sign an NDA with Bob Goldstein.'

'Which she had decided not to sign?' asked Ruth.

'Yes. I wanted her think about the consequences of taking on a man like him.'

'So, you met her to try and persuade her to sign the NDA?'

'I suppose so, yes.'

'What did she say?'

'She was adamant that she wasn't going to sign it, and told me that she had talked to her publicist about approaching tabloid newspapers with the story.'

Lucy leant forward in her seat. 'And you felt that was a dangerous thing to do?'

'Yes. I told her it was professional suicide.'

'Were you worried that this was going to ruin your career too?'

Josh shifted uncomfortably in his seat. 'I ... I don't know. Yes. Goldstein Films are big players and very powerful. Tash was my client.'

'So, her decision to go to the papers was effectively going to damage your career?'

Josh lowered his eyes to the floor, his left leg jigging nervously. 'Yes. You could put it like that.'

'You must have been angry with her for not taking your advice?' Lucy suggested.

Josh scratched his face as he shook his head. 'No. I thought it was a brave thing to do. It was the right thing to do after what had happened.'

'You just told us it was professional suicide, Josh. Which one was it?'

'Both. It was ... brave ... but naïve.'

Lucy could see that they weren't going to get him to admit that he was angry with Tash.

'How would you describe your relationship with Tash?' Ruth asked.

'What do you mean? I was her agent.'

Lucy looked up from the pad where she was taking notes. 'Were you friends, or was it just an agent-client relationship?'

'I'd like to think we were friends,' he replied.

'So, you were close?'

Josh frowned. 'What does that mean?'

'Were you attracted to her?' Lucy asked.

'No,' he snapped, 'I told you that when you came to my office. Tash and I were friends and that was it. I'm happily married.'

Ruth and Lucy exchanged a look – it didn't seem like they were going to get anywhere with their current line of questioning.

'What time did you have drinks with her?' Ruth asked.

'Soon after six, maybe six thirty.'

'Was it just you two?'

'A few people came over to say hello.'

Lucy looked at him. 'Can you tell us who they were?'

'Erm, Adrian Michaels, who is a commissioning editor at the BBC. Tessa Levi from Channel 4. A script development person, but I can't remember her name ...'

'Did they sit and have a drink with you and Tash?' Ruth asked.

He shook his head. 'No. They just came over to say hello. A bit of chitchat and that was it.'

'So, while you were in Soho House you spent the majority of your time with Tash?'

'Yes.'

'Anyone else you can think of?'

'No.'

'Marcus Jankel?'

Josh's face visibly reacted. 'Yes, he came over.'

'You didn't mention him.'

Josh shrugged. 'I forgot. I go in there a lot.'

'How would you describe your relationship with Marcus Jankel?' Lucy asked.

Josh took a few seconds to respond. 'I know him from school. I see him around sometimes.'

'Were you friends?'

'No. We weren't friends,' he answered, a little too quickly.

Ruth looked at him. 'Did you know he was having a relationship with Tash?'

'Yes,' he replied as he moved in his seat and sat up straight.

'What did you think about their relationship?'

'It was none of my business, was it?'

'You never offered an opinion to Tash about her relationship with Marcus?'

'No.' Josh shook his head. 'I don't understand why you're asking me about this?'

'You still haven't really told us about your relationship with Marcus Jankel,' Lucy said.

Josh frowned. 'I don't have any relationship with him.'

'Do you like him?'

'What?'

The question seemed to have thrown him.

'It's a simple question Josh. Do you like him?'

'No, I don't like him,' he announced with a flash of irritation.

'Why not?'

'He's very full of himself.'

'Are you jealous of him?'

'God, no!'

'Why do you say that?'

'Marcus believes he's superior to everyone. He treats women badly. And he's ruthless and vindictive in getting what he wants.'

'So, you think that Marcus could do with being taking down a peg or two?' Ruth asked in her well-rehearsed throwaway tone.

'I suppose so.'

'In fact, you might even enjoy seeing him getting his comeuppance?' Ruth asked.

'Maybe.'

Interesting that he's not denying it, Lucy thought.

Ruth looked down at her notepad. 'The last time we spoke to you, you said that you left Soho House at around nine and that you were home by ten.'

'Yes, I'd had a lot to drink that night so I got that wrong,' he admitted.

'We spoke to your wife, Jane,' Lucy said.

'I know,' he mumbled quietly. 'She told me.'

'She remembered that you came home very drunk after midnight.'

He shrugged. 'It's all a bit of a blur actually.'

Ruth gestured to her notepad. 'Just to clarify, you were drinking all night in Soho House. You got a cab from there and arrived home just after midnight. Is that correct?'

'Yes. I must have just lost track of time.'

Ruth shot a look over at Lucy – *he's lying through his teeth.*

Lucy frowned. 'You didn't go anywhere else for a drink?'

He shook his head. 'No. I must have been there longer than I thought.'

'The funny thing is, Josh, Soho House has a record of you ordering a cab to South London at nine.'

Got you, dickhead!

Lucy watched as his face drained of colour and he lowered his gaze to the floor.

She turned to Ruth. 'DC Hunter, how long do you think it takes in a cab from Soho to South London at nine o'clock at night?'

'My guess would be just over half an hour.'

Lucy fixed Josh with a stare. 'So, Josh. That means that you are lying to us ... again. And you have two and half hours of unaccounted time that you need to tell us about.'

After a few seconds he raised his eyes and stared blankly – first at Lucy, then at Ruth.

'Josh,' Ruth said.

'What?'

'You need to tell us where you were on Monday between nine and midnight.'

'I can't,' he said in a virtual whisper.

'Why not?'

Silence.

'I ... just can't,' he repeated, his voice breaking.

Is he crying?

Lucy wondered if this was the moment that he was going to crumble and admit he had murdered Tash.

'Josh?'

'I was with someone.'

'Who were you with?' Ruth asked.

He wiped a tear from the corner of his eye and shook his head.

'Come on, Josh,' Lucy implored. 'Just tell us who you were with.'

'No ...'

'Josh?'

There was a silent pause as he tried to compose himself.

'I was with ... my assistant,' he said almost breathlessly.

'You're having an affair with your assistant?' Ruth asked.

How bloody original, Lucy thought.

'Okay ... And what's her name?' Lucy asked.

'Hugo. His name is Hugo Allerton.'

Bloody hell!

Lucy looked over at Ruth – they weren't expecting that.

CHAPTER 12

GAUGHRAN AND HASSAN had tracked down the name of the cabbie who had taken Tash home. He was based at a black cab rank office in Gerrard Street, at the heart of London's Chinatown.

As Gaughran stepped off the wet pavement to move around a stationary group of tourists, he was struck by the kaleidoscope of sounds, smells and colours. He loved Chinatown, which had been at its present location since the early 1970s. It relocated from Limehouse near the East End docks, where it was originally established in the early 1900s to cater for Chinese sailors from the cargo ships. The name Chinatown conjured up all sorts of images. The seedy and sinister opium dens that were visited by Sherlock Holmes and Dorian Grey. The evil Chinese drug barons as depicted in Sax Rohmer's Fu Manchu stories with their dangerous Chinese femme fatales.

A cadence of different Chinese dialects filled the air as several young men walked down past a restaurant chattering loudly. The shop and restaurant fronts were a tapestry of red and gold splashes. Banners with ornate black Chinese lettering hung from lampposts. The air was thick with the rich smell of roast duck, Chinese spices mixed with the stench of rubbish, and disinfectant.

'Over there.' Hassan pointed across the road to a taxi office.

Along the pavement outside were five iconic London black cabs, their yellow *Taxi* signs glowing to show they were available for hire.

The glass door to the office was open slightly. Inside were four middle-aged men, drinking tea and reading tabloid newspapers.

That's about right, Gaughran thought to himself as he took out his warrant card.

'Looking for a Terry Grey,' he explained as one of men glanced up quizzically from his paper.

The cabbie looked over his shoulder at a large man with a shaved head who was sitting at a table at the back of the office. 'Terry,' he called.

'Yeah?' he replied in a thick Cockney accent.

'These fellas are looking for you,' the cabbie said with a wry smile. 'Old Bill.'

Gaughran and Hassan approached, took two nearby chairs and sat down.

'You Terry Grey?' Hassan asked.

Terry put down his paper, leant back in his chair, and folded his sizeable tattooed arms across his chest. 'Yeah,' he said defensively.

Gaughran said quietly, 'We'd like to talk to you about a fare you took on Monday night?'

'Okay.'

Hassan reached into his pocket and pulled out a photo of Tash. 'Do you remember picking this woman up about nine o'clock on Monday?'

Terry gave the photo a cursory glance and then shook his head. 'I don't think so.'

'It was on account. Pick up was from Soho House in Greek Street,' Gaughran said. 'There might have been an older woman with her.'

Terry sat forward and peered at the photo more carefully. 'Yeah, yeah. I remember them now. The older woman was a Yank. Bit full of herself.'

Gaughran nodded with a knowing smile. 'Sounds about right.'

Hassan gestured to the photo. 'Can you tell us where you dropped this woman?'

'Yeah, a flat in Peckham. Don't normally go that far south, but I picked up a fare going back to town so it didn't turn out too bad.'

'And you saw her go into her flat?'

'Yeah.'

'Did you notice anyone around when you dropped her home?' Gaughran asked. 'Anyone hanging about? Or anyone sitting in a car?'

Terry shook his head. 'No. I didn't see anyone.'

'You're sure?'

'Yeah.' Terry's face then dropped. 'Christ, she's not that actress that was murdered the other night, is she?'

'Yes, I'm afraid so. Tash Weston.'

'Just been reading about her in The Sun. I didn't recognise her. They had a photo of her from one of her films.

When they said it happened in South London, I didn't put two and two together, you know? That's terrible, that is.'

Terry's expression turned to one of shock now he realised it was Tash that he had taken home.

'You found the fella that done it yet?'

Hassan shook his head. 'Not yet.'

'I hope you bang him up for the rest of his natural. Bastard,' he growled. 'She was only young, 'bout the same age as my daughter.'

'How did she seem on the journey home?' Gaughran asked.

'Yeah, she was all right.' Then he frowned. 'Tell a lie. She and this Yank had a bit of row in the back. It had all calmed down once we got south of the river.'

'Did you hear what they were arguing about?' Hassan asked.

'Not really. I was listening to the radio.'

Gaughran locked eyes with him. 'Terry, we think you might have been the last person to have seen Tash alive, so anything, however small, might really help us.'

'Eh? How can I be the last one to have seen her alive?'

'We believe that she was murdered between the time you dropped her home and around midnight.'

'What about the other passenger? The Yank?'

What's he talking about?

'We've spoken to her. She told us that you dropped her at her home in Battersea, and then went on with Tash to Peckham?'

'No, no, she's having you on. I dropped them both at the young lady's flat in Peckham.'

What?

'You sure about that?'

'Positive. I sat and watched them both go in through the front door. By the time I turned my cab around, the light up on the first floor had come on ... What she telling you that for, eh?'

Gaughran exchanged a look with Hassan – it was a good question. Why had Barbara York told them she had been dropped at home in Battersea, and why had she gone back to Tash's flat?

RUTH AND LUCY WERE back in the tenth-floor offices of the UCA Talent Agency in central London. Even though Josh Harriot's admission to his affair with Hugo Allerton had seemed utterly convincing, they needed it to be confirmed by Allerton himself. Harriot had already lied to them once about where he had been on the night of the murder.

Ruth flashed her warrant card at the young woman behind the reception desk. 'We're looking for Hugo Allerton.'

The young woman seemed a little concerned at the sight of the warrant card. 'I'll just check where he is for you.' She made a call as Ruth and Lucy looked around the main reception area. There were posters of films, television shows, and plays that the clients of UCA had been involved in. It all seemed very glamorous.

Ruth wondered what it must be like to work in such a world. No one ever got hurt, or attacked, or killed for real. There were no genuine tears of grief or loss. Everything was make-believe and made up, like the little plays that she and her brother had created when they were young. Obviously, there was great skill and talent needed to produce a film, but essentially nothing was real. She tried to imagine what it would be like to be an actress. The main stress of the day would be making sure you got your lines right and then gave a decent performance in front of the camera. Then there would be all that waiting around in the trailer. She couldn't work out if it would be a blissful relief to have so little to worry about, or would it just grate that the days were so lacking in real substance or worth.

'Hi there,' said a voice. It was a man in his mid-20s, blonde, tall and very smartly dressed.

'Hugo Allerton?' Lucy asked.

He nodded tentatively. 'Yes.'

'We're police officers,' Lucy said quietly. 'If we could go somewhere private, there's a couple of things we'd like you to clarify to help us in our current investigation.'

'Really? Okay, we can go to the meeting room over there, if that's all right?' His voice was a little camp and Ruth's gaydar immediately picked up on his sexuality.

'That would be great.' Lucy gestured for him to lead the way.

They entered the large meeting room which had a huge oval table surrounded by around a dozen black and chrome chairs. The glass walls that surrounded the room were covered by large venetian blinds.

Hugo sat down nervously and looked at them. 'How can I help?'

Lucy took out her notebook. 'We understand that you're Josh Harriot's assistant?'

'That's right.' Hugo sat forward on his chair.

'And how long have you worked for him?' Ruth asked.

'About eighteen months. Is this about what happened to Tash? It's just that you didn't really say.'

'If you let us ask the questions please, Hugo,' Lucy said with a smile.

'Oh, yes, of course. Sorry.' He squirmed a little in his chair.

'Can you tell us where you were on Monday night?' Lucy asked.

Hugo blinked nervously. 'I was at home.'

'Where's that?'

'I share a flat with friends in Brixton.'

'And you were home all night?'

'Yes.' He seemed somehow relieved at the straightforward nature of the questions.

'Did you see anyone else?'.

'I saw my flatmate, Ed.'

'What was Ed doing?'

'He spent most of the evening in his bedroom. He's studying for a doctorate.'

Ruth caught his eye. 'Did you have any visitors?'

Hugo shook his head. 'No.'

Lucy tilted her head in an effort to appear confused. 'You're sure about that?'

He laughed nervously. 'Yes. Of course.'

Lucy raised an eyebrow and pointed to her notepad. 'That's strange because when we spoke to Josh, he said that he had come to your flat at about ten o'clock on Monday evening.'

Hugo pulled a face as if he had no idea what they were talking about. 'No. He must have been confused.'

Lucy leaned forward, her expression changing to one of irritation. 'Hugo, as you know we're investigating Tash Weston's murder. So, if Josh is lying about being at your flat at the time she was murdered, we need to know. And if *you're* lying to us, then you would be obstructing a murder investigation which is a criminal offence.'

His eyes darted nervously around the room. He had managed to back himself into a corner and now he was scared. Ruth assumed that Josh had told him that their affair needed to be kept a secret from everyone.

Hugo's breathing was becoming shallower as he clasped his hands together.

'Hugo,' Ruth said in a gentle tone. 'Was Josh at your flat on Monday night?'

He stared down at the floor and nodded.

They waited for a few seconds so that he could compose himself.

'Can you tell us what time he got there?'

Hugo looked up at her. 'It was about ten o'clock.'

'And what time did he leave?'

'Around midnight.'

AS THE LIFT DOOR OPENED, Gaughran and Hassan strode out and headed for the reception area of Goldstein

Films. Gaughran wanted to know why Barbara York had lied to them. Was she involved in Tash Weston's murder? If the time of Tash's death was somewhere between ten and midnight on Monday, then York would have been in her flat very close to the time of the murder.

Taking his warrant card from his jacket, Gaughran went over to the receptionist. 'Is Barbara York in?'

The receptionist appeared flustered. 'I'll just check for you.'

Gaughran raised an eyebrow. 'I'm not asking if she wants to see us, I'm asking if she is in the building. And given that you're about to call through to her, I will assume that she's sitting in her office.'

As they turned and walked away, Hassan glanced back over his shoulder. 'It's all right. We know the way.'

They marched down the carpeted corridor that was lined with film posters, and arrived at Barbara York's office. Gaughran knocked loudly on the closed door and opened it without waiting for a reply.

A very startled Barbara York glanced up from her desk, frowned, and took off her reading glasses. 'What the hell is going on?' she thundered.

Gaughran calmly closed the door and fixed her with a stare. 'There appears to be some discrepancies in the account you gave us about your whereabouts on Monday night.'

'You can't just come barging in here!' Getting up from her seat, Barbara was clearly flustered and very angry. 'I thought I made myself very clear. If you want to speak to me, then we will go through official channels and I will have my lawyers present.'

'That's absolutely fine, but you lied to us about where you were at the time of Tash's murder. We know that you went back to her flat in a taxi - very close to the time that she was brutally killed. Obstructing a murder investigation is a serious criminal offence.'

Barbara shrugged. 'You can't possibly think that I had anything to do with what happened to her.'

Hassan gestured to the door. 'We'd like you to accompany us to the station for an interview under caution. If you feel you would like to have legal counsel present we can arrange that for you, or you can provide your own.'

She shook her head. 'I'm not going anywhere with you.'

Gaughran let out a sigh as he glanced over at Hassan. 'You can either come with us immediately, or I'm going to arrest you, cuff you, and take you through reception. Either way, you're coming with us.'

'You wouldn't dare!'

Hassan looked at her. 'He's not joking.'

'This is ridiculous!' Barbara snapped with a sneer. 'If you touch me, I'll sue you and you'll both be out of a job.'

Gaughran shook his head and took the cuffs from his belt. 'Barbara York, I'm arresting you on suspicion of obstruction and perverting the course of justice in a murder investigation. You do not have to say anything, but anything you do say can be taken down and used as evidence in a court of law.'

RUTH WAS SITTING AT her desk as Lucy approached with two coffees. They'd just arrived back at Peckham nick after their interview with Hugo Allerton.

'What did you think?' Lucy asked as she sat down and handed Ruth her coffee.

'Ta,' she said, taking the coffee. 'Well, Hugo has confirmed that Josh did eventually tell us the truth about where he was till midnight on Monday. He's meant to be a happily married man, and that explains why he lied to us. He didn't want anyone to know he was having a homosexual affair with his assistant.'

Lucy nodded. 'You could see that he was totally broken when he told us. I don't think you can fake that.'

'What about Marcus Jankel?' Ruth said thinking out loud. 'He told us that Josh was obsessed with Tash. If Josh is a closet homosexual, how does that work?'

Lucy paused for thought. 'Maybe he's bi-sexual?'

Ruth wasn't convinced. 'I can't see how he could be obsessed with his female actress client, while carrying on a secret affair with his male assistant.'

'No, that doesn't sound very likely,' Lucy agreed.

'Which means that Jankel was lying to us.'

Lucy shrugged. 'Maybe he got his wires crossed?'

'No, he didn't get his wires crossed Lucy. He made it very clear that Josh Harriot was fixated on a client who had just been murdered. That was a deliberate attempt to get Harriot firmly on our radar.'

'I guess ... I don't know what he was thinking.'

'You sound like you know him,' Ruth said.

There was something a little bit off about Lucy and the conversation they were having. Ruth sensed that there was something Lucy wasn't telling her but she had no idea what it might be.

'What is it with you and Marcus Jankel?' Ruth asked.

Lucy instantly bristled. 'What do you mean?'

'He seems to have done a bit of a number on you.'

'I don't know what you're getting at Ruth,' Lucy snapped. 'I just said I thought he was sexy. And he has a watertight alibi for the time of Tash's death. That's it.'

Ruth was about to continue when she saw one of the technicians from Forensics approach holding a VHS tape.

'We've been trawling though the CCTV footage from Coldharbour Lane,' he said. 'We think we've got someone who matches the man described by the victim.'

'That's great,' Lucy said. 'I'll come and take a look.'

Ruth watched her go and wondered what was going on with her.

CHAPTER 13

'WHERE IS SHE?' BROOKS asked as he and Gaughran marched down the corridor.

'She's waiting in Interview Room 2. Two very heavy looking American lawyers have just turned up and they're in there with her now. She said that she was going to call the American Embassy.'

'Bloody hell!' Brooks exclaimed with a wry smile. 'She sounds like a little treat.'

'I think she's very used to getting her own way, Guv.'

'Well that's women for you, Tim,' Brooks quipped.

Gaughran laughed. 'True.'

They turned right and continued past the canteen on the ground floor.

'Why do you think she lied to us?' Brooks asked.

'Either she was too scared to admit that she was at the murder scene and hoped we'd accept her alibi ... or she was directly involved in Tash's murder.'

'Motive?'

'Tash was threatening to blow the lid off Bob Goldstein's sexual assault on her and go to the papers. And my guess is that this wasn't the first time a young actress or assistant had been victim to his criminal behaviour. Maybe it was going to open a can of worms and bring Goldstein Films crashing to the ground.'

'So they killed Tash to shut her up?'

Gaughran shrugged. 'Yeah, maybe.'

They arrived at Interview Room 2 and went in. Barbara York was in deep conversation with one of the lawyers, both of whom were dressed in smart suits, and she deliberately didn't look up at them as they entered.

Before Brooks and Gaughran had time to settle into their seats, the older of the two lawyers peered across the table at them. He had thick bushy eyebrows, swept-back hair and a sharp, charcoal Armani suit.

'Our client is willing to fully cooperate with this police investigation on the understanding that she will be immune from the charge of perverting the course of justice,' he explained. His accent was New York, but less pronounced than Barbara's.

This wasn't the usual type of interview that Gaughran had become used to at Peckham police station. In fact at least 90% of the suspects that they arrested or charged had their legal representation provided for them by the duty solicitor who covered several South London police stations.

Brooks scratched his cheek as he looked across the table directly at Barbara. 'We have no interest in pursuing the charge in question. But you were with the victim in her flat close to the time she was brutally murdered. You lied to my officers about that. My only interest is to find who did this to Tash and get some kind of justice for her and her family.'

THE IMITATION OF DARKNESS

After a few seconds, Barbara cleared her throat. 'I was in Tash's flat for about fifteen minutes, twenty at the most. She called me a mini-cab and I left.'

'Why did you go inside?' Gaughran asked.

'I was trying to convince her not to break the story about what happened between her and Bob.'

'Bob Goldstein?' Brooks asked to clarify.

'Yes. I thought I was close to getting her to change her mind, so I pretty much invited myself in.'

'And did you?'

Barbara frowned. 'Did I what?'

'Change her mind?'

'I think so. I couldn't believe it when I saw the news the next morning. I kept thinking that if I'd have stayed, she might still be alive. Then I wondered if I would have been killed too.'

There was a short silence as Barbara's poignant comment hung in the air.

'And if we needed the details of the cab you took home, you would be able to provide that for us?' Gaughran asked as he scribbled in his pad.

'Yes, of course.' Barbara's tone had softened a little. Gaughran wondered if realising that she might have been in danger herself had given her a little perspective.

'Was there anyone else in Tash's flat when you went inside?' he asked.

'No. She mentioned a couple of times that she had an audition the following morning and she was going to get an early night. I assured her that I wasn't going to stay long.'

'Did you have a drink?'

'No.'

'We believe that after you left, someone Tash knew came to the flat and murdered her. Did she say anything about anyone coming over?'

'No. Like I said, she'd told me she was tired and wanted an early night.'

'What about phone calls? Did she receive any phone calls while you were with her?'

Barbara started to shake her head but then remembered something. 'Actually, yes. Someone called her cell phone when she was in the taxi.'

'Did she speak to them?'

'Yes.'

'Did you hear what they talked about?'

'No, not really, but she was laughing. It sounded quite flirty.'

Gaughran looked up from his notepad. 'And there were no other calls?'

'She had another call while I was in the flat. She took it in the other room but she was only gone for a few seconds and then she came back. I didn't hear what they talked about and she didn't mention it.'

'And when you left, as far as you knew, Tash intended to have an early night?'

'That's what she told me,' Barbara muttered very quietly. 'That poor, poor girl.'

IT WAS LATE AFTERNOON and Brooks had called an impromptu briefing for all the CID officers who were currently at Peckham nick. Having seen the CCTV footage of the suspect in Coldharbour Lane, Lucy had immediately gone to Brooks, even though it made her feel uncomfortable. She felt incredibly guilty about her evening with Marcus, and their kiss. Only a few hours earlier, Brooks had taken the last of his things from the house. She was beginning to wonder what on earth she was doing. Maybe she'd just been drunk and emotional. There was part of her that wanted to resolve not to have any more contact with Marcus - yet another part was longing for a text or a phone call.

'Listen up everyone,' Brooks said as he went to the centre of the room. 'We have the CCTV footage of Coldharbour Lane from Monday night. Lucy?'

Lucy moved over to the VHS player where the footage she had paused earlier was visible on the large television screen. 'Forensics trawled through a few hours of this until they found this man.' She pressed play and the footage showed a tall, handsome man with long hair and a goatee beard leaving a newsagents. He stopped and lit a cigarette. Lucy paused the tape. 'We think this might be the person that Tash thought was stalking her.'

'He's definitely got that Antonio Banderas look,' Ruth said.

Lucy pressed the play button again. 'Okay, so our suspect checks his watch, crosses the road and turns down Southland Street. The timecode shows that it's 10.27pm.'

Brooks walked over to a large map of Peckham on the wall and pointed to Southland Street. 'From here, it's a ten-minute walk to Banfield Road where Tash lived. We also have the CCTV footage from outside King's College Hospital. Lucy ...'

Lucy swapped the VHS and played the footage which showed the car park at King's College Hospital and the road beyond. 'So, this is a continuation of Southland Street. And I think this figure walking past in the same direction is our suspect. If you check the timecode, it's 10.33pm. It's about a five- or six-minute walk from Coldharbour Lane. It's very likely that this is our man, and he's about thirty seconds from Tash's flat.'

Gaughran frowned. 'I know this puts him very close to the flat at the time of the murder, but it doesn't explain how he got inside or drugged her.'

'And are we assuming that he just grabbed the tie that Jankel claims he'd left in the flat and strangled her with it?' Hassan asked.

Lucy shrugged. 'I guess.'

'How about this?' Ruth suggested. 'We know Tash was reckless and impulsive. Barbara York leaves in the taxi. Tash looks out of the window to watch her go, and spots our suspect walking past. She goes out, strikes up a conversation and invites him in?'

Gaughran scratched his chin. 'I don't buy it.'

'Neither do I,' Hassan said.

'What if someone else drugged her in Soho House in the hope that it might lead to some kind of sexual encounter?' Lucy suggested. 'They didn't count on her leaving for an early night. Barbara York leaves the flat and the drugs start to make Tash feel dizzy. Our suspect knocks on the door and notices that she's very unsteady on her feet, so he pushes his way in.'

Brooks nodded. 'So the date rape drug and her murder aren't linked?'

'It's possible,' Ruth agreed, 'but what about the similarities between the scene of the murder and the television drama?'

Lucy shrugged. 'Maybe our suspect had seen it when it was aired. It's locked away in his mind. He attacks Tash in her flat and decides to recreate what he's seen on television.'

Brooks let out a sigh. 'There's something we're missing here. There are too many coincidences for my liking.' He pointed to the screen. 'But there's something very suspicious about this man. Let's see if we can find him and bring him in.'

IT WAS A SLOW HAUL from Peckham nick down to Coldharbour Lane. The rush hour traffic was dense, and roadworks were making the journey frustrating.

'We could have walked this quicker,' Ruth quipped.

Lucy didn't respond for a few seconds. Then she blinked and said, 'Yeah, I know.'

Whatever was going on with her, Ruth wasn't going to push her anymore. She would open up to Ruth when the time was right and there was no point in falling out about it.

Looking ahead, she saw that a couple of coaches were sitting in the bus lane with their hazards flashing. The traffic inched forward again, like cattle moving towards a narrow gate. Grabbing a cigarette, Ruth wound down the window and got a waft of the icy traffic fumes. She gazed out at the pavements where the yellow streetlamps had bleached the colour from the shop fronts. The deep thud of rap music came from a stationary car that was illegally parked on double yellow lines.

As she tapped the ash from her cigarette, she tried to imagine what the scene would have looked like at the turn of the century. The road would have been populated by horse-drawn omnibuses and the odd Hansom cab. There had also been a tram that went all the way up to Vauxhall, via Camberwell. She imagined what those commuters would have made of the scene in front of her. A sense of awe and wonder at the shapes and noises of the vehicles. She also thought how ironic it was that their journey across from Peckham might well have been a lot faster ninety years earlier.

She flicked her cigarette end out onto the wet tarmac and closed the window. She glanced at the London sky ahead of them. It was late afternoon, dusk, and the bright red sky was darkening over the capital.

'Here we go,' Lucy said as she pulled the car over and parked outside A & K Newsagents, the shop they had seen their suspect coming out of on the CCTV. It had a red Coca-Cola awning and a glass door that was wide open.

As they got out of the car, the bitter wind picked up and swirled litter around the pavement. They made their way inside the shop where the air was thick with spices, and something very sweet that Ruth couldn't identify.

A tall Asian man peered at them over the counter.

'We're from Peckham CID,' Lucy explained, showing him her warrant card. 'We're hoping you can help us with something.'

'Okay,' the shopkeeper said with a nod.

She took out a Polaroid photo that she had taken from the CCTV footage. It showed the suspect leaving the shop, with the date and time visible at the bottom.

'Do you recognise this man?' she asked, handing him the photo.

He took out his reading glasses, put them on, and peered at the photograph. 'Oh, yes.'

'Do you know his name?' Ruth asked.

He shook his head. 'No, sorry.'

'But you've seen him here in your shop?'

'Yes.'

Lucy took back the photograph. 'Does he come in here a lot?'

'Oh yes,' the shopkeeper said. 'Most days.'

'What does he buy?'

'Cigarettes. Sometimes beer or bread.'

'Is there anything else you can tell us about him? Does he have an accent?'

'Yes, but I don't know where he is from.'

Ruth asked gently, 'But if you had to make a guess?'

'Turkish maybe ... or Moroccan. Something like that.'

'Does he come in at the same time of day?'

The shopkeeper shook his head. 'No. Sometimes it is very early, just as I'm opening.'

'What time's that?'

'I open at six, but sometimes he comes in later. Maybe ten o'clock.'

Ruth and Lucy looked at each other. That pattern of behaviour didn't help them at all.

'I think he works shifts.'

Ruth's ears pricked up. 'Why do you say that?'

'I think he said something about it once, that he was late for his shift.'

Glancing around the shop, Ruth noticed a small CCTV camera positioned high above the cigarette display unit behind where the shopkeeper was standing.

Bingo!

'You've got CCTV?' she asked, gesturing to the camera.

'Yes.'

'We're going to need to see the footage from Monday of this week. Do you have it here?'

He shook his head. 'No, sorry. My brother takes the tapes home. But I can bring it in tomorrow morning if that would help you?'

Ruth smiled at him. 'Yes. That would be incredibly helpful.

CHAPTER 14

IT WAS GONE 10PM BY the time Ruth came through the front door. She was exhausted and had a banging headache, but the blanket of warmth from her flat instantly brightened her mood. Shiori had agreed to pick up the girls, bath them and put them to bed. Ruth still had no idea if, or when, she was going to confront her about her suspicions. If she was honest, she was far too tired to cope with any emotional confrontation.

As she took off her overcoat and hung it on the row of hooks by the door, the scent of spicy food wafted up the hallway from the kitchen.

Is Shiori cooking? Ruth thought. *She never cooks.*

It was a running joke that when it was ever Shiori's turn to cook, she either paid for a takeaway or bought M&S food that just needed to be shoved in the oven. Ruth wasn't complaining. Either one of those was fine by her.

'Erm, are you actually cooking?' Ruth asked with a wry smile as she went into the kitchen.

'Lebanese spiced lamb flatbreads and couscous salad,' Shiori said triumphantly as she came over and gave her a kiss.

'Lebanese? How bloody middle class are we?' Ruth said, rolling her eyes.

Shiori poured a glass of white wine and handed it to her. 'You *are* middle class darling. You're a detective.'

Ruth took a swig of wine, hoping that alcohol might take away her pounding headache. 'I don't feel very middle class.'

'Just sit down - dinner will be about twenty minutes,' Shiori said with a smile.

She's acting a bit weird, Ruth thought.

'What have I done to deserve all this then?' Then she looked at Shiori and couldn't help herself. '... or are you feeling guilty about something?' she asked.

'Oh that's nice,' Shiori said jokingly, 'does there have to be an ulterior motive just because I'm cooking for my girlfriend?'

Is she overcompensating for something? And why is she so bloody happy?

'Drink your wine and relax,' she continued. 'I'm going to have a quick shower and then we'll eat.'

'Okay,' Ruth said indifferently. Her headache was still bothering her.

She watched Shiori leave the room and took a large swig of wine.

Why is she having a shower?

She got up from the sofa and marched over to one of the kitchen cupboards where she hoped there was some paracetamol. There wasn't.

There's some in the bathroom cabinet, she thought to herself.

She went upstairs and headed towards the bathroom where the shower was already running.

'Hi, I'm just coming in to get some paracetamol,' she called as she opened the door.

The noise of the shower must have drowned out her voice as Shiori didn't respond.

As she went to the cabinet, Ruth said again. 'It's just me getting some paracetamol!'

'Okay!' Shiori called back.

As Ruth opened the mirrored door, she saw the reflection of Shiori behind the bright blue shower curtain.

Shiori moved briefly from behind the curtain at the end of the bath and leant down to pick up a bottle of shampoo from its edge.

Her back was visible for only a second, but Ruth could see that there were long, thin red marks across the skin.

She took the paracetamol back into the kitchen and swallowed a couple with a mouthful of wine.

Her head was spinning from what she had just seen. She wasn't an idiot. In fact, she was an experienced detective.

Shiori had had sex with someone fairly recently. It explained her strange mood, her decision to have a shower, and the red marks on her back.

IT HAD TAKEN LUCY JUST over forty minutes to get from South London to Portobello Road at the heart of Notting Hill, even though it was only nine miles. As the icy wind picked up, she pulled up the collar of her coat and felt the air sting her face. She turned left down Elgin Crescent and passed the blue frontage of 'Neal's Yard Remedies' which, as far as she knew, sold overpriced soaps and bath oils. Then a designer furniture shop and an estate agents. She peered in the window and noticed the price for one of the beautiful Georgian Notting Hill houses - £499,999.

Half a million for a house? How the hell does anyone afford that?

As she turned right, she saw the restaurant that Marcus Jankel had invited her to. Osteria Basilica. Feeling a little nervous, she pushed open the door. Inside she was surprised to see that it was relatively simple and rustic. For some reason, she had assumed that Marcus would have invited her to some fancy restaurant with white linen and sparkling glass everywhere.

'You're late,' a voice said gently.

She spun around to see Marcus giving her a sexy grin. He leaned towards her and kissed her on both cheeks.

'Very continental,' she said as she raised an eyebrow.

He pulled a seat out for her, and a waiter arrived to take her coat and hand her a menu.

'By the way, you look stunning,' Marcus said as he sat down opposite her.

She hesitated before speaking. 'I nearly didn't come tonight.'

'Why's that?'

'My DCI still thinks there's something oddly coincidental about your involvement in Tash's murder. So does my partner, Ruth.'

'Well there is, isn't there?' he said. 'A young woman, whom I had a casual relationship with, was murdered in the same way as I described in a script I wrote nearly three years ago. She was killed with my tie. That's incredibly creepy and weird, but I feel like I'm also a victim in all of this too.'

'You think that there's someone out to get you?' Lucy asked as Marcus poured her a glass of wine.

'Don't you? Someone did this and put me directly in the firing line. That's really scary because I wonder if they're going to do something else? I know it sounds paranoid, but I've started watching to see if anyone's following me.'

Lucy took some olive bread and broke it with her fingers. 'Who do you know that would want to destroy you like that?'

Marcus shrugged. 'I told you to look at Josh Harriot for starters.'

'He's got a watertight alibi.'

'Right, I see ... Well, I've ruffled a few feathers in the film and television business but I can't see anyone resorting to this length to get back at me.' He poured them both some more wine. 'I've been playing it through in my head. I don't understand it.'

'Before you ask, I can't start discussing the finer details of the case with you.'

Marcus gave her a knowing smile. 'You shouldn't be having dinner with me or kissing me either.'

Lucy laughed. 'I know. And that's why I nearly cancelled.'

'So, it if was a copycat, it couldn't have been an intruder. And that means that Tash must have known her murderer well enough to sleep with him.' He studied her face for a reaction to his theory.

'I told you. I'm not discussing it with you.'

'No, but from your reaction, I was getting close. There's something else isn't there?' He poured some water into both of their water glasses. 'I know. I've got it. If someone had drugged Tash, then they could have recreated the scene from my script without needing her to be compliant ... How am I doing?'

'I'm still not saying, but you would make a very good detective.'

'Yeah, and that would be a proper job,' he said.

'Writing isn't a proper job then?'

Marcus snorted. 'God no. Making up stuff for characters to say or do. It doesn't mean anything. It's utter nonsense. If you ever go to an awards ceremony, you would think these people had cured cancer or had spent their lives doing humanitarian work on the frontline of a war zone. All they did was have their make-up done, learn some lines, repeat those lines and go back to the trailer. Jesus!'

'Then why do you do it?'

'Affirmation, status, ego, self-pity, lack of self-esteem ... take your pick.'

'So, you're completely aware of why you do it?' Lucy asked with a frown.

'Of course. I see an expensive therapist every week so that I can be self-aware. I'm the classic abandoned child who went to boarding school. I fear that my parents didn't love me, that I'm not good enough, that I'm worthless. Therefore I strive to be a high achiever in the glamorous world of film and television to prove to my parents, and everyone else, that I'm worth loving, that I'm good enough. Of course, the person who needs to believe that most is me. And money, fame, and success don't fill that hole in the soul.'

Lucy blew out her cheeks. 'Bloody hell! It's all going on, isn't it?'

'Oh yeah,' he replied. His flippant self-analysis had clearly upset him a little. 'And it's bloody hard work sometimes.'

'Carrying all that around?'

He nodded, and for a moment Lucy could see the vulnerability behind his eyes. He then snapped himself out of it and said in a tone that seemed to verge on anger, 'Poor old Marcus, eh? BAFTA winning writer, house in Notting Hill, season ticket to Arsenal, private members' clubs, first-class flights ... You name it, I've got it.'

Lucy reached over and touched his hand. 'None of that means you're happy though, does it?'

'It should do though, shouldn't it?' He turned his hand over and held hers.

Lucy felt a flicker of excitement at the touch of his hand and feel of his skin.

Right now, I just want to take you to bed.

He gave her a quizzical look.

'What?' she asked.

'You don't buy into any of that bullshit, do you?'

She shrugged. 'I'm just a working-class girl from South London.'

He leant forward and rubbed his thumb gently across the back of her hand. 'And that's why you're so special. You see all of this for what it is. And it makes you so much more attractive because you see it with such fresh eyes.'

Lucy smiled. The wine had relaxed her, and being with Marcus was making her feel warm and fuzzy all over.

'Are you a good kisser?' she asked him moving closer.

'What?'

'You kissed me last night, but I've forgotten whether it was any good.'

He raised an eyebrow. 'Really?'

'Really.'

'I can try again?'

Lucy nodded. 'Yes, just to be on the safe side.'

He leant in and kissed her softly on the mouth. His breath was warm and smelled nicely of alcohol. Putting his hand to her face, he kissed her harder and their tongues touched for a second before he moved back and gazed at her.

'What do you think?'

Lucy gave him a sexy smile. 'I think we should skip dinner.'

CHAPTER 15

GAUGHRAN HAD BEEN WAITING outside the Dulwich and Sydenham Golf Club for nearly an hour. After two pints with Syed, he had decided to bite the bullet and try to make contact with his father. He knew that confrontation wouldn't work and so he was going to be as conciliatory as his ego would allow him to be. He had done nothing wrong but he wanted to understand why his father was acting as if he had.

The BBC radio news was covering the latest allegations of President Clinton's affair with Monica Lewinsky. Gaughran knew and cared little about American politics. In fact, he made a point of avoiding politics altogether – it just didn't interest him. However, having seen Monica Lewinsky, he did wonder why the most powerful person in America had picked her to have an affair with. She was a bit podgy and funny-looking. If she had looked like Cindy Crawford or Elle McPherson, he might have understood – but she didn't.

Tuning the radio to see if he could find any sport, Gaughran gazed out from the golf club car park and north towards central London. The skyline glimmered like Emerald City, promising glamour and money. The lights of the Post Office Tower winked rhythmically over to the northwest.

Eventually he found a radio channel discussing football. With the exception of a recent defeat to Everton, his team Chelsea had been on a decent winning streak. Their manager, the Dutch maestro Ruud Gullit, was by far the coolest manager in the Premiership, Gaughran thought. The man had dreads, and he wore loafers with no socks in the dugout. Oh, and he was voted the best footballer on the planet twice in the late 80s, as well as winning the much-coveted Ballon D'Or.

Gullit had also led his team to Wembley the previous May where they had won the FA Cup. Gaughran hadn't managed to get a ticket, but he had watched the game in a pub on the Fulham Road, along with thousands of other Chelsea fans. It had been Chelsea's first trophy since the early 70s when Gaughran was still a baby, and the street party around Stamford Bridge had gone on into the early hours.

A set of headlights broke his train of thought, as a car swept into the car park and headed over towards the club house. It was a white BMW 4x4.

Who the bloody hell is that and why are they driving so fast?

A short while later a figure emerged from the clubhouse carrying clubs.

It was his father.

Even though he wasn't unsteady on his feet, Gaughran could tell that he'd had a few drinks.

A middle-aged woman got out of the car. She was all blonde hair, fake tan and nails.

To his horror, the woman ran straight over to his father, put her arms around him and snogged him for several seconds.

What the fuck is going on?

His father opened the boot and tossed the golf clubs inside. It wasn't the first time he'd done that.

I can't believe that fucker is having an affair. What a selfish prick!

1

CHAPTER 16

Friday 30th January

AS RUTH SIPPED HER coffee and listened to Brooks' morning briefing, she could still feel the anxiety in the pit of her stomach. Koyuki's comments about her parents 'snogging', combined with what she had seen of Shiori in the shower, had convinced her that she was back with her husband Jerry. It was a horrible thought after all he had put her through. It wasn't a surprise that there was still an attraction, even love, between them. They had been married and they had Koyuki. But betrayal was betrayal and it was hard to take.

Trying to put the thoughts out of her mind, she glanced over as Brooks made his way to the scene boards and pointed to a photograph. 'Josh Harriot now has a strong alibi for where he was at the time of Tash's death. Ruth?'

Ruth sat up in her seat and gathered her thoughts. Her mind was still foggy and jumbled from her concerns over Shiori. 'Yes, Guv. We interviewed Hugo Allerton, who is Harriot's assistant at UCA Talent Agency. He confirmed what

Harriot told us. He arrived at Hugo's flat around ten o'clock and left around midnight.'

'And you believed him?'

Ruth nodded. 'They both seemed very emotional about the affair. There was nothing to suggest that either of them was lying to us.'

'Lucy?' Brooks said, glancing over at her.

If anything, Lucy had been acting even more out of character than the previous day, but Ruth wasn't going to probe just yet.

'Yes, Guv. Harriot was in bits when he revealed his affair with Allerton. My instinct was that they were both telling the truth.'

'Okay,' Brooks said with a nod. 'So that puts Harriot out of the frame for now. Tim, can you fill in the team with the latest on Barbara York?'

'Sure Guv. We brought her in for interview yesterday. She admitted that she had gone with Tash Weston back to her flat in an attempt to persuade her not to go to the press with her story about Bob Goldstein's sexual assault. When she thought she had managed to change Tash's mind, she got a mini-cab home at about ten thirty.'

Brooks shrugged. 'From the crime scene that we found at Banfield Road, do we think someone like Barbara York is capable of murdering Tash in the way that we found her?'

'If the drugs had incapacitated Tash while Barbara York was at her flat, she could have staged her murder to look however she wanted it to,' Gaughran suggested.

Brooks nodded. 'Okay. First thing to do is to track down the mini-cab company and check if she really did leave the flat around ten thirty.' He pointed to a photo of Marcus Jankel. 'He still bothers me. I know we have a witness who saw him arrive home at the time of Tash's murder, but he was having a relationship with her and the murder is a copycat of something that he made up.'

'Doesn't that rule him out?' Lucy asked.

'Not every killer is a criminal mastermind, Lucy,' Gaughran pointed out.

'Come on. He's got a degree from Oxford. Someone staged Tash's murder to replicate his script ... and he has an alibi.'

Gaughran raised an eyebrow. 'You seem very keen to defend him, Lucy. Has someone got the hots for Mr Jankel?'

'Piss off, Tim,' she retorted. 'I just don't believe he would deliberately put himself in the middle of all of this.'

'Unless that's part of the thrill?' Ruth suggested.

Brooks rubbed the nape of his neck. 'I don't know. I'd like us to do some more digging on him as I want to know why his name keeps cropping up ... Ruth, I think you've got something to show us?'

'Yes, Guv.' She took the VHS tape she had picked up from the owner of A&K Newsagents and placed it in the player. She had cued it up earlier and found the precise moment that their suspect had walked into the shop on Monday night to buy cigarettes.

'Okay, so this is our suspect here,' she said, pointing to a figure entering the shop. 'And then thirty seconds later, we get a nice shot of him buying cigarettes.'

She paused the image. There was their suspect. He was olive-skinned, handsome, with long, shoulder length black hair, a goatee beard and wearing a battered leather jacket.

'How do we find out who he is?' Brooks asked.

Lucy shrugged. 'We know that he goes into this newsagents at dawn or around ten o'clock most days. We need to set up surveillance on the shop until he goes in.'

'What about some kind of press release with that image?' Hassan suggested, pointing to the screen.

Brooks shook his head. 'If he sees that image, he'll know we have the CCTV from the shop. And he might suspect that we're staking out the shop and not go there ever again.'

It was good a point Ruth thought as she grabbed the Polaroid camera from her desk.

'Say cheese,' she joked as she took a photo of the screen. And then something occurred to her as she studied the image. 'He's wearing some kind of ID badge on his shirt.'

'What?' Brooks moved closer to the screen and stood next to Ruth.

The image was grainy but as Ruth squinted she could make out three letters at the top of the badge. White letters against a blue background.

'NHS,' she said reading aloud. She looked at Brooks. 'What's the betting our suspect works at King's College Hospital?'

Brooks smiled and nodded. 'Good work, Ruth.'

RUTH AND LUCY HAD PARKED outside King's College Hospital and were now marching towards the main entrance. It was cold, and Ruth felt the first touches of sleet on her face and the tip of her nose.

'If our suspect works with medical supplies, he might have access to something like Rohypnol, or whatever the pathologist said it was,' Lucy suggested.

'Flunitrazepam,' Ruth corrected.

'How did you remember that?' Lucy asked as they went through the automatic sliding doors that led into the hospital.

'I worked a case when I was in uniform. We went to what we thought was a routine death of an old lady who had died in her sleep. When they did the PM, they found Flunitrazepam in the tox report. Turned out the landlord wanted vacant possession of the flat back but she had refused.'

'So he killed her?'

'Yep. He popped in for a cup of tea and to collect the rent. While she wasn't looking, he put the stuff in her tea. He left and she died in the chair she was sitting in.'

'Bloody hell, that's cold. How did he get it?'

'He was a surgeon.'

Lucy's eyes widened. 'What? Are you kidding?'

'No. I wish I was. He was a neurosurgeon at St George's. Got a life sentence. He assumed there would be no tox report but the coroner decided to be thorough and ordered one because she hadn't turned seventy.'

Lucy was still shaking her head as they arrived at the main reception.

'Hi there. Peckham CID,' Ruth said, showing the receptionist her warrant card. 'We're trying to track down someone we think might work here?'

The receptionist nodded and pointed to a corridor on the opposite side of the building. 'You'll need to go to our Human Resources department. It's just down there.'

'Thanks.'

As soon as they were in the corridor, they saw an open door marked *Human Resources – Main Office*. A woman was typing away at a computer and seemed oblivious to their presence.

'Hi there,' Lucy said getting out her warrant card. 'We're from Peckham CID. We're trying to trace someone who we think works here.'

The woman looked up, nodded and went to close the door. 'Sorry, I was miles away. Come and sit down. I'm Jo.'

All three sat down in some chairs that were arranged around a low coffee table.

'Have you got the name of the person you're trying to trace?' Jo asked.

'No,' Ruth said as she pulled out the Polaroid photo, 'but we do have this.'

Jo took the photo, studied it and shook her head. 'Sorry. I don't recognise him. Why do you think he works here?'

Ruth leaned over and pointed to his badge. 'This has NHS printed at the top, and this CCTV was taken up on Coldharbour Lane not far from here.'

Jo nodded. 'That does look like one of our badges but we employ over eight thousand people here. It's going to be hard to track someone down just with that photo.'

Lucy looked at her and said, 'We're investigating a murder, so it's really important that we find him.'

'Okay, give me two minutes. Can I take this?'

'Sure,' Ruth said.

Jo got up and breezed out of the office.

Lucy pulled a face. 'You know, he might not even work here. The Lambeth Hospital is only a couple of miles away. He might work there.'

Ruth nodded – they really were looking for a needle in haystack. It seemed as if the surveillance operation on the newsagents was going to be their best bet. And that meant endless hours in a car.

Jo came back in and shook her head. 'I'm really sorry. I've asked around and no one seems to recognise him. He might not even work in this hospital.'

'Yeah, we've just thought of that,' Ruth said as she got up. 'Thanks anyway.'

Ruth and Lucy wandered back down the corridor and out into the main lobby.

'We didn't show the receptionist the photo,' Lucy said. ' She sees most of the staff coming in.'

Ruth nodded as they headed back to the desk. 'Worth a try.'

The receptionist smiled and said, 'Hello again. Did you find it all right?'

'Yes thanks,' Ruth said. 'I wonder if you could look at this photograph and tell us if you recognise the man?'

'I'll give it a go.'

Ruth showed her the photo but she shook her head. 'No, sorry. I don't know him.'

Ruth and Lucy gave each other a slightly dispirited look. Such were the frustrations of methodical police work.

Then something occurred to Ruth and she turned back to the receptionist. 'Can you tell me what time you start on reception here?'

'I get in for ten every morning.'

'And what time do you leave?'

'Six on the dot,' the receptionist replied looking a little confused.

Ruth turned to Lucy with a raised eyebrow. 'She's not here when he comes in.'

Lucy nodded and looked at the receptionist. 'So, who works here before you in the morning?'

'A woman called Jill,' Jo said, and then pointed to the small shop across the way that sold newspapers, soft toys and sweets. 'She works in the shop for the rest of the day if you want to speak to her.'

Ruth and Lucy turned, crossed to the shop and saw a middle-aged Afro-Caribbean woman behind the till.

'We're looking for Jill?' Lucy said as she fished out her warrant card.

'That's me, darling. Have I done something wrong?'

Lucy smiled. 'No, nothing like that.'

Ruth took out the picture and showed it to her. 'Do you recognise this man?'

'Yeah, that's Hadir,' she said with a frown. 'Been up to no good, has he?'

Ruth forced a smile. 'We're not sure yet.'

'You know Hadir, do you?' Lucy asked.

'Oh yeah. He makes me laugh. Funny man,' Jill chortled. 'His family are a long way away, so I try and look out for him, you know?'

Do you know where he works in this hospital?'

Jill nodded and pointed to the floor. 'Down there.'

Ruth frowned. 'I'm not following you.'

'In the basement, where the bodies are,' Jill whispered.

'He works in the mortuary?' Lucy asked.

Jill nodded. 'But he doesn't work today. It's his day off.'

CHAPTER 17

THE NIGHT SKY WAS BLACK overhead as Ruth and Lucy walked up the weed-strewn garden path in Dunedin Road. It was the address they had been given for Hadir Benali by the HR department at King's College Hospital. The road was only a two-minute walk from where Tash Weston had been murdered, and its location explained why Tash had spotted Benali in the area on several occasions. The ramshackle house was narrow, with a front door that looked like it hadn't been painted since the 1960s. Patches of green moss had grown on the brickwork where the old drainpipe was broken.

Lucy knocked on the door and they waited. As she exhaled, her breath was white and visible in the icy air.

She turned to Ruth. 'Do you remember when you used to do that at school?'

'What's that?'

'Get a pen and pretend to smoke when your breath condensed in the cold air.'

There was still no answer from the door, so she knocked again.

'I started smoking when I was thirteen, so I didn't need to pretend,' Ruth said with an ironic laugh.

'Thirteen? Bloody hell! I'm surprised you've got any lungs left.'

'It's true. I'm a medical miracle.'

Lucy put her finger to her lips. She could hear movement from inside the house somewhere.

Ruth whispered, 'Someone in there?'

Lucy nodded. There was the noise of a door closing towards the back of the house.

Pushing the letterbox open, she peered inside. All she could see was a dark hallway covered in junk mail. She got a strong waft of marijuana.

'I can smell weed,' she whispered. 'And I don't think he's coming to the door any time soon.'

'You think he's gonna do a runner?'

'If he's our man, then it's quite possible.'

Ruth pointed to a passageway to their left that looked like it ran down the side of the house. 'Let's try round the back then.'

'Oh great. The one day I wore a slight heel,' Lucy groaned as she pointed to her shoes. She moved over to the passageway where an iron gate was open by a few inches. As she pushed it open further, the rusted hinges made a low metallic groan.

Christ, this is all a bit Hammer Horror, she thought acerbically.

They crept slowly down the side of the house, pushing their way through the thick overhanging undergrowth that barred their way. Now that they were out of the range of the streetlights they were in total darkness.

Taking out her torch, Lucy clicked it on and then stopped just short of walking straight into a disused fridge that rested against the mouldy side wall of the house.

'Bloody hell!' she muttered.

'Having fun?' Ruth quipped as she clicked on her own torch. They continued to weave and duck through the low hanging branches, and eventually made their way through into a tiny, derelict back garden.

Waving her torch around, Lucy saw that the garden was cluttered with old furniture, a stained mattress, a broken ladder, pots of paint and bags of rubbish. The cold winter air was thick with the stench of decay.

They moved quietly across the back of the house. All the lights inside had been turned off so it was in absolute darkness. Relying only on the light of their pocket torches, they squatted and looked around.

Lucy strained to listen. Except for the wind rustling in some nearby trees, it was silent. Then a soft whoosh of a distant car like a veiled whisper.

There was a back door to what she assumed was the kitchen.

Reaching up slowly, she pushed down its cold, metal-levered handle – it was locked.

Bollocks!

There was a noise from inside.

Lucy and Ruth exchanged a look – *there's definitely somebody in there.*

Then another noise. They froze.

In the distance, there was the sound of sirens.

Suddenly, a dark figure leapt from a ground floor window and sprinted across the garden.

Jesus Christ!

'Stop! Police!' Lucy shouted.

Before they had time to react, the hooded figure had climbed the four-foot brick wall and pulled themselves over the mesh fencing that was above it.

By the time Lucy and Ruth reached the wall in pursuit, he had dropped down to the other side and was off.

As the figure sprinted right to escape along the alleyway, Lucy caught sight of his profile.

Hadir Benali.

'It's him!' she growled as she pulled herself up the mesh.

A jagged piece of wire stuck into her thumb. 'Shit!'

She hauled herself to the top of the mesh fencing, heaved herself over, and dropped down into the alleyway. Ruth did the same.

'That's much better than the last time you did that!' Lucy said as they turned to pursue Benali.

'Where the hell was that?'

'Hammersmith.'

Benali was fast, and putting an increasing distance between them.

'Shit!' Lucy shouted as she started to breathe heavily. It had been a long time since she had done any meaningful exercise.

'Keep going,' Ruth panted.

There was light up ahead and Lucy could see that there were steel railings where the alleyway came out onto the main road.

'Stop! Police!' Ruth yelled.

Benali looked back for a second and then vaulted the railings and darted left.

The muscles in Lucy's legs were starting to burn. She clenched her fists as she powered on. If this was the man who had brutally murdered Tash Weston, then she wasn't going to let him get away. *Fuck that!*

As they reached the railings, they glanced left.

Benali was weaving in and out of people who were making their way along Denmark Hill. It was rush hour and the traffic was moving slowly.

Lucy thought there was over a hundred yards between them.

How the hell are we ever going to catch him?

They scrambled over the railings and continued to pursue him north on Denmark Hill. In the distance they saw Benali stop a teenager on a mountain bike, wrestle him to the ground, and ride off along the pavement on the bike.

'Great!' Lucy growled as she slowed down.

Ruth doubled over with her hands on her hips. 'We're never going to catch him now,' she gasped between breaths.

Lucy sucked in air – her whole body ached. 'That really hurts!'

As they watched Benali cycle away, a gang of teenagers, all hoods and baseball caps, blocked his path and surrounded him. There was an argument going on, and a moment later someone pushed Benali to the pavement aggressively.

''Ave that, bitch boy! You wanna go?'

'Oh bollocks!' Lucy said. 'I think he stole the wrong kid's bike.'

As one of the youths kicked Benali in the head, Lucy and Ruth broke into a sprint.

'Shit!' Lucy exclaimed.

'I just hope they don't kill him before we get there,' Ruth shouted as they ran.

Benali was being kicked and punched from all sides. It was a shocking and frenzied attack.

Grabbing their warrant cards, Lucy and Ruth approached quickly.

'Oi, leave him alone!' Lucy bellowed.

'Nah, he nicked dat bike, fam,' one of the teenagers shouted, kicking Benali in the chest.

'Hey! Get away from him now ...' Ruth yelled, 'or I'll nick the lot of you!'

There was a lot of mumbling, swearing, and kissing of teeth as the youths backed away.

Lucy went over to where Benali lay motionless on the pavement. He was unconscious, but he had a pulse. 'We need the paramedics here, and fast.'

AN HOUR LATER, RUTH and Lucy were sitting in a corridor in A&E. Benali had regained consciousness before the paramedics had arrived, but he needed checking out thoroughly in hospital. Ruth had handcuffed him to the trolley bed – they were taking no chances of him running again. She sipped from a bottle of water as she was still recovering from the foot chase earlier.

The air was filled with a cacophony of sounds. The steady bleep of monitors, phones ringing, nurses talking in raised voices, and the groan of a drunken patient who was sprawled across three seats opposite them.

For a moment, it took her back to when her father had had a cardiac arrest in the middle of Northcote Road Market. He had been raced to St George's in Tooting. She had sat with her mother and brother in seats just like these, waiting while the staff had worked on him. But it was no use. They found out later that his heart had stopped when he fell, and had never started again. Her father had been an old-fashioned man, born during the Second World War. He smoked like a chimney, liked a drink, and ate whatever he fancied - usually covered in butter and salt. The fact that he hadn't made it to seventy wasn't therefore a shock, but her mum was utterly lost without him and she never really got over it.

'How is he?' Lucy asked as a doctor approached.

'Concussed. I think he's got some fractured ribs and a possible broken wrist.'

'Is he up to talking?'

The doctor pulled a face as if to say, *Can it wait?*

'We're investigating a murder,' Ruth explained very quietly. 'It would only take five minutes, but it's really important.'

'Okay, but only five minutes.'

'Are you keeping him in overnight?' Lucy asked.

'Yes, I'd like to keep him under observation given his head injuries. We'll probably move him to a ward upstairs in about half an hour.'

'Okay. Depending on what he says, we may need to get a uniformed officer to sit with him overnight.'

'I'll let the ward sister know,' the doctor said as he turned and walked off.

Ruth and Lucy got up and made their way to the first cubicle where Benali had been taken. It had been cordoned off with blue curtains.

Pulling back the curtain slowly, Ruth could see that Benali's face was already swollen around the jaw. He had a black eye and a nasty graze on his temple.

'How are you feeling?' she asked as she and Lucy sat on the two orange plastic chairs beside the trolley bed.

Benali said nothing.

Lucy held up a wallet in a small evidence bag. 'We retrieved this wallet from you before the paramedics arrived.'

'That is mine,' he said angrily in a thick, North African accent. 'You must give it back to me!'

Ruth looked at him and said quietly, 'Hadir, we found an ID card in your wallet that shows that you work in this hospital? Is that right?'

He nodded. Despite his injuries, his face was symmetrical, his nose straight and his mouth full. He was very handsome, just as Tash Weston had described the man she thought was stalking her to her friend Jane Sinclair.

Lucy moved her chair a little closer to the trolley bed. 'Why did you run from us, Hadir?'

'I didn't know who you were. I was scared.'

'You were scared of two women knocking on your front door? Really?'

'Maybe you were council people? Or immigration people? I don't know.'

'Are you in this country illegally?'

'No, no, of course not.'

'Then why did you run? We identified ourselves as police officers twice, but you continued to run.'

'In my country, if the police come knocking at your door, then you run,' he explained. 'You do not wait to see what they want.'

'But you're not in your country, Hadir,' Ruth pointed out.

'Sometimes it is the same here,' he said wearily. 'The police here are corrupt and racist too.'

Ruth delved into her pocket and pulled out the Polaroid of the man buying cigarettes from the newsagent's. 'Can you look at this photograph, please?'

He peered at the image for a few seconds.

'Is that you?' she asked.

'Yes.'

'Can you tell us where you went after you had bought those cigarettes?' Lucy asked.

Benali frowned as if it was a strange question. 'I went home.'

'Can anyone vouch for you?'

'Sorry?' Benali said with a frown. 'I don't understand.'

Ruth looked at him. 'Do you live with anyone else? Or is there anyone who can prove that you did go straight home?'

He shook his head. 'No. I live on my own. My family are in Tangiers.'

'And you're sure you didn't go anywhere else before you went home?'

'No, no. I don't understand why you ask me this question,' he groaned as he shifted and then winced in pain.

Lucy pulled a photograph of Tash Weston from her pocket and held it up for Benali to look at. 'Do you recognise this woman?'

Benali frowned. 'No. I don't know her.'

Ruth was watching Benali like a hawk but he hadn't reacted when he saw the photo of Tash.

'You've never seen her before?'

'No.'

'You're sure about that?'

'Yes, I have never seen her before.'

'You don't know where she lives?'

'No.'

'And you've never been to her flat?'

'No. Why are you asking me about her?' he asked in an irritated voice.

Lucy stared at him dubiously. 'Because she was murdered last Monday night very close to where you live. And she reported that a man fitting your description had been following her and had been outside her home.'

Benali was shaken. 'No, that wasn't me. I promise you. I have never seen that woman before. I have a wife and children back home in Morocco.'

'Okay,' Ruth said. 'We have applied for a warrant to search your home, Hadir. Are we going to find anything there that you might want to tell us about now?'

He shook his head, but he still seemed scared. 'You will find nothing. I promise you. I have nothing to hide.'

Ruth exchanged a look with Lucy – she wasn't sure they had the right man.

CHAPTER 18

RUTH GAZED UP INTO the dark night sky for a few seconds. The stars seemed tiny, like spilled sugar across a black awning. The icy wind tousled her hair and she pulled up the collar of her coat against the freezing cold. Her ears had become numb and she was regretting not bringing her woollen hat. She and Lucy were once again standing on the front doorstep of Hadir Benali's house. This time they had three uniformed officers with them to help with the initial search, plus a SOCO team that was on standby in case it turned out to be a crime scene.

Having knocked to make sure no one was in, one of the uniformed officers stepped forward with a door lock opening tool and went to work. About thirty seconds later, the latch to the front door was open and they all went in.

Ruth snapped on her blue forensic gloves over her frozen fingers. She was taking no chances when it came to contaminating any evidence.

As she stepped forward inside the house, her foot slipped a little on the mountain of junk mail and food delivery leaflets that lay on the hall floor. The house smelled dank, with an underlying aroma of weed and spicy food. She reached for the light switch and turned on the solitary light bulb that hung from the flaky ceiling.

There was a door on the left which she assumed led to some kind of living room. She entered slowly. The room was sparse. In the far corner was an old television, a VHS recorder and some VHS tapes in a small pile. On the right was a large armchair covered with an olive-colour patterned material. An ashtray on the floor was filled with cigarette butts and the roaches from spliffs.

'Home sweet home,' Lucy muttered under her breath.

Several pictures and photos had been sellotaped to the wall in an attempt to make the room more homely. To one side, a large picture of the city of Tangiers, with its ancient city walls and port. Beside that, a picture torn from a magazine of the Moroccan footballer Mustapha Hadji, dressed in the distinctive dark green strip of the Moroccan national team.

Scanning the room, Ruth could see that there was virtually nothing else of interest. She looked at the uniformed officers and said, 'Can you guys have a look upstairs?'

The officers nodded, turned, and proceeded out into the hallway and up the stairs, their boots thundering on the wooden steps as they went.

Ruth and Lucy moved slowly down towards the back of the house where there was a small and basic kitchen. The smell of spices was almost overwhelming. As Ruth searched the cupboards, she saw bags of couscous, dried fruit, nuts, lentils, and tins of sardines that had red Arabic writing on them.

She could hear the boots of the officers searching upstairs. So far, they had found nothing incriminating which reinforced her gut feeling that they had the wrong man.

As Ruth and Lucy went out into the hallway, one of the officers came down the stairs.

'Anything?' Ruth asked.

He shook his head. 'All the rooms are empty except one bedroom where he sleeps. There's a mattress on the floor, some books, and a pile of clothes. That's it.'

Lucy pulled a face. 'We haven't got anything to justify getting SOCOs in here, have we?'

Ruth shook her head. 'No.' But then something occurred to her. 'These old Victorian houses have cellars, don't they?'

'I don't know,' Lucy said. 'I can't see one.'

The officer nodded. 'Yeah, most of the houses in Peckham have a basement or cellar of some kind.'

'Well, where is it?' Ruth began to examine the wooded panels that ran along the wall under the staircase.

Lucy shrugged. 'Maybe these houses just don't have one?'

'It's normally around here,' Ruth said as she continued her inspection.

She took out her pocket torch and shone its beam on to the wood as she worked her way down the wall towards the kitchen. She stopped for a moment. There was a tiny gap in the wood of about three or four millimetres. Running her hand over it, she felt a small wisp of cold air against her palm.

She turned to Lucy. 'It's here.'

'What?'

'There's something here.'

Taking two steps back and using her torch, she could see the faint outline of a doorway.

Bingo!

She walked forward, shoved the wooden panel and felt the movement of the door.

'I need something to prise this open,' she said as the other officers came down the stairs.

Lucy turned, went to the kitchen, and returned a moment later with a metal fish slice. 'Will this do?'

'Perfect,' Ruth said, as she wedged it into the gap and levered with the slice.

Out of the wooden wall, a door opened.

'Ta da!' she said triumphantly.

A narrow wooden staircase led down into the darkness of the cellar. The air was damp and thick with the smell of oil and paint.

'Oh great,' Lucy grumbled.

'What's wrong?'

'If this was a film, this is the part where the audience would say, "What are you going down there for? You're going to find lots of dead bodies or a girl in some homemade cell who has been kept there for the past ten years."'

One of the officers let out a little laugh at Lucy's comment.

Ruth frowned. 'Don't joke. God knows what we might find down here.'

Holding onto the wobbly wooden handrail, she stepped carefully down each step, peering into the blackness and using her torch to look around.

The ceiling was low, and thick wooden pillars jutted from the floor to hold it up.

Ruth spotted a light switch on the bare brick wall and clicked it on. A dim bulb at the far end threw a murky light across the space. It was cluttered with old cardboard boxes stacked from floor to ceiling, shelves, paint pots, and a stepladder. Against another wall was an old mahogany wardrobe.

There was a sudden noise from behind the stack of boxes.

'What the fuck was that?' Lucy asked nervously.

They all froze and listened again.

Ruth's heart started to beat a little faster.

Was someone or something hiding behind there?

Focussing her torchlight on where the noise had come, Ruth moved forward a couple of paces.

There was another noise. It sounded like someone moving against cardboard.

'Do you want me to have a look?' whispered one of the officers.

Ruth ignored his request and, as she took another step, she saw a pink tail and a dark shape scurry behind the shelving unit.

'It's all right, it's a rat,' she said.

'Oh good. I love rats,' Lucy quipped.

For the next few minutes, Ruth, Lucy and the officers searched the contents of the boxes, shelves and the wardrobe.

'Anything?' Ruth asked.

'Nope,' Lucy said. 'I'm starting to wonder if we're wasting our time with this bloke.'

Ruth was thinking the same thing, and had begun to run the other suspects through her mind. Maybe it was someone who just hadn't been on their radar at all?

'Why's that chair there like that?' Lucy asked, pointing to a battered wooden chair with a burgundy seat cover. Underneath it was what appeared to be a crumpled orange towel.

'No idea.' Ruth didn't know what Lucy was getting at.

'It's facing the wardrobe, and it looks like it's been placed there deliberately.' Lucy went over to the chair and then glanced at the mahogany wardrobe that was resting against the wall. Flicking some cobwebs from the brickwork, she shone her torch behind. 'There's something on the wall here.'

Ruth went over. 'What is it?'

'I can't see,' she said as she gestured to one of the uniformed officers. 'Constable, could you give us a hand to move this away from the wall?'

'Of course,' he replied.

Ruth and Lucy grabbed one side of the wardrobe while the officer took the other. Ruth was surprised at how light it was. She and Lucy could have moved it on their own – it just looked heavy.

They pulled the wardrobe away, then turned to look at the space it had occupied. Ruth's face dropped, and her stomach turned.

Oh my God!

They were looking at a large cork pinboard about five feet square attached to the wall.

And it was covered in a picture collage of Tash Weston.

'Jesus Christ!' Lucy exclaimed.

CHAPTER 19

AN HOUR LATER, RUTH and Lucy arrived back on the Hetton Ward at King's College Hospital. They had contacted Brooks to tell him what they'd found, and had handed the house over to the SOCO team.

Most of the photos of Tash had been cut from film or fashion magazines. However, there were over half a dozen that had been taken from outside Tash's flat showing her inside. Lucy was convinced they had the right man now.

As she and Ruth walked along the hospital corridor, her phone buzzed with a text. It was from Marcus.

I need to see you. Last night was incredible. I understand if you're busy. X

Lucy gestured to the ladies' toilets. 'I'll be two minutes.'

Ruth smiled and nodded. 'I'll wait here.'

'Don't flirt with any nurses,' Lucy joked, but she was feeling guilty about deceiving Ruth.

The toilets were empty and she marched into a stall and locked the door behind her. Taking her phone, she wondered what to type.

'Okay. But work is mental. I'm not going to be finished until late.'

She would leave the kiss off the text for the time being.

I don't care. I'd really like to see you tonight. I'm a real night owl! X

Lucy couldn't help but smile at his text. It reassured her that it was worth seeing him. She thought for a second. If she went to his place, then she could control when she left.

'I'll be at yours just after ten?'

'Brilliant! X"

Feeling upbeat at the prospect of seeing Marcus, Lucy strode out of the toilets and noticed Ruth frowning at her.

'What's wrong?' Lucy asked, looking down at her trousers playfully. 'Have I tucked my jacket into my knickers?'

Ruth laughed. 'No. You've just got a strange look on your face.'

They began to walk down the corridor towards the ward.

'Yeah, that's just my face,' Lucy joked. 'I'm stuck with it, I'm afraid.'

Ruth rolled her eyes. 'That's not what I meant, silly. You just looked ... smug.'

'Smug? Oh thanks!'

'Or like someone had told you a joke in the toilets,' Ruth said. 'It's not important.'

'Oh, well I've been dying for a wee for about an hour, and now I feel a lot better.'

'Which is more information than I required, but thank you anyway,' Ruth snorted.

They arrived at the nurses' desk on Hetton Ward and showed their warrant cards.

'We're looking for Hadir Benali,' Lucy explained. 'I think he's got one of our officers with him?'

A very attractive nurse, late 30s, nodded with a serious expression and pointed to the corridor on their left. 'Yes, he's down there in one of the single rooms.'

'Thanks,' Ruth said, and grinned at Lucy as they headed down the corridor. 'Now I would have definitely flirted with her.'

'So would I, and I'm straight,' Lucy joked. She spotted a young male uniformed officer sitting on a chair outside a room.

'Here we go.'

'Evening Constable,' Lucy said. 'Any problems?'

The officer shook his head. 'Not a peep.'

Lucy gestured to the room. 'We're about to arrest this suspect, so we're going to need an officer here all night.'

'No problem, I'll talk to my Sarge.'

Ruth and Lucy opened the door and saw Benali in a hospital bed. His right hand was cuffed to the side of the bed and he was staring up at the ceiling.

Lucy closed the door behind them.

'Hadir Benali?' Lucy said. 'You are under arrest on suspicion of the murder of Natasha Weston. You do not have to say anything, but anything you do say can be taken down and used in a court of law. Do you understand what I've just said to you?'

He was silent for a moment, then very slowly he turned his head and stared at them.

'Yes,' he mumbled with a strange look on his face.

'We've searched your house and found your collection of photos of Tash Weston in the basement. Is there anything you want to tell us about that?'

Benali smirked. 'It's not illegal to have those pictures, is it?'

'It could be illegal to take photos of someone inside their house,' Ruth replied.

'I don't think so,' he said with a little laugh.

This isn't funny, you prick!

His arrogance was starting to get right up Lucy's nose.

'We know you were stalking Natasha Weston in the weeks leading up to her murder,' she said. 'You need to tell us what happened last Monday night, Hadir.'

Benali looked up at the ceiling again and rubbed his nose. He didn't seem distinctly fazed by being charged with murder or by what they had discovered in his home.

'How did you get into Tash's flat?' Lucy snapped. 'Did you force your way in?'

He gave a little sigh of irritation. 'Why don't you ask her that?'

Ruth and Lucy exchanged a look. *What the fuck is he talking about?*

'Why don't we ask who?' Lucy asked, unable to hide her frustration.

'Poor little Natasha. You say that I am following her. You say that I force myself into her flat. You say that I have killed her. So, just ask her. Simple.'

'We can't ask her, can we? She's dead,' Lucy almost yelled at him.

Benali turned his head slowly and stared at her. This time there was something quite unnerving about his cold expression.

'Exactly,' he said in a calm but conceited tone. 'You cannot talk to that whore, because she is dead.'

Lucy could have quite happily walked over and punched him in the face. She took a deep breath – she didn't want Benali thinking that he had somehow got to her.

'Why do you think she is a whore, Hadir?' Ruth asked without a trace of emotion.

'Why do you think?' Hadir shrugged. 'Isn't it obvious?'

Ruth shook her head. 'No, it's not. So, enlighten me.'

'They are all little whores, little bitches,' he sneered. 'Parading themselves. She knew exactly what she was doing. And that is why she is dead.'

'Did you kill Natasha Weston, Hadir?' Ruth asked.

He shook his head and smiled. 'No, of course not. She brought it on herself, as if she had done it with her own hand. But it was God's hand. God Almighty!'

Lucy looked again at Ruth – it seemed that Benali might be suffering from some kind of mental illness.

'Hadir, you will remain in this hospital until later today,' Ruth explained. 'You will then be transferred to a holding cell at Peckham police station. We will be interviewing you again tomorrow. If you wish to have legal counsel present, we can organise that for you. Do you understand?'

Benali looked at them both with distain. 'You will find no evidence of my wrongdoing. I can promise you that. I have destroyed anything that might lead you down that path, I can assure you.'

CHAPTER 20

IT WAS NEARLY 10PM by the time Lucy arrived in Ruston Mews. Her head was filled with thoughts about what they had found in Benali's home, and their conversation with him in the hospital. Neither she nor Ruth were certain if he had made some kind of confession but the evidence against him was mounting.

Lucy reverse-parked into a small space and nodded in satisfaction. Before getting out of the car, she leaned over to the passenger seat and grabbed a cold bottle of Pinot Grigio white wine that she'd bought on the way. She needed a drink.

As she walked down the mews, her heels clicked noisily on the cobbled surface. The air was fresh and cold. Taking a deep breath, she tried to clear her head of the stresses of the day. What she should have done is gone home, had a hot shower, drunk half a bottle of wine, and gone to bed. But her motto was that you can sleep when you're dead, and that life was too short not to take a few chances.

She gazed up at the narrow mews cottages and their tiny first-floor balconies. The house next to Marcus' had been painted in candyfloss-pink, and the balcony was adorned with a variety of plants and hanging baskets.

She arrived at Marcus's front door and rang the buzzer.

After a few seconds, she rang again but there was no reply.

She glanced down at her watch. It was 9.55pm. Technically she'd said she would be there after ten.

Looking around for signs of his car, she spotted someone at a first-floor window of the house opposite. A man with his top off, pulling on a sweater.

It was Marcus!

What the fuck is he doing?

She couldn't believe her eyes. She had arrived early only to spot him getting dressed in the house opposite.

Are you fucking kidding me? What a wanker!

A moment later, the front door to that house opened and Marcus appeared. He kissed a dark-haired woman goodbye on the cheek and came jogging over the road without a care in the world.

Lucy could hardly contain her rage.

To her astonishment, he gave her a cheery wave when he saw her standing on his doorstep.

'Hi, hi,' he said with a smile. 'Sorry. Have you been waiting there long?'

Lucy gritted her teeth, took two steps forward and slapped him hard across the face.

THWACK!

'Jesus Christ!' he yelped.

She might have overdone it as the skin on her hand actually stung from the force.

'You wanker!' she growled.

Holding his face, Marcus looked at her wide-eyed and shocked. 'What the fuck are you doing?'

'I can't believe that I've turned up here only to watch you getting dressed having shagged your neighbour. So, fuck off you needle-dicked little twat!'

Turning on her heels, Lucy felt tears well up in her eyes. She felt so utterly humiliated and broke into a jog towards her car.

'Wait! You've got it all wrong,' Marcus shouted as he ran to catch her up. 'Oh my God. I wasn't shagging Polly. She's an osteopath - she's treating my lower back.'

Lucy shook her head. 'Nice try but that's bollocks.'

'Seriously,' he said, putting his hand on her arm.

'Don't touch me!'

'Come on, let's go and ask her.' He gestured to Polly's house.

'She's not going to admit to shagging you, is she?' Lucy snapped, but part of her was wondering if he might be telling the truth.

'Well, she's also gay. And she's sitting in there watching TV with her girlfriend, Nell.'

Lucy took a few seconds to calm down.

Oh God, have I just completely overreacted.

Marcus had a little smile on his face. She could see he was dying to laugh.

'This is not funny,' she said, but it was starting to sound like she might have got the wrong end of the stick.

'Look, I can see how you might have got the wrong idea ... Sorry.'

Polly had appeared on the balcony and looked down. 'Everything all right, Marcus?'

Oh God. She must have heard me shouting. That's really embarrassing.

'Fine,' Marcus said as he looked up. 'This is Lucy who I was telling you about?'

'Oh yes. Hi,' she replied with an accent that wouldn't have been out of place at Buckingham Palace. 'I don't know what you see in Marcus. He's a total arse!' she laughed.

'Yes, thanks Polly.' Marcus rolled his eyes.

'Hi there,' Lucy said very quietly.

Polly smiled at her, then looked at Marcus. 'If your back goes into spasm again, you know where I am.'

'How's Nell?' he asked.

'Fine. She wants the recipe for your goat's cheese and watermelon salad.'

'No problem.'

Polly gave Lucy a wave. 'Well, nice to have met you. I'd better go. Ally McBeal's on and Nell's got a thing for Calista Flockhart.'

Marcus laughed. 'I'll see you guys soon.'

For a few moments, Lucy looked at him uncertainly.

'I think I might owe you an apology,' she said, trying to stifle a laugh.

'You think?' You nearly broke my jaw. I'm not some crackhead from Peckham.'

Lucy laughed. 'I'm not taking back the wanker bit though.'

He pulled a face that feigned offence. 'Oh, and why not?'

'You've got a recipe for a goat's cheese and watermelon salad. That makes you a wanker,' Lucy quipped.

He smiled. 'Welcome to Notting Hill.'

'Are you going to invite me in?' Lucy asked, pointing to the door.

'It depends on whether or not you're going to assault me again,' he replied, fishing out his keys as they walked towards his house.

'And that depends on whether you behave yourself,' she said with a sexy grin.

He unlocked the door, they went in, and began to kiss passionately in the small hallway at the bottom of the stairs.

Marcus stopped, put his hand to her face and smiled. 'Needledick? Really?'

Lucy raised an eyebrow. 'I can't remember. You'll just have to remind me.'

He pushed her slowly back onto the stairs as they grappled with each other's clothes.

RUTH GULPED DOWN THE remainder of her wine and poured herself another glass. Not only had it been an exhausting day, but she was expecting Shiori to come through the front door any minute now and she had resolved to confront her.

Taking another long swig, she then reached for the packet of Marlborough Lights, took one and lit it. She wandered over to the patio door and opened it. The air outside was freezing but it felt nice against her face. She pulled a garden chair over, sat down and gazed up at the dark winter sky.

Across to the east, she saw a strobe of blue light as a train from Balham station switched from diesel to the overhead electric lines. The distant, rhythmic sound of the carriages on the track felt reassuring. It had been the background sound to most of her life. She had grown up on an estate in Battersea, and her bedroom window overlooked train lines that went behind Battersea Power Station up to Vauxhall and Waterloo. They weren't noisy enough to wake her or be intrusive, in fact they formed a lovely cadence of reassuring sound.

In the darkness, the large tree that grew against the wire fence at the bottom of her tiny garden seemed far bigger than she knew it was. In one place, the trunk had grown around one of the metal posts, the folds of wood wrapped around it like the lips of a giant mouth.

'What are you doing out here, it's freezing!' a voice asked.

It was Shiori.

Ruth felt herself tense as she turned to look at her. 'However mad it sounds, I wanted a blast a fresh air and a ciggie.'

'And nearly a bottle of Merlot,' Shiori said with a raised eyebrow.

Condescending bitch, Ruth thought, although it was going to be easier to confront her if she was in one of her pompous moods.

'I'll come in,' Ruth said as she stubbed out her cigarette, 'there's something I need to talk to you about.'

'Oh God, that sounds ominous,' Shiori laughed.

Yeah, you won't be laughing in a minute, you lying cow.

As they went inside, Shiori frowned at her. 'Everything all right?'

'No,' Ruth said as she gestured to the sofa. 'Shall we sit down?'

'Okay ...' Shiori was already sounding nervous.

Ruth stared at her, took and breath and asked, 'Are you sleeping with Jerry?'

'What?' Shiori said, her eyes widening.

Ruth sat forward. 'I'm going to try and be calm about this. I know you're sleeping with Jerry. Please don't deny it.'

Shiori blinked rapidly as her eyes darted around the room nervously. Ruth knew she was weighing up whether to continue lying or to come clean.

'Please don't lie to me, Shiori,' Ruth implored her. 'I think you owe me that. Do the right the thing and just tell me the truth. I already know anyway.'

Shiori looked away briefly. 'Yes I am ... and I'm sorry.'

Even though she already knew, Ruth still felt sick at hearing it from Shiori's mouth.

'How long?'

'A few weeks.' Shiori looked down at her hands and fiddled with the rings on her finger.

'Do you still love him?'

She shrugged. 'I don't know. I guess so.'

'Guess?' Ruth shook her head. 'Don't you know?'

'It's so complicated,' Shiori said getting up and moving towards Ruth.

Ruth raised her hand to stop her. 'I'd prefer it if you just stayed there. If you're leaving me, I don't want to be near you.'

Shiori reached up to her face and wiped away a tear. 'We have Koyuki together. She needs a father.'

'A father who is a workaholic and a cheating wanker. Those were your words, not mine, Shiori.'

She nodded. 'Jerry's not perfect. But he wants us to try again.'

Oh God, she really is leaving me.

'And that's it?' Ruth asked with an angry shrug. 'He wants to try again and you're going to give up what we have together and go back to him? Just like that.'

'I want Koyuki to grow up in a normal family with a mum and dad,' Shiori said as she sniffed and wiped more tears from her face.

'Jesus Christ! If 'normal' means Koyuki will have a father who is shallow, materialistic, and cheats on her mother, then good luck.'

'That's not fair!' Shiori snapped.

'You were sleeping with him behind my back!' Ruth growled. 'Don't take any moral high ground with me.'

Ruth got up from the sofa, went over to the table, and unscrewed another bottle of Merlot. She saw Shiori looking at her.

'It sounds like you've made up your mind,' Ruth said, 'but I don't want you knocking on my door in a couple months when you've found out he's screwing his assistant again.'

LUCY TRACED HER FINGER over Marcus' face and wiped a bead of sweat from above one of his dark eyebrows. The cold sheet of his bed felt refreshing across her legs.

'You've got that whole dark mysterious poetic look, haven't you?' she said quietly as she gazed into his chestnut eyes.

'Byronic?'

'Bionic?' Lucy asked deliberately. She didn't know what Byronic meant exactly.

He laughed. 'No, although bionic sounds good. Steve Austin, we can rebuild him, the Six Million Dollar Man.'

Lucy smiled. 'Actually, I used to have a thing for Lee Majors. He looked a bit like if Elvis had had a younger brother.'

Marcus snorted. 'God, you've really given that some thought.'

'And Byronic is named after Lord Byron?' Lucy asked, hoping she hadn't made a mistake and now appeared stupid.

'Exactly,' he said, sounding surprised.

'Don't patronise me, Mr Public School Boy,' she grinned. 'I'll have you know that we studied a lot of Byron in Sacred Hearts Catholic School in Camberwell.'

'Of course. You told me you were a lapsed Catholic.'

Lucy laughed. 'Very lapsed after what we just did!'

He looked at her with a serious expression. 'So, are we okay? I find it very hard to get close to people and then, when I do, I push them away and self-destruct.'

'Yeah, I didn't need to be Dr Freud to work that out.' She leaned in and kissed him on the mouth.

Marcus got out of the bed. 'I'm going to have a shower.'

She glanced at the native American tattoo that he had on the back of his left shoulder. 'You know that only rock stars and bikers can pull off tattoos?'

'It's all part of my attention-seeking nature and need to rebel.' Marcus laughed as he disappeared into the bathroom and closed the door.

Lucy lay back on the pillows and realised she hadn't thought about Harry for several hours. It was a huge relief and she allowed herself a little smile. She had no idea if she and Marcus had any future yet, but he was fun, interesting, and very sexy.

Grabbing one of Marcus' t-shirts from the floor, she put it on and wandered around the bedroom. There was an old walnut table on which was a pile of books – *The Beach, Captain Corelli's Mandolin, Angela's Ashes* and *Enduring Love*. She was surprised that she had heard of all of them. She'd assumed that Marcus spent his time reading complex literature that you needed an English degree to understand.

On the walls were a series of framed posters from art exhibitions and plays. A Howard Hodgkin exhibition at the Tate Britain. Anna Karenina by Helen Edmundson at the National Theatre in 1996.

As she looked down, Lucy noticed that on the left-hand side of the table there was a framed photograph of a young girl, aged about eight. The photo appeared old, and had possibly been taken in the 70s or early 80s. Below that, there were two drawers with ornate brass handles.

She could still hear the shower running, and glanced at the bathroom door to make sure it was fully closed. Being a detective, she was naturally inquisitive – or nosy – and she couldn't help but slide open one of the drawers and look inside. There was a row of ornately-decorated silver Victorian pill boxes. She took one in her hand and carefully removed the top to reveal a small lock of blonde hair. She wondered if it had anything to do with the photograph. Inside another of the pill boxes was a different lock of hair, this time auburn.

That's quite weird, she thought to herself.

Before she had time to look further, the shower stopped. She replaced the boxes and quietly closed the drawer. What the hell were the locks of hair? Past girlfriends? That would be really creepy. It wasn't as though she could now ask him without confessing that she had rummaged through his stuff.

Before she had time to jump back into bed, the bathroom door opened. Marcus was standing there looking gorgeous with dark, wet tousled hair, and a white towel around his waist. Lucy was worried that he would wonder what the hell she was doing.

Oh shit!

She smiled at him, trying to gauge his reaction.

'Snooping through my stuff?' he asked.

For a couple of seconds, she couldn't work out if he was annoyed but she had to play along.

'Hey, I'm a detective. What did you expect?' she said in a breezy tone.

He smiled. 'If you find a severed finger, it's been planted.'

Lucy laughed, and her eye was drawn back to the photograph of the young girl.

'My sister, Hettie,' he said.

'It's all right, I wasn't going to pry.'

'It's fine ...' A sombre expression formed across his brow.

'Are you close?'

He paused before replying. 'She died, so ...'

'Oh God, I'm so sorry for bringing it up,' Lucy whispered, hoping the earth would open up and swallow her.

'No, no, it's fine.' He looked at her reassuringly. 'If I didn't want to talk about her, then I wouldn't have put her photo there.'

There were a few awkward seconds as Lucy looked at him. 'Do you mind me asking what happened?'

He rubbed his face and cleared his throat. 'She got knocked off her bike when we were kids in Germany.'

'Oh no. That's horrible.'

'Actually, it was only a few days after that photograph was taken.'

There was another silence.

'I've got a sister and I don't know what I'd have done if something like that had happened to her,' Lucy said with empathy.

He nodded and sat down on the edge of the bed. 'I saw it happen.'

'That must have been terrible.'

'Thing is, I insisted on taking her out on the new bike she'd got for her birthday. I was a year older than her and I could ride without stabilisers. My parents warned us to be careful. Hettie lost her balance, came off the pavement and out into the road. There was this lorry and ...'

'I'm so sorry.' Lucy came over and sat next to him on the bed. 'I can't imagine how you dealt with that. Or your parents.'

'My parents?' he snorted. 'They just blamed me.'

'What?'

'As far as they were concerned, I'd been responsible for Hettie that afternoon. I was meant to be looking after her ... and she died,' Marcus said as his voice began to break.

'It was an accident,' Lucy said as she put a comforting hand on his shoulder. 'They must have seen that later?'

'Later?' he said in a virtual whisper. 'Three months later they packed me off to an English boarding school.'

'Jesus! You were only nine years old.'

Marcus nodded. She could see there were tears in his eyes but he wiped them away and seemed embarrassed. 'Sorry ... I ...'

Lucy put her arm around him. 'Hey, I don't know how anyone could have got through all that.'

'Yeah, well I didn't, did I?' he said with a soft laugh. 'I'm an emotionally retarded sociopath.'

'You're not,' Lucy whispered as she turned his head so that he faced her. 'Trust me. In my line of work I've become an expert on sociopaths, and you're not one.'

Marcus looked at her. 'How did I ever get to meet someone like you?'

They kissed and then rolled back onto the bed.

CHAPTER 21

Saturday 31st January

BROOKS WAS IN MID FLOW when Lucy crept into the back of the CID office. Ruth frowned at her and mouthed *Are you okay?* In the years that Ruth had worked at Peckham nick, she had never known Lucy to be late. Lucy nodded to signal she was alright.

Brooks stopped speaking and looked at her. At first, it seemed like he was just going to carry on but then he said, 'Nice of you to join us, Lucy.'

'Sorry Guv,' she said, pulling an apologetic face.

Ruth was surprised. It wasn't like Brooks to single someone out like that in a CID briefing. For the other members of the team, there was nothing more to this short exchange. However, Ruth knew the subtext of the words and body language between them. It was clear that they weren't going to be able to work together for very much longer if things didn't remain professional.

'As you know, we've made a very significant breakthrough in this investigation,' Brooks stated as he headed over the scene boards and pointed to a photograph. 'We have arrested this man, Hadir Benali, on suspicion of Tash's murder. Ruth?'

Ruth stood up from her seat and composed herself as she reached the boards. 'If you remember, Jane Sinclair told us that Tash believed she was being stalked. She had seen a man walking past her flat, following her home, and he'd even been on the same train as her.' Ruth pointed to Benali's photo. 'We're convinced this is the man. He matches the description that Tash gave Jane, *and* we found this little display of photos of Tash hidden behind a wardrobe in his basement.' She indicated a large photo of the collage.

There were murmurs from detectives who hadn't yet been brought up to speed. This was a huge break in the case.

'Benali is a Moroccan national, and according to his passport he is twenty-eight. We believe that he has family living back in Tangiers. He works as a hospital porter in the mortuary at King's College Hospital.' Ruth went over to the map of Peckham. 'Benali's flat is here, so you can see that he was only two minutes from where Tash lived in Banfield Road.'

'Have we interviewed him yet?' Gaughran asked.

'Not officially. As most of you know, he was attacked while he was trying to escape from us. It seems that he stole a bike from the brother of a member of the Peckham Young Guns.'

Gaughran snorted. 'That wasn't very clever.

The Peckham Young Guns were part of the notorious Peckham Boys gang who had been a violent presence in SE15 since the 1980s.

'Maybe we should get the Young Guns to patrol the streets round here,' Hassan joked. 'People are a lot more afraid of them than they are of us.'

Ruth gave a wry smile at the thought. 'Benali was kicked unconscious and taken to King's College Hospital. He was suffering from concussion, but he was released this morning and he's currently in a holding cell downstairs.'

Brooks looked over at her. 'You and Lucy okay to interview him under caution straight after this?'

'Yes, Guv,' Ruth replied. 'Last night, Benali was babbling and not making much sense. We'll need to have him psychologically assessed.'

Gaughran rolled his eyes. 'Please don't tell me *diminished responsibility*? You're having a laugh, aren't you?'

'We haven't even charged him yet, Tim,' Brooks said. 'Let's see how it plays out first, eh?'

'Unfortunately, I doubt that Jane Sinclair's testimony and the collage we discovered in his basement are going to be enough to charge him,' Ruth said.

Brooks shook his head. 'No, it won't. We'll need more to reach the CPS threshold. We have to find something concrete to link him to the crime scene.'

Hassan glanced over and said, 'Guv, first batch of forensics arrived back this morning. They've got unidentified DNA on the victim's bed. They've tested it against the elimination sample and there was no match.'

Brooks' face brightened a little. 'Do we have Benali's DNA on the system?'

'Not yet,' Ruth explained. 'But we can do.'

Brooks nodded. 'Right, let's fast-track it.' He glanced down at his watch. 'I don't think we're going to get an extension to hold him with what we've got so far. That means that he's walking out of here early evening, so we need to get a shift on.'

'And he's a flight risk,' Gaughran added as he looked up. 'We don't want him sodding off back to Morocco and disappearing there.'

'Anyone got anything else?' Brooks asked.

Hassan indicated he had something. 'Bob Goldstein's office lied about him being out of the country at the time of Tash's murder. They told us he was in a meeting in New York. I've checked the passenger list. He did have a first-class seat booked last Monday morning, but he didn't travel.'

'Right,' Brooks said, but Ruth could see that he thought it was an unwelcome distraction.

'What d'you want us to do, Guv?' Hassan asked.

'Find out why he lied to us, but don't waste too much time on it at the moment.'

Hassan nodded. 'Yes, Guv.'

Brooks took a breath and cast his eyes over the team. He was fired up. 'Right, listen everyone. Benali is our prime suspect and I want us to nail the bastard. You saw the crime scene and you saw what someone did to Tash Weston. So, we're working round the clock on this. I want Benali's phone records, bank records, CCTV, medical information. Talk to the people he works with. Anything and everything. I mean it. If he took a shit in the last week I want to know where, why, and for how long. Somewhere, he'll have made a mistake. We've got to find it before he's released. Okay, let's do some great work out there everyone!'

RUTH AND LUCY WERE down in the evidence room, sifting through the boxes of belongings that the SOCOs had taken from Benali's flat. Luckily, he had very few possessions so it was a relatively simpler task than it sometimes proved. However, they hadn't managed to find anything out of the ordinary yet.

'Smell like condoms, don't they?' Lucy commented as she looked at the blue forensic gloves she was wearing.

Ruth raised an eyebrow. 'I can't remember. It's been a while. In fact, it's been about twenty-five years.'

'Oh yeah,' Lucy muttered, not wanting to say that for her it had been about twelve hours.

'Not like you to be late,' Ruth said.

Lucy knew she was fishing for a longer conversation, but she wasn't in the mood. In fact she was tired and feeling guilty for keeping her ongoing tryst with Marcus Jankel a secret from her. 'Roadworks and a broken-down bus, that's all.'

Before their conversation could continue, Lucy pulled a dark green tobacco tin from the box and opened it. Inside she spotted a small key that was attached to a blue plastic fob. Looking at is closely, she could tell that it wasn't a door key like a Chubb or a Yale.

'What do you think this is?' she asked, holding it up.

Ruth held out her hand. 'Let's have a look.'

Lucy gave her the key, and Ruth examined it. 'One of those cash boxes?'

Lucy shook her head. 'It's too big for that.'

'A safe?'

'I don't think so.'

The door opened and Brooks came in. 'Right ladies, Benali has had his hour with the duty solicitor. The police doctor has given him the once-over and declared him physically fit for interview.'

'Okay, Guv,' Lucy said. It felt so weird to be in the same room as Harry and trying to act normally after all they had been through. On top of that, she'd had sex with someone only a few hours earlier and was feeling incredibly guilty.

Ruth showed the key to Brooks. 'Any idea what this might be for, Guv?'

Brooks took it from her and studied it for a moment. 'I was going to say it's a garage key, but my guess is that it's for one of those storage facility places that seem to be springing up all over.'

Ruth nodded. 'There's one just behind the Queen's Road Tyre Centre.'

Brooks handed the key back to Ruth. 'Take it with you when you interview Benali and ask him about it. If it's significant, it might really rattle him.'

'Yes, Guv,' Ruth said and looked over at Lucy. 'We'll go along there now.'

CHAPTER 22

'MR GOLDSTEIN WILL SEE you now,' said the receptionist.

Gaughran and Hassan had only just arrived at Goldstein Films, although this time they were on the floor above the main reception.

Before they had time turn the corner into his office, Goldstein appeared with a huge smile.

'Hey, hey, how's it going?' he boomed in his deep New York drawl. 'Sorry to have kept England's finest.'

Goldstein was a bear of a man. He was so barrel-chested that someone had quipped that he must have swallowed a fire extinguisher. He was only five eight or nine tall, with a pug nose and small piggy eyes, but he made up for his lack of height with sheer physical presence.

He beckoned them to follow him into his office, then closed the door and gestured to the chairs that were on one side of his enormous desk.

'Can I get you something. Tea?' he asked, with a slightly mocking emphasis on *tea*. 'I guess I can't tempt you with something stronger. Not while you're on duty, unless you want to end up in the Tower.'

Goldstein laughed as he sat back in his chair.

Gaughran and Hassan exchanged a brief glance – *Is this guy for real?*

'Mr Goldstein, we ...' Gaughran began.

'Bob ...' he corrected him. 'Everyone calls me Bob. Except my mother who calls me Robert, especially when I'm in trouble.'

'We just wanted to clarify a couple of things as part of our investigation,' Hassan explained.

'Of course.' Goldstein nodded with a suitably solemn face, which Gaughran didn't believe for one second. 'It was such terrible news. I still can't believe what happened to Tash. She was just so young, so talented.'

Yeah, but that didn't stop you trying to sexually assault her, did it? Gaughran thought.

Hassan fished out his notebook and opened it. 'We had a fax from your lawyers to tell us that you were in New York last Monday. Is that right?'

Goldstein nodded. 'I believe that a fax was sent over, yes.'

Gaughran stared at him defiantly. He wanted Goldstein to know that he wasn't intimidated by him. 'And *were* you in New York?'

Goldstein smiled arrogantly. 'I have a very strong feeling that you know I wasn't.'

'We checked the passenger list,' Hassan said.

Goldstein shrugged. 'Of course you did. It's your job to do stuff like that.'

'So, why did you lie to us about your whereabouts?' Gaughran asked.

'I wouldn't have put it quite as crudely as that. I think there was a communication failure between my assistant and my lawyers. An innocent mistake.' He held up his hands and shook his head. 'Lawyers, huh? You wanna know how a lawyer sleeps?'

Gaughran raised an eyebrow. He wasn't sure what Goldstein was getting at.

'First he lies on one side, then he lies on the other,' he chortled. 'It's a joke ... So, yeah, I did have a flight booked to New York. Then something came up, so I had to stay here. Happens all the time. I'm sorry if that's caused you any problems.'

'Can you tell us where you were on Monday evening?' Hassan asked.

'I have a suite at The Savoy. I'm guessing I was there.'

'Can you prove it?'

'Can I prove it?' Goldstein laughed. 'Can you prove I wasn't?'

'We don't know yet,' Gaughran chipped in, fixing him with a stare.

This Yank is starting to get right up my nose.

'Hey, I'm joking,' Goldstein said, chortling again. 'The staff probably knew I was there. I must have used the phone or room service. I'm sure if you contact The Savoy, they can find someone who saw me there.'

Although he seemed very sure of himself, Gaughran noted that to all intents and purposes, Goldstein didn't yet have an alibi for the time of Tash's murder.

Gaughran sat forward. *Let's see how he deals with this ...*

'We understand that there was some kind of legal dispute between you and Tash Weston?'

The expression on Goldstein's face hardened as he smoothed his hand over his chin. He glared at Gaughran for a few seconds and then forced a smile. 'You know what fellas, it's been great talking to you this morning. And I'm glad that we've been able to clear up the little misunderstanding about where I was on Monday but—'

'Except, Bob,' Gaughran interrupted, 'you haven't cleared up where you were on Monday. Not to my satisfaction anyway. You have an unsubstantiated alibi, that's all.' Gaughran was enjoying seeing Goldstein rattled.

Goldstein ignored him and spoke to Hassan. 'Like I said, it's been good to have this little chat. I hope you understand that I'm a very busy man, so I'm sure you can see yourselves out.' He then glared at Gaughran. 'If you would like to continue this conversation, then it would be best for you to contact my legal team to arrange a convenient time for us to meet.'

'Thank you for your time,' Gaughran said, giving him a cold smile. 'We'll be in touch.'

HADIR BENALI WAS NOW dressed in a grey tracksuit as his clothes had been taken for forensic analysis. He had also been swabbed for his DNA. The bruising around his right eye had now changed to a dark mauve colour and there was so much swelling that he could hardly see out of it.

Christ, he looks like he's done ten rounds with Mike Tyson! Ruth thought.

Lucy held the end of her biro between her teeth and leant forward to click the red button on the recording machine. As the long electronic beep sounded, Ruth opened her folder and slid one of the files over to Lucy.

Ruth cleared her throat before speaking. 'Interview conducted with Hadir Benali, 1.20pm, Peckham Police Station. Present are Detective Constable Lucy Henry, Duty Solicitor Simon Gregg and myself, Detective Constable Ruth Hunter.' She glanced over at Benali. 'Hadir, do you understand that you are still under arrest?'

'Yeah,' he mumbled, staring down at the table.

She flicked casually through the contents of her folder and took out a photograph of the collage of pictures they had found in Benali's cellar. She placed it on the table and then turned it around to show him. 'Hadir, I have here an image of a board of pictures that we found hidden in the cellar in your home. Can you tell us about it?'

Benali started to bite his nails, avoiding any eye contact.

'For the purposes of the tape, the suspect has not replied to the question.'

She slid the photograph further across the table so that it was directly in front of him. 'Hadir, could you look at this photograph for me?'

He let out a sigh, sat back on the chair and looked up at the ceiling.

Oh great, is this all we're going to get out of him today? Ruth thought, feeling frustrated at his childish behaviour.

'For the purposes of the tape, the suspect has refused to look at the photograph which shows a noticeboard covered in images of Natasha Weston,' Ruth said, unable to mask the slight weariness in her voice.

Lucy sat forward in her seat and frowned in Benali's direction. 'Does the name Natasha or Tash Weston mean anything to you, Hadir?'

He folded his arms, sat lower in his chair and continued to gaze up at the ceiling.

'Hadir, does the name Natasha or Tash Weston mean anything to you?' she asked again using a sterner tone.

Benali's eyes seemed to be roaming around the ceiling as if he hadn't heard the question.

'For the purposes of the tape, the suspect has not answered the question,' Ruth said.

She took another image from her folder and held it out towards him. 'Hadir, this is one of several photographs we found at your home. They are all of Tash Weston inside her flat and have been taken from the road outside. Can you tell us anything about them?'

Benali smacked his lips against each other noisily but continued to study the ceiling.

Jesus, he's really annoying me.

'Did you take those photographs, Hadir?' Lucy asked.

Lucy and Ruth exchanged a look of frustration. 'For the purposes of the tape, the suspect is refusing to answer the question.'

Ruth fished into her folder again and pulled out a small transparent evidence bag. It contained the key on the blue fob that they had spotted earlier. 'Hadir, we found this key at your home. Could you tell us what it's for?'

Benali's expression changed. His body visibly tensed as he sat up. He then lowered his head very slowly and stared at the evidence bag that Ruth was holding.

Now that's got his bloody attention, Ruth thought.

'Do you recognise this key, Hadir?' she asked. 'We found it in your house.'

For a few seconds, Benali just frowned and stared at the key. He then turned and glanced at the duty solicitor.

'I'm going to tell you what I think, Hadir,' Ruth said. 'I think that this key is for a storage unit that you have rented. And in that storage unit, I think there are things that you have hidden and don't want anyone else to see. Is that right?'

Benali glared at her and gritted his teeth.

'So, what I think we should do is go and find that storage unit. Then we can bring whatever is in there back here, and then you can tell us all about what we've found. How does that sound?'

Suddenly, Benali shot up out of his chair and launched himself across the table in an attempt to grab the key from Ruth's hand.

Ruth managed to get out of his way while Lucy slammed him down onto the table and cuffed his hands behind his back as he struggled.

'I think we can add assaulting a police officer to the charges,' Lucy said under her breath.

The very shocked duty solicitor looked at them. 'I think my client could do with a break so I can talk to him and calm him down.'

Ruth nodded. 'I think that's a very good idea. In fact, I suggest that he goes back to one of our holding cells to cool off for a bit.'

CHAPTER 23

GAUGHRAN AND HASSAN went downstairs and approached the receptionist in the main lobby of Goldstein Films. Gaughran showed his warrant card and smiled. 'Hi there. Barbara York ordered herself a mini-cab on your account on Monday night, between ten and eleven o'clock. We'd like the details of the company that she would have used for that journey please?'

The receptionist nodded. 'Of course. I'll just look that up for you.'

Gaughran was aware of someone approaching. He turned around to see Barbara York coming their way.

Hassan raised an eyebrow. 'Here we go.'

'I thought you had been asked to leave these offices,' Barbara growled.

'I've no idea what you're talking about,' Gaughran said, readying himself for a verbal onslaught.

'I think Bob made it very clear that you were not welcome here?' she sneered.

'Listen, we're British police officers conducting a murder investigation,' Gaughran replied with the hint of a smirk. 'We don't need to be made to feel welcome. We'll go where we want and we'll leave these offices when we're ready. Do you understand that?'

'You must have a search warrant?' Barbara said with condescending raise of her eyebrow.

'Hey, if you want us to go and get a search warrant, we can come back here with a dozen police officers and rip this place apart,' Gaughran retorted, trying to control his temper.

After a few seconds, Barbara let out an audible sigh. 'Bob is very upset about the nature of the conversation you've just had with him. He agreed to see you on the understanding that he would explain where he was on Monday night and nothing else.'

Gaughran held her gaze. 'It's up to us to decide what is and what isn't relevant to our investigation. Frankly, it's none of your business what we talked to *Bob* about.'

'How dare you speak to me like that,' Barbara said bristling. 'This is the second time you have thrown your weight around and made wild accusations in these offices. As far as I'm concerned, this is harassment and I'm going to make sure your Chief of Police knows about your unacceptable behaviour.'

'We don't have a Chief of Police,' Hassan said quietly.

'What?' Barbara said, virtually spitting out the word.

Gaughran was finding it hard not to show how much he was enjoying watching Barbara 'losing her shit'. 'He was just pointing out that the Metropolitan Police doesn't have a Chief, we have a Commissioner. His name is Sir Paul Condon. I can write it down for you if you like.'

'Are you trying to be funny?' she snarled.

'No.'

Hassan indicated the receptionist. 'We're waiting for some information and then we'll be on our way.'

Barbara glared at them. 'Make sure that you do.'

She turned and stormed away.

Gaughran glanced at the receptionist who gave him an apologetic smile. 'I'm guessing that Miss York isn't the easiest person to work for?'

'She's just very protective of Bob,' the receptionist replied in a virtual whisper. 'And God help anyone who crosses him because they'll have her to contend with. But, of course, I didn't tell you that.'

Gaughran laughed. 'Tell me what?'

WHILE THEY GAVE BENALI some time to cool off, Lucy and Ruth made their way over to 'The Storage Place' that was located just off Queen's Road, close to Peckham High Street. Benali's reaction to seeing the key had convinced them that he had something to hide – they just hoped that the key did belong to one of the storage units.

They parked in the customer car park and got out of the car. Ruth finished her cigarette, tossed it to the floor, and stubbed it out with her heel.

'Shiori's been shagging Jerry,' Ruth said as they approached a Portakabin marked 'Reception'.

'What?' Lucy said, her eyes widening. 'Are you kidding?'

'I wish I was.'

'I thought he'd cheated on her and was generally a total prick?'

'Yeah, correct on both counts,' Ruth said, rolling her eyes.

'So, what the hell is she doing?' Lucy asked.

'That's the million-dollar question.' As Ruth said it, she realised that she wasn't as upset about Shiori being unfaithful as she thought she might be.

'Are you alright?'

'Yeah,' Ruth said, sounding surprised by her own answer. 'I don't know why. I've had my suspicions for a while now. I thought I'd be very angry and upset, but I'm not really. I don't think we were ever going to be soulmates for life.'

Lucy shrugged as they reached the office door. 'Maybe it's for the best then?'

'Maybe.' Ruth opened the door and glanced inside. The office smelled of stale cigarette smoke and stewed tea. A middle-aged man had his feet up on the desk and was reading a copy of *The Sun*.

'Can I help, love?' he asked, peering over the top of the paper.

Love? Really? thought Ruth. *It's 1998 for God's sake!*

She held out her warrant card. 'DC Hunter, Peckham CID. We were wondering if you could help us with something?'

'Oh right.' He swung his legs to the floor, sat up straight, and put down his paper. 'What do you need?'

Christ, he's changed his tune now he knows we're coppers.

As they approached the table where he was sitting, Ruth spotted an old man sitting over in the corner rolling up a cigarette. On the wall beside him was a West Ham FC pendant and scarf, and the obligatory calendar of a woman with her breasts showing.

Nice. That doesn't make me feel uncomfortable at all, she thought sarcastically.

Pulling the evidence bag from her pocket, she went over and showed the key to the man. 'We're trying to trace whatever this key fits. Clearly, it's not for a door. We don't think it's for a safe. Our DCI seemed to think it might be for a storage unit.'

The man fished his glasses from the top pocket of his shirt and peered at it. 'If it is, it's not one of ours I'm afraid.'

Ruth looked at Lucy in frustration. Brooks had seemed pretty certain the key came from a storage facility, and this was the only one in the area.

'You're sure?' Ruth asked.

'Yeah, it's too small.' He turned towards the old man in the corner who had just popped his roll-up into his mouth. 'Pat, come and have a look at this for us, will you?'

Pat got to his feet and doddered over from where he had been sitting. 'What we looking at then?'

Ruth showed him the key in the evidence bag.

'What d'you think?' the man asked him.

Pat inspected it for a few seconds. 'Yeah, it's a locker key.'

'Locker?' Lucy asked.

'You know, the lockers you get at the swimming baths or at a school.'

Ruth had a thought. 'What about lockers you might get if you worked at a hospital?'

Pat shrugged. 'I suppose so.'

Ruth nodded and said, 'Thanks.'

As she and Lucy began to head for the door, Pat pointed to the paper on the table. 'This anything to do with that actress that got murdered a few nights ago?'

'Sorry. We can't really discuss any ongoing cases,' Ruth said as she opened the flimsy Portakabin door.

'Yeah, well I hope you find whoever done that to her and string him up.

CHAPTER 24

RUTH AND LUCY HAD ARRIVED at King's College Hospital thirty minutes ago only to receive a phone call from Brooks. Time had finally run out and Benali had been released from Peckham nick pending further enquiries. They had no choice but to plough on and find the evidence they needed. They were now in the basement of the hospital with one of the maintenance men, having established that the key did indeed belong to one of their lockers. Certain staff were allocated a locker in which to store their personal possessions, and Hadir Benali had been assigned locker number 237.

'They're just up here,' the maintenance man said in a thick Scottish accent.

'Sounds like you're a long way from home?' Ruth said.

'Aye, Fort William.'

'I went around there on holiday as a kid,' Lucy said. 'Isn't it near Glencoe?'

He nodded. 'Aye. Not far.'

The basement was large and windowless and had very low ceilings. It was beginning to make Ruth feel claustrophobic. She seemed to have suffered from a form of claustrophobia ever since she could remember. There had been an incident at school when she was ten, when the school bully, Tracey Harding, had pushed her into a small store cupboard and then put a hockey stick in between the two handles. Everyone burst into fits of laughter before disappearing for their lunch break. Ruth had been stuck in there for nearly half an hour until Mr Kelly had found her. She wondered if her fear of enclosed spaces stemmed from that. A few years ago, Tracey Harding had been nicked in Clapham Junction for robbery and assault. When she received a custodial sentence, Ruth had a little vindictive laugh to herself.

As they turned a corner, a huge bank of grey metallic lockers loomed into view.

'Here we go,' the maintenance man said.

Ruth raised an eyebrow. 'Now, that's a lot of lockers.'

'Over two thousand.'

Glancing at the numbers, Ruth and Lucy walked down the rows until they found what they were looking for – number 237.

Ruth took the key from the plastic evidence bag and hoped to hell that there was something very incriminating inside the locker.

She put the key in the lock but it didn't turn. She tried again. Nothing.

'It doesn't seem to want to unlock,' she grumbled, and then handed it to the maintenance man to have a go.

He pushed it back into the lock, wiggled it, and then took it out. 'No, it's not the right key.'

Ruth frowned. 'But it is a key to one of your lockers?'

'Oh aye, it's one of ours. It must be for another locker down here, but I could nae tell you which one. It'd take you a week to check them all.'

Ruth had a thought. 'Wait there. I've had an idea.'

'Where are you going?' Lucy asked as Ruth turned and headed back the way they had come.

'I'll be five minutes. Promise,' Ruth said as she broke into a jog.

She arrived at the lifts, pressed the button and got in.

A few seconds later, the doors opened on the ground floor and she got out. Turning right, she jogged across the main entrance lobby of the hospital and into the shop. It was a long shot, but it had to be worth a try.

She spotted Jill putting out packets of crisps on an empty shelf and went over. 'Hi Jill. I'm DC Ruth Hunter. Do you remember me from yesterday?'

'Of course I do!' Jill said and gave her a beaming smile. She then gestured to the shelf. 'If you want cheese and onion you're out of luck 'cos they didn't deliver any.'

Ruth smiled. 'I'm fine thanks. You said that Hadir was a friend of yours?'

'That's right,' she said. 'I think he must be sick or something 'cos I ain't seen him at work for a couple of days now.'

'Have you ever let him use your locker?'

Jill frowned. 'Yes. Why you asking me that?'

'So, he has the key to your work locker downstairs?'

'Yes, dear,' Jill said, looking utterly confused. 'Hadir lost his and he didn't want to get into trouble, so I gave him mine. You won't tell anyone, will you?'

Ruth shook her head. 'It's fine. Don't worry about it. What number is your locker?'

'It's 175.'

'Thank you.'

'Is Hadir all right? He's not in any trouble is he?' Jill asked.

'Thanks for your help,' Ruth said. 'I've got to go now.'

Ruth made her way back to the lift and returned to the basement. A few minutes later, she arrived, slightly out of breath, where Lucy and the maintenance man were waiting with bemused looks on their faces.

'What's going on?' Lucy asked.

'175,' Ruth said, trying to get her breath back.

'What?'

'That key fits locker 175. Jill, who works in the shop. It's her locker.'

'How did you know that?'

Ruth shrugged. 'Just a lucky guess.'

'Yeah, well from the looks of you, you need to cut down on your smoking,' Lucy joked as they made their way to the lockers again and soon found locker 175.

Pushing the key into the lock, Ruth twisted it. There was a metallic clunk and the door opened.

'Bingo!' Lucy said as they peered inside.

At the bottom of the locker was a small black gym bag. Ruth pulled out her forensic gloves, snapped them on and took out the bag.

She crouched down and unzipped it.

As she opened the bag she could see several pairs of women's sexy knickers. There was a small cuddly toy, a size 5 pair of pink trainers, and a notebook that had a name embossed in gold on the front – *Natasha Weston*.

Got him!

As she delved further into the bag she found more photographs of Tash inside her home that had also been taken from the road.

Ruth looked up at Lucy. 'I think we've got the bastard!'

CHAPTER 25

RUTH AND LUCY WERE sitting in their car, which was parked close to the main entrance of King's College Hospital. They had their man – they just needed to make sure he didn't get away.

'Control to Alpha Zero, over,' said the crackly voice of a computer aided dispatch operator back at Peckham nick.

Ruth pushed the red button on her Tetra radio. 'Alpha Zero receiving, go ahead Control.'

'We have two uniformed units at target location, rear entrance is secure, over.'

'Received Control. Will advise, out,' Ruth said and put her radio down. She felt relieved that both the main and rear entrance to the hospital were now secure. A quick visit to the reception and HR had established that Hadir Benali was already back at work. All Ruth and Lucy needed to do was to wait for Brooks to talk to a magistrate and the CPS and get the arrest warrant over to them.

'I wonder why Benali didn't do a runner?' Lucy said.

'Maybe he thought we'd never find that locker, and without the contents he might have guessed that we'd never be able to charge him.'

Lucy nodded and frowned. 'I wonder what happened that night?'

'I can't work out how he got into her flat,' Ruth said.

'I wonder if Tash left the door open or unlocked when Barbara York left? If she was out of it on that ...'

'Flunitrazepam...'

'Yeah, that,' Lucy said. 'Then maybe she wasn't thinking clearly.'

'He might have rung the doorbell and just forced his way in if she was completely out of it, and that would explain why there were no defence wounds.'

'We've never found that four-leafed clover necklace, have we?'

'No, I was hoping it was going to show up in Benali's locker.'

'So was I. Any doubts that we've got the right man?'

'Not anymore,' Ruth said as she shook her head. 'Last night, when I couldn't sleep, I remembered a case I read about in the papers a few years ago. An American actress called Rebecca Shaeffer, I think it was. She was in some big American TV series and this young guy stalked her for a couple of years. When he saw her latest film, in which she sleeps with this bloke, he thought it was real. He got into a rage and went round and killed her on her doorstep.'

'That's horrible.'

'It's frightening how obsessed people can get,' Ruth said, and then checked her watch. 'Brooks should be here in a minute.' She fished a cigarette out of her packet and lit it.

'I slept with Marcus Jankel last night,' Lucy said quietly.

What!

Ruth turned to look at her. 'You did what?'

Lucy squirmed. 'I slept with Marcus Jankel. I really like him.'

'You really like him? He's right in the middle of our murder investigation!'

'No he's not,' Lucy said. 'Not anymore.'

'Are you insane?' Ruth snapped.

Lucy gestured to the hospital. 'We've got our man. What's the problem?'

Ruth snorted. 'Don't give me that! You know you could have jeopardised the case by sleeping with him.'

'But I haven't,' Lucy said.

There was an awkward silence which was broken by Brooks appearing next to them in a car. He got out and knocked on Lucy's window. She buzzed it down.

'Late Christmas present.' He held up the arrest warrant for Benali. 'Let's go and get him, shall we?'

'We're not finished talking,' Ruth muttered under her breath to Lucy as they got out of the car.

'I am,' Lucy snapped.

The three of them marched over to the front entrance, showing warrant cards to the security guard as they went inside.

They got to the lift. The doors opened and they got in.

There was an uneasy silence as Ruth reached over and pressed B for the basement where they knew Benali worked.

Ruth stared over at Lucy but she avoided her gaze. She was still fuming from what Lucy had just divulged.

'Wheeling dead bodies around all day,' Brooks said, raising an eyebrow. 'Bit of a cliché, isn't it?'

'Better than him working on the maternity ward, I guess,' Lucy joked sardonically.

The doors opened and on the wall in front of them were signs to various departments that were located in the basement.

A sign for the *Chapel of Rest* and one for the *Mortuary* indicated they were to the right.

As they turned into the corridor, Ruth saw a figure in a dark blue polo shirt and black trousers drinking tea on a bench seat.

Benali!

'Isn't that …?' Lucy said under her breath.

'Yes,' Ruth said as they got closer.

Brooks took the lead as Benali glanced up at them. He didn't seem very surprised to see them.

'Hadir Benali. I have a warrant here for your arrest. I'm arresting you on suspicion of the murder of Natasha Weston. You do not have to say anything, but anything you do say can be taken down and used against you in a court of law. Do you understand what I've just said to you?'

'Of course,' Benali said with a creepy smile. He put his tea down on the floor and got up. He went to reach inside his trouser pocket when Brooks raised his hand to stop him.

'What are you doing?' Brooks snapped.

They didn't want him bringing out a weapon.

'I'm getting my phone,' Benali said with a shrug. 'I'm allowed to ring my solicitor, aren't I?'

'You can do that when we get back to the station.' Brooks began to take the cuffs from his belt.

Suddenly, Benali punched Brooks straight in the face.

CRACK!

Before any of them could react, Brooks had crumpled to the floor and Benali sprinted away down the corridor.

'Bloody hell!' Ruth yelled.

'Jesus,' Lucy growled as she went over to see if Brooks was okay.

Brooks groaned and sat up nursing a bloody nose.

'You okay?' Lucy asked crouching down.

'Don't bloody stop, Lucy!' Brooks exclaimed. 'Just get after him!'

Ruth and Lucy turned and sprinted after Benali, who was now halfway down the corridor.

As they sped along, they turned a corner only to see that the corridor now split left and right.

And there was no sign of Benali anywhere.

'Fuck!' Lucy said.

Ruth stopped in her tracks. 'Which way did he go?'

'No idea,' Lucy said with a shrug.

'You go left, I'll go right,' Ruth said, already breathless. 'And be careful.'

Lucy gave her a quizzical look. 'Hey, when am I ever not careful?'

'Last night, for starters,' Ruth said as she took off to the right.

'Oi, that's below the belt,' Lucy yelled as she went the other way.

Ruth thundered down the corridor, went around a corner and spotted Benali running ahead towards a set of double doors. Several nurses and a doctor jumped out of his way as he yelled at them.

Setting off in pursuit, Ruth was trying to work out where she was in the hospital.

It's like a bloody rabbit warren down here, she thought.

She watched as Benali ran towards some big red metal doors that were marked with a green *Fire Exit* sign. From where she was, she could see a large notice that had been attached to them that read *Not In Use.*

Benali ran at the doors, hitting them with all his weight but they didn't move. Turning around, he saw Ruth heading his way and tried another set of doors to the left.

Ruth saw him push them open and disappear inside.

Bollocks! What's in there?

Thirty seconds later, Ruth arrived at the doors which read *Mortuary – Authorised Staff Only.*

Great! The mortuary!

Sucking in breath, she stopped running and began to try and get her breath.

Jesus, I'm unfit.

As she made her way inside, she continued trying to get her breath back as she noticed the huge drop in temperature.

The mortuary was in virtual darkness, except for a tiny amount of light thrown out by fridges at the far end. The air was freezing cold and smelled of disinfectant and chemicals.

Walking slowly, Ruth gazed into the darkness to see if she could see where Benali was hiding. Her shoes clicked noisily on the solid floors, instantly giving away her position.

Reaching down slowly, she slipped her shoes off and padded across the floor in her socks, making no sound at all.

God, that's better. Now where the bloody hell has he gone?

She paused and listened.

Nothing but the distant hum of the refrigeration units.

Ruth clicked her Tetra radio and spoke very quietly, 'Alpha Zero to Control, over.'

'This is Control, go ahead Alpha Zero.'

'I'm pursuing suspect Hadir Benali who has escaped from custody. I believe that the suspect is in the mortuary area of King's College Hospital but I have lost visual contact. Request backup, over,' she said as her breathing began to return to normal.

'Control, received. Will advise, stand by, over.'

Ruth moved again slowly, slightly crouched, her eyes scanning the darkness for any sign of movement.

She stopped again and listened. The faintest sound of a footstep over by one of the metal gurneys where the bodies would be laid out for post-mortem examinations.

We can't stay in here all bloody day.

'Hadir?' Ruth said very quietly.

Nothing.

She began to cross the floor to where she had heard movement.

Where the hell is he? If he jumps out and attacks me, I'm in trouble.

The sound of more movement and of doors opening in the corridor startled her for a second.

'Hadir? Just come out from wherever you're hiding. You're not going to get away,' Ruth said gently.

However, she was beginning to feel very uneasy. As she stood motionless in the darkness, all she could hear was the thudding of her heart against her chest.

Her radio crackled loudly, 'Control to Alpha Zero, back-up is en route, ETA five minutes, over.'

She was startled momentarily.

There was a noise from the far side of the mortuary.

Ruth squinted and could see Benali maneouvering his way along the far wall.

'Hadir! Stop there. Please. I want you to talk to me!' she said in as calm a voice as she could muster.

After a few seconds, Benali stopped and stared at her.

She moved tentatively towards him. She could feel her heart beating faster and faster. Only she stood between him, the doors out to the corridor and his escape. He was young and physically strong, but she had faced tougher odds.

He glared at Ruth. 'Leave me alone!' he growled as he raised his right hand.

Something glinted in the darkness.

He was holding a large surgical knife.

Shit! That's not good.

Ruth held up her hand to try and calm him. 'Hadir, just stop whatever it is you're thinking of doing. Just take a moment.'

Inching closer and closer, she was trying to work out how she was going to disarm him without getting injured.

She glanced around nervously to see if there was anything she could grab to incapacitate him.

Ruth moved another few inches.

There were a few bottles on a surgical tray but nothing that looked like it might help her.

'Stay there!' Hadir roared as he waved the knife at her.

Ruth slowed her approach. It seemed like he was about to explode. 'Okay, okay, but what about your family back in Tangiers?'

Benali shook his head. 'Whatever happens, they won't ever see me again. I will spend my life in prison.'

'Hand youself in to me now. Plead guilty to Tash's murder. If you behave and rehabilitate yourself, you could serve twelve to fifteen years,' Ruth explained. 'You will get to see your family again. If you harm me and try to get away, it will be very different.'

Benali gave an ironic laugh. 'I will not plead guilty to that woman's murder, Never!'

'Why not?'

'She brought that upon herself. I didn't do anything to her,' Benali growled.

'Did you force your way into the flat, Hadir?' Ruth asked.

He shook his head and snapped aggressively, 'What are you talking about? You don't get it, do you?'

'What don't I get? Tell me,' Ruth said very quietly.

Benali was working himself into a frenzy. 'I loved her! She ... I wanted her to just love me.'

Ruth could see that Benali had tears in his eyes. She approached him cautiously and reached out. 'Come on, Hadir. Just hand me the knife. Please.'

Hadir looked like all the fight had left him as he sighed.

She reached out again. 'Come on.'

He nodded sadly but a second later he exploded in rage. 'No, no, no! I don't think so. If I go to hell, then you must come with me!'

He leapt forward and swung the knife towards Ruth's throat.

She darted back, sensing the movement of the blade which had missed her by millimetres.

Taking two steps further back, Ruth frantically searched for something to defend herself. She grabbed a metal surgical tray as Benali attacked again.

The blade smashed against the tray as she held it up, knocking the knife from Benali's grasp.

She was now backed against the wall as Benali came for her again.

Shit! Now what?

She glanced down at the bottles of liquid that she had seen earlier.

As the blade of the knife swept towards her chest, she managed to deflect Benali's arm away.

Glancing down at the bottles, she saw a label – *Potassium Chloride.*

She quickly grabbed the bottle with her right hand and lifted it, intending to swing it towards Benali's head, but the sweat from her palm caused her to lose her grip. The bottle slipped from her grasp, and she watched as it sailed through the air and crashed against Benali's jaw.

Thwack!

Benali staggered.

Ruth prayed that the force had been enough to hurt him.

For a second, she locked eyes with him. He was stunned.

But not enough for her to be safe.

Shifting her bodyweight with her hips, she swung her fist and hit him with an almighty right hook in the middle of his face. She felt his nose crack under her knuckles.

Benali's eyes rolled as he lost his balance and fell backwards into the metal gurney, and then onto the floor.

A red hot searing pain shot through Ruth's right hand and knuckles.

Jesus, that hurt!

She took a few steps forward and looked down at him. He was barely conscious and he wasn't going anywhere.

Where the hell did that come from?

The doors flew open and Lucy raced in followed closely by Brooks.

'You okay?' Brooks said as he approached.

'Just about,' Ruth said, taking a breath.

CHAPTER 26

IT WAS LATE AFTERNOON as Ruth glanced up from her desk in CID and saw Brooks approaching. He plonked a coffee down in front of her. 'Thought you could do with that? You okay?'

'Yes, Guv,' she said with a wry smile as she flexed her right hand. 'My knuckles are killing me though.'

'Peckham's next welterweight champion, eh?' Brooks joked but she could see his eyes lacked their usual sparkle.

He headed out to the middle of the CID office. 'Okay everyone, listen up!' He waited as detectives stopped chattering and turned their attention towards him. 'As most of you know by now, we have arrested Hadir Benali for Tash's murder. I've spoken to Forensics. Not only have they lifted Benali's fingerprints from Tash's front door, they've also got his fingerprint on a photograph inside Tash's flat. That puts him inside. Combined with his collection of Tash's possessions and the stuff we found at his home, the CPS have agreed that we have reached threshold.' Brooks smiled at the team who couldn't help let out collective sighs of relief and the odd handclap. 'I'm pleased to tell you that we will be charging Hadir Benali this evening with Tash's murder.'

Ruth let out a sigh and said, 'Thank God.'

She looked over at Lucy who nodded back. They had got their man and now they could try and get justice for Tash and her family.

'You've done a brilliant job on this case and I know how passionately you all felt that we had to find Tash's killer and bring him to justice,' Brooks said. 'But let's not take our eye off the ball now. We need to build as strong a case against Benali as we can before we hand it over to the CPS. I also want all loose ends tied up. I do not want his defence team finding anything on one of the other suspects and using that to cast doubt in the jury's mind. So, there's lots to feel positive about, but there's also lots of work still to do.'

'You buying drinks at The Greyhound later then, Guv?' Gaughran asked with a cheeky grin.

It was Peckham CID tradition that when they secured a major arrest or conviction, they went to the pub and the DCI bought several rounds of drinks.

'Of course. If memory serves me right, Tim, I've never seen you at the bar in there anyway,' Brooks quipped.

There was laughter from the detectives, especially Hassan.

'What are you laughing at Syed?' Gaughran grinned. 'Everyone knows you're tighter than a nun's fanny.'

There was more laughter.

Brooks put up his hands. 'Right, guys. Let's settle down. You can save the handbags for the pub. Anything I need to know at this stage?'

Hassan frowned at some papers he was sifting through and said, 'Guv, I've looked at Tash's landline phone records.

She did receive a phone call at 10.23pm, which is the phone call that Barbara York mentioned in her interview.'

'Have you got the number?' Brooks asked.

'Yeah. I then traced it with 02. Turns out it's a mobile phone belonging to that Hugo Allerton.'

'How long did the call last?' Brooks asked.

'Just over a minute, so a conversation took place.'

Brooks was puzzled. 'You and Tim go and have a chat with him first thing tomorrow. It might have been that he was just too scared to say that he had spoken to her that night. But check it out.'

'Yes, Guv,' Hassan said.

Ruth signalled that she wanted to speak. 'Front desk took a phone call this morning, Guv. Possible eye witness who saw Benali in Banfield Road around the time of the murder. Her memory was triggered when she saw the story in the newspaper.'

'Good. Again, first thing tomorrow, you and Lucy go and see if she's viable,' Brooks said. 'That reminds me. As you're aware, this is a high profile case and there will be a lot of journalists sniffing around for an angle on the story.' Brooks looked over at Gaughran. 'Do not get pissed and start shooting your mouth off to any Tom, Dick or Harry who asks you about the case.'

'Why are you looking at me, Guv?' Gaughran asked defensively.

Brooks raised an eyebrow. 'No idea, Tim.'

Gaughran smiled. 'Still no word about which mini-cab firm picked up Barbara York from Tash's flat.'

'Chase that up. I don't want anything popping out of the woodwork once we've charged Benali,' Brooks said. 'Anything else, before I send you lot off to go and get pissed up?'

'Don't suppose it matters, Guv,' Gaughran began, 'but you said that you remembered Ruston Mews in Notting Hill from somewhere. I've remembered why you'd know it.'

'Englighten us.' Brooks said.

'Up until 1954, Ruston Mews was named Rillington Place.'

For a second, Ruth had trouble remembering the significance of Rillington Place. Then it hit her. Number 10 was the infamous house there where serial killer John Christie had murdered eight people.

'Yeah, that's it.' Brooks nodded. 'For you youngsters who don't know the significance, 10 Rillington Place was the notorious house where John Christie gassed and murdered eight people. He hid his wife under the floorboards, three bodies were wallpapered over, and five buried in the garden.'

'Well it turns out that No. 8 Ruston Mews is next to where 10 Rillington Place stood until the council pulled it down in the 50s. I think it's weird that Marcus Jankel lives there, especially given what he writes about.'

'I guess it's only weird if he bought the house in Ruston Mews for that reason,' Brooks said with a shrug as he glanced down at his watch. 'Okay, five o'clock. Get your coats, first round is on me!'

As Ruth grabbed her coat she looked over at Lucy who was deep in thought. She wondered if Gaughran's research had spooked her.

'You coming to The Greyhound?' she asked Lucy.

'Yeah, I'll be there in a minute,' Lucy said with a forced smile. 'Just a couple of things I need to do here first.'

Ruth nodded, but something about Lucy's response made her suspicious.

What's she up to?

THE CID OFFICERS HAD been drinking for a couple of hours and things were starting to get raucous. They normally did when they got a result. Ruth finished her wine. She wasn't really in the mood to join in the celebrations. The discovery that Shiori had been sleeping with her ex-husband was still on her mind. Even though Ruth realised that Shiori was never going to have been the love of her life, they were close and she thought that they loved each other, in the immortal words of Prince Charles, *Whatever love means.* However, she couldn't help but feel rejected and wonder what she had done wrong to drive Shiori back into the arms of her odious ex-husband. She had spent the last couple of days over-analysing everything. Was she not intellectual enough for Shiori, who was an Ivy League educated journalist? Maybe their love life just wasn't exciting enough? And then the most damning of all those thoughts. Deep down, was Ruth a person who just wasn't worth loving? That was a crushing thought. but it was one she'd had many times. The evidence was there after all. Her husband Dan, Ella's father, had cheated on her many times and then moved to Australia with his girlfriend. Now Shiori had drawn the same conclusion and had gone back to her husband. What was it that made it so hard for people to continue loving her and wanting to be with her?

Stop with this terrible self-pity, will you? she said to herself.

She looked at her watch and saw that it had just gone seven. She would return to the office, sort through some paperwork, and chase up a few leads that still needed looking at. It was better than going back and sitting alone in her flat in Balham.

Out of the corner of her eye, she saw Lucy at the bar on her own. They hadn't said more than two words to each other since Benali's arrest at the hospital.

Ruth moved past a few CID officers and approached Lucy at the bar. 'You okay?'

Lucy nodded. 'It's been quite a week, hasn't it?'

'You staying here for the duration?' Ruth asked.

'No,' Lucy gestured to the detectives at the bar. 'They've already started the obligatory nob gags. I heard them discussing tits, so I came over here before I kicked one of them.'

Ruth laughed. 'Yeah, well they have a few pints, and then all political correctness goes out of the window. It's like being at a Bernard Manning stand-up show.'

'Where you off to?' Lucy asked. 'Haven't you got to collect Ella?'

Ruth shook her head. 'She's at a friends for a sleepover.'

'So, you're footloose and fancy free?' Lucy pulled a face. 'Sorry, I didn't mean ... you know. Sorry.'

'Shut up!' Ruth said with a smile. 'This is me you're talking to. I'm not pining and wishing I could be with Shiori, so don't worry about it ... You going home in a minute then?'

Lucy shrugged. 'I'm not sure yet.'

What does that mean?

'Oh, okay ...' Ruth said with a frown.

'If you're asking me if I'm seeing Marcus Jankel later, then I don't know.'

'It's none of my business, is it?'

'No, it's not, and if you remember, we've got someone arrested, locked up and charged with Tash's murder.'

'Okay, point taken. I'm just going on my instinct.'

'I don't think it's that, do you?'

'What does that mean?' Ruth asked. She didn't like Lucy's tone.

'Come off it, Ruth. You've always been a bit of an inverted snob. You vote Labour, you're a member of UNISON, and you judge anyone with a middle-class accent as being a posh twat. That's why you don't like Marcus. You think he's privileged.'

Ruth shook her head. 'No, it's not that. The only reason we're not looking at him is because a neighbour gave him an alibi, and it's a pretty flimsy one. And what about the whole Rillington Place thing? Don't you find that creepy?'

'I understand that you're feeling a bit shit about yourself Ruth, but please don't take it out on me,' Lucy snapped as she grabbed her coat and bag. 'I'm off to shag my serial killer boyfriend.'

Ruth watched as Lucy walked purposefully towards the doors and left the pub.

CHAPTER 27

IT WAS GONE 9PM AND Gaughran was sitting in the back of a mini-cab which drew up outside his house in a small cul-de-sac to the south of Peckham. He had received a text from his mum, Celia, asking if he was about, so he told her to come round just after nine.

'That's four quid, mate,' the taxi driver said as they stopped.

'Here's a fiver and keep the change.' Gaughran handed him the money as he got out.

True to form, his mum was sitting in a car parked on his drive. She was always early. One of her pet hates was being late, and ever since Gaughran was a kid he knew she would prefer to be half an hour early for something and wait, than cutting it fine. She just found it too stressful.

As she got out of the car, Gaughran smiled and gave her a wave. It was good to see her, although he did worry about the reason for her visit.

He walked up the drive and she gave him a hug and a kiss. 'Hello, Tim.'

'You all right, Mum?' he asked as he gave her a hug and then opened his front door and ushered her in. He couldn't help but think of seeing his dad with his mistress at the golf club. Looking at his mum only made him more angry.

'Christ, you smell of beer,' she said.

'Work do,' he explained with a smile. 'I left them to it.'

'Oh, it's nice and warm in here,' Celia said.

'You stopping?' Gaughran asked as he put on the downstairs lights. 'You wanna pop your coat up there?'

'Oh yes.' He could tell she was nervous as she took off her coat and scarf and hung them up. 'You gonna make me a coffeee then with that fancy coffee machine?'

'Course,' he replied as they went into the kitchen. 'If I'm honest, I've hardly used it.'

Celia frowned. 'Thought it cost you a bomb.'

'It did!' Gaughran snorted. 'I could have bought a bloody car for what I paid for it.'

'Yeah, well if you're like your dad, you're probably at work most of the time.'

I'm nothing like Dad, he thought to himself.

Gaughran clicked on the Bialetti coffee maker. He'd had at least five pints so his head was fuzzy, but a strong coffee would do the trick.

'You don't normally pop round,' Gaughran said. 'Everything all right?'

'I need to talk to you about something, Tim'

Gaughran immediately assumed that something was wrong with either her or his father. Maybe they were ill, or worse?

'What's wrong?' he asked anxiously.

'It's your dad's 65th birthday on Monday,' Celia said by way of an explanation.

Gaughran frowned. 'I'm not buying him a bloody present, if that's what you're asking me?'

Celia looked at him with a nervous expression on her face. 'I wondered if you want to drop in? We're having a few people round.'

Gaughran gave her a wry smile. 'Mum, you are aware that I haven't been in your house, or spoken to Dad, for over seven months?'

'Yeah, course I am,' she said.

'I'm confused, Mum,' Gaughran said, but he was relieved that neither of them had a life threatening illness.

'He wants you to come over,' Celia explained in a virtual whisper.

'Dad does?' Gaughran asked with a dubious raise of his eyebrow.

'Yeah.'

'He said that?'

'Yeah.'

'But he didn't have the balls to come round and ask me himself?' Gaughran said, feeling a surge of anger.

'No, you know what he's like,' Celia said with a shrug. 'He's a stubborn bugger.'

'Yeah, well that's a polite way of putting it.' Gaughran tipped a large spoonful of ground coffee into the machine.

'Would you, love?' Celia asked with hopeful smile that nearly broke his heart. 'Please.'

Gaughran nodded. 'Yeah, I'll come. But I'm doing it for you, not him, okay?'

The look of relief on his mum's face was clear to see. 'He'll be made up to see you, even if he doesn't say it. And so will I.'

Gaughran's thoughts turned to what he had witnessed at the golf club two nights earlier. He had no plans to tell his mum what he had seen – it would devastate her.

'Dad all right is he?' he asked.

'Never better actually,' she replied with a smile. 'Still spends half his life up the golf club with your Uncle Les but it must be doing him some good, 'cos I've never seen him so happy.'

Gaughran nodded. 'Yeah, well as long as you're all right Mum.'

She laughed. 'You know me, Tim. Take it as it comes.'

Gaughran grabbed two white china coffee cups and saucers from the cupboard. 'We'll go all posh shall we?'

'Yeah, why not, eh? Push the boat out,' she said with a beaming smile.

Gaughran knew that all she really wanted was for him and his dad to get along, and for the family to be back together like it used to be. Unfortunately, it wasn't quite as simple as that but he couldn't explain any of it to her.

'I think I've got those Italian coffee biscuits somewhere,' he said. 'The ones with the red label.'

'You don't mean Lotus Biscoffi, do you?'

'Exactly,' he said as he opened more cupboards to find them.

'Tim?' his mum said quietly.

'Yeah?'

'So, I can tell your dad that you will come then?'

'Yeah, of course. It'll be nice to see everyone, and maybe me and Dad can find some time to have a little chat, eh?'

She smiled. 'Yeah, I know he'd like that.'

Yeah, he might not when I get fucking through with him, Gaughran thought.

CHAPTER 28

LUCY AND MARCUS WERE in bed together at his house in Notting Hill. They had been making love and planned to go out for a late dinner.

'Thai, Korean, Moroccan, Goan?' Marcus said, listing where they could eat.

'You know what I fancy?'

Marcus grinned. 'If it's anal, then I have to draw the line there. I don't do stuff like that in the first week.'

Lucy laughed and slapped him. 'Oh my God! I can't believe you just said that!'

'Sorry, probably crossing the line, humour wise.'

'Definitely,' Lucy said, pretending to be more shocked than she actually was. 'I *was* going to say fish and chips.'

Marcus smiled. 'Great fish place up on Ladbroke Grove. Although if you want curry sauce I'm going to have to ask you to leave right now.'

Lucy pulled a face. 'No. Curry sauce is definitely all sorts of wrong.'

'Phew, I'm so glad you said that.' He laughed as he leaned over and moved a whisp of hair from her face. 'You really are quite beautiful.'

As Lucy leant in and kissed him hard, he rolled over on top of her. They began to kiss more passionately and she felt his hands stroke her inner thighs.

'I thought we were getting food,' she whispered.

'It's open until midnight,' he whispered back.

'Oh, good,' Lucy said with a grin.

Reaching down the side of bed, Marcus took hold of his dressing gown and pulled the long cord from its waist. 'Want to make things more interesting?'

Does he mean tie me up? Isn't it a bit soon for that kind of thing?

'I don't know,' Lucy said. Part of her was turned on by the thought, but she also feared that it would make her vulnerable.

Marcus smiled and went to put the cord back. 'It's okay. Don't worry ...'

'It's fine,' Lucy said, pulling him closer to her. 'I want you to do it.'

'Sure?'

'Yes,' she gasped as she stretched her hands up towards the wrought iron bedhead.

'Really?'

'Get on with it,' she giggled.

Marcus entwined the cord around her wrists, looped it around again, and tied her hands tightly to the top of the curved bedhead.

He's done that before she thought. It made her feel uncomfortable.

For a few seconds, Lucy felt calm but the dawning realisation that she was now tied to the bed and therefore totally vulnerable scared her.

Marcus could do anything and she would have no way of stopping him.

'What do you want me to do?' he whispered as he kissed the skin around her knees and thighs.

Lucy didn't reply – she didn't know what to say.

He sat up and then stared directly in her eyes.

In the half light of the bedroom, there seemed to be something very different about the expression on his face. Or was it just the light.

'Why did you let me do that to you?' he asked. His voice seemed to be far more matter of fact now, almost as if he was angry that she had allowed him to tie her up.

'Because you asked me to,' Lucy said softly, as she felt her heart rate starting to increase.

Something's not right here. What's he doing?

Marcus frowned. 'But that's completely reckless. You hardly know me.'

'I think I do,' Lucy said uncertainly. Her breathing was becoming more rapid and shallow.

He laughed. 'I could literally do anything to you right now and there is nothing you could do about it. You might scream, but then again I could gag you.'

There were a few seconds of silence.

Lucy's heart was thumping against her chest. She remembered what had happened to Tash, the drama that Marcus had written, and what Gaughran had told them about Ruston Mews.

Jesus! I'm having a panic attack!

'Untie me right now!' Lucy yelled, pulling her hands and twisting.

Marcus loomed over her and stared down.

'I said untie me!' she shouted.

She could see the expression on his face. He looked surprised at her reaction.

'Sorry,' he mumbled as he untied the cord. 'Sorry, here you go. God I'm really sorry.'

Feeling the cord loosen, she pulled her hands free and glared at him. 'You stupid wanker!'

'Sorry, I didn't mean to scare you!'

'What the fuck was all that?'

'I was messing about,' Marcus said as he winced. 'I'm really sorry. I'm an idiot.'

Lucy got off the bed and started to grab her clothes from the floor. 'You're a prick. And I'm leaving.'

He put his hand on her shoulder. 'Lucy, I'm really sorry.'

She flinched. 'Don't touch me, Marcus!' She was angry with herself for allowing him to tie her up and make her feel so vulnerable.

'Please don't go,' he pleaded. 'I feel really bad.'

'You acted like a twat!' Lucy said as she felt herself starting to calm down a little.

'I did. A complete twat,' he agreed.

Lucy continued to get dressed. 'I'm still going.'

He sat up on the bed, pulled the sheet around him and looked at her. 'Well, for what it's worth, I think I love you.'

What did he just say?

'What are you talking about Marcus?' Lucy asked with a frown. Even though it was a crazy thing to say, she couldn't help but feel flattered. 'You've only known me for a few days.'

He shrugged. 'Okay. I guess what I meant to say was that I've never felt like this about anyone before.' He moved over, took her hand and traced his finger over it. 'And I think I could be falling in love with you.'

Lucy looked down into his big brown eyes. The orange from the streetlight threw a warm hue over the room.

He gave her a little boy lost look. 'Please stay.'

'Why should I?'

He smiled at her and took both her hands in his. 'Because I will run up to Ladbroke Grove and get us fish and chips. We'll crack open a very smooth Italian red. And then we'll sit here in bed and watch a great old black and white movie ... How does that sound?'

'You understand that you're still a total twat?'

'Absolutely.'

Lucy couldn't help but smile at him. 'Yeah, that does actually sound really nice.

CHAPTER 29

Sunday 1st February

WITH A STRETCH AND a yawn, Ruth leaned back in her chair, finished her toast, and took a sip of her second coffee of the day. It was only 7 am and it was a Sunday! She remembered in the past having to explain to various 'romantic' partners that major crime investigations didn't just stop for the weekend.

She had a long statement to type up in which she had to describe in detail what had happened at the hospital the previous day. Benali had been injured inside the mortuary so she had to demonstrate that she had used *reasonable force* in his arrest. Given that he was attacking her with an eight-inch surgical knife, it wasn't going to be difficult to show that she had acted in self-defence. However, she had known other officers who had been hauled through investigations by the Police Complaints Authority, PCA, even when *reasonable force* and self-defence were blatantly obvious.

'You're in bloody early,' Brooks commented as he entered the office. 'We can take our foot off the gas a bit now we've got Benali bang to rights.'

Ruth smiled and pointed to her paperwork. 'Yeah, I thought I'd get ahead of the game with this lot.' She tilted her head in query. 'Sore head this morning, Guv?'

Brooks shook his head. 'I left them to it. Wasn't really in the mood.'

'Yeah.' Ruth gave him a sympathetic smile. 'Sorry to hear about you and Lucy.'

'We'll be all right,' he said unconvincingly. 'She sent me a text this morning. She's taking the day off as holiday. Said she wants to catch up on some sleep. Don't blame her.'

'Oh right,' Ruth said, but she knew that Lucy probably wasn't at home.

'You okay to talk to that eye witness on your own? I can come with you if you want?'

'I'll be fine, Guv.'

'I'll see you at briefing then,' he said as he headed for his office.

Ruth watched him go. He cut a sad figure as he went and she felt a little sorry for him.

She got up from her desk and grabbed one of the reports which now needed photocopying in triplicate. As she passed Lucy's desk she couldn't help but glance down at the notepad beside her phone. She had been suspicious last night when Lucy had left the pub abruptly, and wondered if there was anything to indicate what she had been up to.

Her eyes were drawn to a name that was scribbled down in biro – *Polly Margaret Baker*. The name was familiar, but why? Then she realised. It was the name of the neighbour who had seen Marcus Jankel arrive home at the time of Tash's murder. Her witness statement effectively gave him a watertight alibi. Beside the name was written a date – 23rd January 1968. Was that Polly Baker's date of birth? That would make her thirty, wouldn't it? More importantly, why was Lucy taking an interest in her now? Was she having her own suspicions about Jankel? Even though it seemed highly unlikely that he was involved in Tash's murder, maybe Lucy was starting to check up on him.

Glancing around the empty office, Ruth noticed that one of the computers was linked to the Police National Computer, PNC, and the Home Office Large Major Enquiry System, which was amusingly called HOLMES after Sir Arthur Conan Doyle's famous literary London detective. On major crimes such as murder, HOLMES allowed senior investigating officers to check and coordinate a range of intelligence sources.

She sat down at the keyboard and typed in Polly Margaret Baker's name and the possible date of birth into the PNC for a preliminary background check. The screen cursor disappeared and the following appeared on the screen – *Information is Security Protected.*

What the hell does that mean?

Ruth glanced up as someone came into the office. It was Brooks. She turned her chair to face him as he approached.

'Something up, Guv?'

He was holding a fax and didn't look happy. 'This eye witness we've got who says that she saw Benali in the vicinity of Tash's flat at the time of the murder. Shirley Munroe. Apparently she's got form for this kind of thing.'

Ruth stifled a sigh. 'What do you mean?'

'In layman's terms, she's a crackpot. She rings this station every week with information about one crime or another. If we put up a missing poster, she's on the phone within minutes.'

'Bollocks.' Ruth said despondently.

'Bollocks indeed,' Brooks groaned.

It wasn't good news. An eye witness statement would have been incredibly powerful in the prosecution's case against Benali.

'Doesn't look like I'll be paying her a visit then,' Ruth said, and then pointed to the screen. 'Any ideas why this has popped up?'

Brooks peered at the message. 'Who are you looking at?'

'Polly Baker. She's the neighbour who claimed to have seen Marcus Jankel at the time of Tash's murder.'

'And you're doing a PNC check because …?'

Ruth raised her shoulders. 'Just tying up loose ends. I thought I'd check her out.'

'Why?'

'Just trust me on this, Guv. I think she's worth looking at.'

'Okay. If you think she's a loose end, then let's have a look at her.' Brooks sat on the chair next to her. 'Security Protected usually means there's some risk attached to their identity.'

'Meaning?'

'Sometimes they're a police informant. Could be in witness protection. As a DCI I can have a look for you on my login if you want?'

Ruth nodded. 'Thanks Guv.'

Brooks logged in and she passed him the piece of paper with Polly Baker's full name and date of birth. A few seconds later, a screen of information appeared.

Brooks frowned. 'For starters, her name isn't Polly Margaret Baker. She was given that name in 1975.'

'What's her original name?' Ruth asked, looking at the screen.

'It won't tell me that here. I'd have to make a phone call to find out,' he said as he pressed another button and more information appeared. He puffed his cheeks and then exhaled. 'Bloody hell. At the age of eight, she was convicted of the murder of her parents in Germany. Because of her age, she was unable to stand trial and was sent to Windsor where she had maternal grandparents, Peter and Mary Baker. That explains why she was renamed Polly Baker, I guess. She's been in the UK ever since.'

'Isn't Marcus Jankel originally from Germany?' Ruth asked thinking out loud.

Brooks nodded in agreement. 'Something here doesn't add up, does it?'

'No, Guv,' Ruth said as she shook her head. 'Maybe I should go and have a chat with Polly Baker?'

CHAPTER 30

'I'M GOING TO MAKE YOU breakfast in bed,' Lucy said as she flung back the duvet.

She had taken a rare day off work and was spending it with Marcus. Life felt good.

'We should go out somewhere today,' he said, leaning back on the pillows and lighting a cigarette.

'Out?' Lucy asked. 'Like where?'

'Why don't we get out of London? I know a fantastic pub on the Thames in Windsor. The Boatman.'

'Windsor sounds nice. Isn't Eton in Windsor?'

'Very good, it is.' Marcus smiled. 'In fact we used to sneak out to The Boatman during lunchtimes when we were in sixth form. I'm pretty sure our housemasters just turned a blind eye.'

Lucy shook her head. 'Yeah, it's when you say stuff like *housemasters* that I realise how incredibly posh and out of touch with reality you really are.'

Marcus laughed. 'Sorry!'

Pulling on a long t-shirt, Lucy pointed down the hallway to the kitchen. 'Have you got eggs?'

'Yes.'

'Anything else?'

Marcus shrugged. 'Spinach?'

'Oh my God. I've never been out with anyone who had spinach in their fridge!'

'You should try it with toasted pine nuts,' Marcus said, smiling. 'Incredible.'

'Such a ponce,' Lucy joked. 'It does mean I could make us Eggs Florentine though.'

'Eggs Florentine? All your working-class credibility just went out of the window,' he quipped.

'I'll be back in ten minutes.' Lucy walked barefoot down the wooden floors towards the kitchen.

How the hell did I remember Eggs Florentine? And what is Eggs Benedict then?

Her eyes were drawn to a large shadowy film poster up on the wall. The film was called *10 Rillington Place* and starred Richard Attenborough. And it was a biopic about the serial killer John Christie!

Oh my God! Why the hell is that on the wall?

She took a step back and felt her stomach lurch.

'Do you want to know something really weird?' said a voice beside her.

It was Marcus.

She almost jumped out of her skin.

'For fuck's sake, Marcus, you made me jump!'

'Sorry. Have you seen it?' he asked, pointing to the poster.

Moving away from him, Lucy shook her head. 'No I bloody haven't!' She wasn't sure if she should be annoyed or scared. And she wasn't about to tell him about the discussion they'd had in CID about Ruston Mews formerly being

Rillington Place, or that the very house she was standing in was only next door to where 10 Rillington Place had been.'

Marcus pulled a face. 'Very creepy. Attenborough is incredible in it.'

Lucy's stomach tensed and she began to feel uneasy.

He touched her shoulder and beckoned her over to a small window. 'This will freak you out. Look out there.'

Wondering if she should just make her excuses and leave, Lucy went over and glanced outside.

'What am I looking at?' she asked, aware of how tense she was now feeling.

'You see there are some new buildings and a communal garden? Just there?'

She nodded and could guess what he was about to tell her. 'Yeah.'

'I know this is a bit weird, but that's where 10 Rillington Place actually was,' he said as he gave a bit of a shudder. 'Horrible if you think about it.'

'Did you know that when you bought this house?' she asked.

'God, no! I think I would have probably thought twice about living next to the site of some serial killer. Funnily enough, they didn't mention it in the details.'

Although she was relieved to hear him say it, she still felt spooked. 'How did you find out?'

'Mrs Walker at No 5 told me. She's been here since the 50s when it all happened, so she gave me all the gory details. According to Polly, she likes to tell everyone about it,' he said with a smile. He looked at her with concern. 'Are you all right?'

Lucy smiled back at him but she couldn't shake the uncomfortable feeling in her stomach. 'Yeah, fine. It's just a bit weird.'

'Sorry,' Marcus said with a furrowed brow. 'I just thought that as a murder detective you would find it interesting.'

She nodded and gave a wry smile. 'Yeah, it is. Sorry. I suppose on my day off I'd prefer to avoid the sites of serial killings, that's all.'

'Yes, of course,' Marcus laughed. 'I tell you what. Forget cooking. I'll go and get the car. We'll have a quick coffee and then go for brunch at the River Café in Hammersmith.'

Lucy nodded. 'Yeah, that's sounds nice. I'll have a quick shower.'

'Great.' He took her in his arms. 'I'm going to make sure you have a lovely day off. Don't worry.'

She took a deep breath and allowed herself to relax a bit.

GAUGHRAN SMILED AT the receptionist at Goldstein Films. 'Yeah, it's us again.'

'I can see that,' she said, returning his smile.

'We seem to be having great difficulty in tracking down a mini-cab that Barbara York used on Monday night, the 26th January. We believe that she rang for a taxi from Peckham to Battersea at about ten thirty. She told us that she called a mini-cab company that your company has an account with?'

The receptionist looked apologetic. 'Sorry. We've got several accounts I'm afraid. Would you like me to ask Barbara and get back to you?'

'No offence, but I've got a feeling that it would be far quicker if we just pop in and ask her right now,' Gaughran said pointing towards where he knew Barbara York's office was.

'Oh, right,' she said, becoming flustered. 'Well I'm sorry but you can't go in there.'

Gaughran shrugged. 'Yeah, you said that last time.'

'It's okay, we know the way,' Hassan said dismissively.

They went through the double glass doors and marched down the corridor to Barbara York's office.

Gaughran knocked and almost simultaneously opened the door.

Sitting behind Barbara's desk was a smart-looking man, late 30s, sharp suit. He was in the middle of a telephone conversation and appeared shocked to see them burst in.

'Eddie?' he spoke into the phone with an American accent. 'I'm gonna have to call you back.'

Where the hell is Barbara? Gaughran wondered.

'Hi there,' the man said with a frown as he put down the phone. 'Can I help you guys?'

Gaughran got out his warrant card and showed it to him. 'We're police officers. We're looking for Barbara York.'

The man nodded and sat forward. 'Oh, Barbara. Right, well she's not here.'

Gaughran gave him a sarcastic smile. 'Yeah, I can see that. Any idea when she'll be back?'

'She flew to New York this morning,' the man explained, 'and I'm now heading up the London office. Is this something I can help you with, or did you need to speak with Barbara specifically?'

'Can I ask why she had to fly back to New York so suddenly?' Hassan asked.

The man shrugged. 'I think it was a personal thing. Family.'

Gaughran nodded. 'And when is she coming back to London?'

'Actually, I don't think she *is* coming back to London. I'm pretty sure Bob said something about her working on some projects out in LA.'

Gaughran let out an audible sigh. 'In that case, we have a problem. We're investigating Tash Weston's murder.'

'Yeah, I read about that.'

'We do need to speak to Barbara so she can help us with our enquiries.'

'I don't know what to tell you?' the man said, leaning back in his chair. 'If you give the New York office a call, I'm sure they could track her down for you. But I guess if she's caught up in this family thing, it might be difficult to get hold of her for the next few days.'

Gaughran looked at Hassan. *What the hell is going on here?*

'I'm sorry I can't be of more help, guys,' he added with a forced smile. He got up from the desk as a signal that it was time for them to leave.

Gaughran fixed him with a stare. 'That's all right. I believe that the London Met and the NYPD have a very good working relationship, especially when it comes to serious crime like *homicide*. I'll let them know that we need to speak to Barbara in connection with our murder case and I'm sure they'll find her for us.'

The man pulled a face. 'If you feel that's the way you want to go on this. But Mr Goldstein is fiercely protective of his employees. You might say that he sees them like a family. And he also has one hell of a legal team. So, good luck.'

RUTH AND BROOKS WERE marching along the corridor to Interview Room 1. Everything had been put on hold as word had come from the duty solicitor that Benali wanted to confess to Tash's murder, and he was happy to sign a statement to that effect. He would be entering a guilty plea when he appeared before a judge at Southwark Crown Court the following morning.

'You think Benali is serious?' Ruth asked. Part of her was still trying to process what they had found out about Polly Baker and if it was connected to Marcus Jankel. She wondered if Lucy's holiday request had anything to do with her wanting to spend time with Jankel.

Brooks shrugged. 'No idea. From what you've told me, I think there is some kind of mental health issue going on with him.'

'Has anyone mentioned diminished responsibility?'

Brooks shook his head as they arrived at the interview room. 'Not yet. He'll need a psychological evaluation to start with.'

They went in and sat down at the interview table. Benali was still dressed in a grey tracksuit and his eye was still swollen and closed.

Ruth leant forward and clicked the red button on the recording machine. The long electronic beep sounded as Brooks opened his files and slid one of them over to Ruth.

'Interview conducted with Hadir Benali, 11.05 am, Peckham Police Station. Present are Detective Chief Inspector Harry Brooks, duty solicitor Simon Gregg and myself, Detective Constable Ruth Hunter.' Ruth then glanced over at Benali. 'Hadir, do you understand that you are still under arrest?'

'Yes,' he mumbled.

'We understand that you would like to tell us what happened last Monday evening?' Brooks said.

Benali was jiggling his leg as he bit the nail on one of his fingers. 'Look, I just want to confess that I killed her, that's it.'

'It's not quite as simple as that, Hadir,' Ruth pointed out. 'We're going to need you to tell us exactly what happened at Tash's flat last Monday night.'

'I was waiting outside for her.'

'What time was that?' Brooks asked, taking a pen from his pocket.

'Ten? I dunno. I have no watch but ten or ten thirty.'

'Okay, so you waited outside Tash's flat,' Ruth said gently, 'and then what happened?'

'She came home,' Benali said as he rubbed his goatee beard and sat back in the chair.

'Had she walked home?' Ruth asked. They had to use the interview to establish whether or not Benali really had murdered Tash, and that meant asking questions where he could trip himself up.

'No,' Benali said with a shake of his head. 'She arrived home in a taxi.'

Brooks glanced up from his notepad. 'So, a mini-cab?'

Benali smiled. Maybe he was starting to become aware of the little traps they were setting for him. 'No, no. A black taxi cab.'

Brooks nodded. 'Okay, a black cab. And she was on her own?'

'No. There was a lady with her. An older lady I think.'

'And what did they do?' Ruth asked.

'They got out of the taxi and they go inside her flat for a while.'

'And all this time you were waiting outside the flat and watching?'

Benali nodded and then a moment later he said, 'Yes.'

'Did you wait outside Tash's flat and watch her often?'

'Yes.' There was nothing in his voice that suggested he thought this was either a strange or shameful thing to do.

Brooks looked up from his notepad. 'Okay, so tell me what happened next, Hadir,' he said.

Benali shrugged. 'The lady left.'

'How did she leave?' Ruth asked.

'A taxi.' Benali smiled and corrected himself. 'A mini-cab.'

'How long do you estimate she was in there?' Brooks asked.

Benali thought for a few seconds. 'Twenty minutes, I think. Maybe half an hour.'

Ruth exchanged a look with Brooks – Benali's statement backed up Barbara York's version of events and there was no way they could have colluded with one another. Benali didn't seem like a regular at Soho House.

'And then what happened?' Ruth asked.

Benali smoothed the goatee on his face and said, 'I went over and I killed her.'

'Okay,' Ruth said. There was something about Benali's matter of fact explanation that was chilling. 'How did you get inside Tash's flat?'

'I walked over and knocked on the door. She opened the door and I pushed. She is small. She is not very strong. Then I dragged her by her hair up the stairs.'

Brooks showed no reaction. 'Okay. And then what happened?'

'And then I killed her.'

'How did you kill her, Hadir?' Ruth asked. No one outside of the CID office and the mortuary knew the specific details of how Tash had been murdered. Thankfully, those details hadn't found their way into any of the stories in the press yet. If Benali knew the elaborate details of the murder, then there would be no doubting he was the murderer.

Benali frowned. 'I do not understand.'

'How did you kill her?' Brooks asked slowly. 'Did you stab her?'

Benali wagged his finger at them. 'No, no, no. Not stabbed. What is the word when someone cannot breathe? Strangle? Yes, I strangled her.'

'With your hands?' Brooks asked.

This is the moment of truth ...

Benali pulled a face as though this was a ridiculous question. 'No, no. Not with my hands.'

Without signalling the importance of what he had just said, Brooks gave Ruth a surreptitious look.

I think we've got our man, Ruth thought to herself.

CHAPTER 31

HAVING SHOWERED AND drunk a freshly-made coffee, Lucy was sitting in an armchair in Marcus' living room looking out along Ruston Mews. He had gone to get the car so they could drive over to the River Café in Hammersmith. If she was honest, she was feeling incredibly sleepy. It wasn't surprising given the intensity of the case she was working on and the emotional rollercoaster of her split with Harry.

Jesus, I can hardly keep my eyes open!

She gave a loud yawn as she looked at the large iron gates that were at the top of the mews, and spotted a beautiful, vintage 1960s Mercedes 190 SL pull in. She squinted and saw that Marcus was driving.

Wow. That is some car! she thought. She hated the phrase but it was a *babe magnet!*

She had forgotten her tiredness. It was exciting to think about the prospect of being driven across London in that car, and eating a gorgeous brunch looking over the Thames with her handsome boyfriend. Was he now her boyfriend? She guessed so. *Now that's a proper day off.*

Taking a deep breath, she shook her head and tried to muster some energy. She watched as Marcus pulled the car up outside.

A few seconds later, he bounded up the stairs and grinned at her. 'Ready to go?'

'Yeah, I'm exhausted, but it's my day off and I refuse to sleep all day.'

'I love your attitude,' Marcus said. 'You can sleep when you're dead, that's what they say isn't it?'

'They do,' Lucy said. 'I saw your car.'

'Oh that old thing,' Marcus joked.

'It must be worth a fortune,' Lucy said as she got to her feet. Her tiredness was making her head swim, and for a moment she felt unsteady.

'Oh God, are you alright?' he asked as he went over to her.

'Yeah, I've been overdoing it. I've had a crazy week. I'm fine,' she said as her head cleared and she regained her balance.

He grinned. 'I didn't like to tell you that I'd drugged your coffee.'

'Ha, ha,' Lucy gave him a sarcastic smile. 'I'll just grab my coat and bag, and I'll be with you.'

Reaching inside his jacket, Marcus pulled out a small navy jewellery box. 'I hope you don't mind, but I got you a little something.'

Has he bought me jewellery? Now my perfect day is complete, she thought.

He handed her the box which had the name *Henry Stephens Jewellery* embossed on it in gold letters.

I've never heard of that shop so I guess it must be very classy!

Opening it slowly, she saw a delicate silver necklace inside.

'Aww, it's beautiful Marcus,' she said, feeling a little overwhelmed by his romantic gesture. 'You didn't need to get me anything.'

'Nonsense. Do you want me to help you put it on?'

'Yes, please,' Lucy said as he took the necklace from her.

He went behind her and gently looped the necklace around her neck and then fastened it.

'Perfect,' he said as he gestured to the elegant vintage wall mirror over the fireplace. 'Why don't you go and have a look in the mirror? It really is perfect.'

Still feeling a little woozy, she took two steps across the patterned rug and looked at her reflection.

She reached up to touch the necklace and realised that it had something very small attached to his centre.

'You really are a big softie at heart, aren't you?'

Marcus laughed and held up his hands. 'Guilty.'

Smiling over at him, she then glanced back at her reflection and noticed a tiny four-leafed clover at the necklace's centre.

A four-leafed clover!

The significance of it made her stomach lurch.

Oh my God!

She could feel her hand began to shake.

'Don't you like it?' Marcus asked with a strange smile. 'I thought you, of all people, would have loved it. You know how much it means.'

A surge of terror swept through Lucy but as she turned to face Marcus her vision began to blur.

'What the hell are you doing?' she asked.

He leant forward and peered at her. 'Yeah, I wasn't joking when I said that I drugged your coffee.'

'I don't understand ...' Lucy said, but her mouth had gone very dry. 'What have you done?'

'Flunitrazepam. It's a little less crude than Rohypnol and totally tasteless. Perfect for someone like me.'

Closing one eye to try and correct her vision, Lucy gasped as she started to lose her balance. 'You need to let me go ...'

'Oh, I don't think you can go anywhere while you're feeling like that,' he said.

She took one step forward and then fell. Marcus stepped forward, caught her under the arms and turned her around so he could lower her into the armchair.

'Whoops. There you go,' he said with a little laugh. Then he looked at the necklace. 'I knew Tash's necklace would suit you perfectly. You really remind me of her, you know that?'

CHAPTER 32

BROOKS AND RUTH WERE continuing to interview Benali but he was being increasingly vague about what had happened on Monday night.

'Can you confirm that before Tash was murdered, you had never been inside her flat? Is that correct?' Brooks asked.

Benali frowned. 'Yes, I thought that is what I told you.'

'Hadir, you seem to be going round and round in circles here,' Brooks said. 'Where were you in the flat when you first attacked Tash?'

Benali acted as if he hadn't heard the question and leant over to talk to the Duty Solicitor, Simon Gregg. For the next minute, they had a whispered but animated conversation.

What the hell is going on? Ruth wondered. She had never seen anything like this before in an interview. She had gone from being certain that they had the man who had murdered Tash, to now seriously doubting that fact.

Gregg cleared his throat, looked over at them with a slightly bemused expression and said, 'My client is no longer willing to confess to the murder of Natasha Weston. He will be putting in a plea of not guilty at Southwark Crown Court.'

Brooks and Ruth looked at each other in utter confusion.

'What?' Brooks thundered, unable to hide his frustration.

There were a few seconds of silence as Brooks and Ruth tried to get their heads around Benali's complete U-turn in the interview.

'Hadir?' Ruth said, still trying to work out what was going on in his mind. 'Can you tell us why you have changed your plea.'

Benali frowned. 'Because I did not murder that woman.'

'But you told us a few minutes ago that you did?' Brooks growled.

'And now I'm telling you I didn't.'

'But we have evidence that suggests that you did,' Brooks said.

Benali shook his head. 'That is impossible because I didn't.'

'Sweet Jesus ...' Brooks rubbed his chin in bewilderment as he reached into one of the case files. He pulled out a photograph of the bag they had found in Benali's hospital locker with Tash's possessions laid out next to it. 'Hadir, this is what we found inside the locker in the hospital that you have the key for.'

Benali nodded. 'Yes.'

'For the purposes of the tape, I am showing the suspect a photograph of a bag containing various possessions belonging to the victim,' Brooks said.

'What is the question?' Benali said.

'You have possessions belonging to Tash. How could you have got them unless you went inside her flat?' Ruth asked. 'That's the question.'

'They have all come from her bin,' he said. 'I check her bin all the time. If there is something in there I want, I take it. The old trainers, the notebook. They were all in her bin.'

'You expect us to believe that?' Brooks snorted.

'I don't care what you believe,' Benali said. 'That is the truth.'

Was that a plausible explanation for how he had her possessions? Ruth worried that it might be. There was nothing in the bag that Tash might not have thrown away. It had just never occurred to them that's how they had come into Benali's possession.

Brooks reached inside the case file and took out another photograph. It was of the cover of a fashion magazine featuring Tash at its centre. 'We found this magazine cover inside Tash's flat. It has your fingerprints all over it, Hadir. How do you explain that?'

'About three months ago, I saw that magazine in the shop so I bought it. I took off the cover, put it in an envelope through her front door with a note asking Tash to sign it for me. I put my phone number on it so she could tell me if she would do that,' Benali explained. 'I never heard back from her. It made me very angry that she would treat me this way. But that is why my fingerprints are on it. It doesn't mean I was in her flat though, does it?'

Shit! Benali's defence counsel are going to have a field day with all this. We can't even prove that he was ever in the flat! Ruth thought.

'Are you now saying that you have never been inside Tash's flat and you did not murder her?' Brooks said, unable to hide his frustration.

'Yes, that is correct,' Benali said as he stared over at Gregg.

'But you were sitting outside Tash's flat on Monday night watching her?' Brooks asked.

'Yes.'

'You saw her arrive home in a cab with an older woman who then left about twenty minutes later?'

'Yes.'

'Did you see anything or anyone else?' Ruth asked.

Benali nodded. 'Yes, of course.'

'What did you see, Hadir?' Ruth asked very calmly.

'I saw the man who *did* kill her,' Benali said.

What? Jesus Christ!

Brooks and Ruth exchanged a look of surprise.

'Can you describe him?'

'Yes. He arrived in this beautiful car. An old Mercedes. I saw him when he got out. He was a tall, handsome man with long hair down to here.' Benali demonstrated the man's hair came down to his shoulder. 'He was smoking a cigarette. He knocked on the door and went inside.'

Ruth looked over at Brooks – *Marcus Jankel.*

CHAPTER 33

AS LUCY REGAINED CONSCIOUSNESS, she found that she was staring up at the corniced ceiling of a room she didn't recognise.

Where the hell am I? What the hell happened?

At first, she wondered if she had been out drinking. Her head was pounding and her mouth was dry.

Did I drink so much that I blacked out?

Then she remembered she was in Marcus' house. For a few seconds, she tried to refocus her vision and clear her head. Her arms were above her head and she was becoming aware of something around her wrists. At first she had assumed that she had slept like that.

My wrists are tied up! What the hell is going on?

As her heartbeat began to race, the hideous memories of what had happened inside Marcus' house a few hours earlier tumbled back into her consciousness like a terrifying nightmare.

Oh my God, I need to get out of here!

She tugged at whatever was being used to bind her wrists to the bedhead. It was no good. Glancing up, she saw that it was the cord from Marcus' dressing gown that he had used to tie her wrists the night before.

Something metallic brushed against the tip of her chin. Looking down, she saw the delicate silver necklace with the four-leafed clover attached. It had been Tash Weston's necklace and now it was round her neck.

The thought of it terrified her.

He's going to kill me like he killed her.

She yanked again at the cord with all her strength but it only got tighter. Raising herself up as best she could, she glanced around the bedroom for something to help her escape. Marcus had made sure there was nothing that could be kicked or knocked over.

Christ, I'm trapped here. Where the hell is he?

Lying back down, she began to wonder how she had been so taken in by Marcus. She was a detective for God's sake. As her mind raced, she realised there might have been clues if she'd been more suspicious or on her guard.

'You've really made things very difficult for me,' said a voice.

It was Marcus.

The sound of his voice made her shudder. They had been so intimate. But when she thought of what he had done to Tash Weston, it made her feel sick.

Raising her head, she could see him sitting in an armchair at the far end of the room, crossed-legged and with a cigarette dangling from his mouth.

'Untie me now, Marcus,' Lucy pleaded with a mixture of anger and fear.

'I can't do that, can I?' He lit the cigarette and blew out a stream of smoke. 'I've fallen in love with you Lucy, which puts me in a terrible dilemma.'

With her pulse now racing, she tried to get her breath as she pulled the cord again. She knew that his *terrible dilem-*

ma was whether or not to kill her. Now she needed to work out how to persuade him to let her go – or at least engineer a moment where she could escape.

'Don't you think I'm in a dilemma too?' Lucy said. 'I'm a police officer and I've fallen in love with someone like you.'

He stood up from the chair and walked towards her slowly. 'Someone like me? You mean a cold-hearted killer?'

'No.' Lucy shook her head. 'I know you, Marcus. I know you're not like that. You told me things about yourself. You let me see your vulnerable side.'

'But I'm afraid I didn't,' Marcus said. He let out a deep sigh. 'None of that was true. It was all just a little act.'

'Of course it wasn't,' she said, hoping to find a way to tap into his emotional weakness. 'You told me what happened to your sister.'

He stared down at her and frowned. 'Poor, poor Lucy. My sister isn't dead.'

'What? Yes, she is,' Lucy insisted. There was no way that Marcus could have faked the story about her death and his parents sending him away. She had seen him crying and totally broken.

'Well, if she is, who was the person you spoke to over there the other night?' he said, pointing to the house across the road.

Lucy thought for a few seconds and then it dawned on her. 'Polly is your sister?'

That's why she was happy to give him a watertight alibi.

'Why did you tell me she was dead?' she asked.

'Because if I had told you the true story of what actually happened that day,' Marcus said, 'you definitely wouldn't have slept with me again.'

'I don't understand. Are you saying she didn't die, and your parents didn't send you away to boarding school?' Lucy tried to make sense of what he was telling her.

'No she didn't die, but they were murdered that day,' he said. ' In fact it was Polly who killed them. Well, Hettie as she was then.'

Lucy arched her brows. What he was telling her was becoming increasingly bizarre. 'When she was eight?'

'I know. Hard to believe isn't it? The German press had a field day when they broke the story.' Marcus said shaking his head.

Lucy glared directly in his eyes. 'It sounds like you're making up another one of your stories.'

'I wish I was,' he said as he came over and sat next to her on the bed. He smiled as he ran his hand over her cheek and brushed a strand of hair from her face.

'Please ... don't touch me,' she said. It was making her flesh crawl.

'I can tell you the truth now. It makes no difference does it? My parents kept us like dogs from the time we could first walk. Worse than dogs. Hettie and I were kept in a tiny room that was no bigger than a cupboard. No light, just a small mattress between us. We had to eat our food out of bowls with our hands. If we complained, we were beaten and locked in that room for days on end. No food, no water, and no toilet. Every day we were made to do household chores and beaten if we didn't work hard enough.'

'Oh my God,' Lucy said under her breath.

'One day, Hettie got hold of a knife in the kitchen and stabbed my mother in her back over and over until she fell to the floor. She bled to death in front of us,' Marcus said gazing into space. 'When my father came in to see what was going on, Hettie stabbed him in the stomach and then in the neck as he lay on the floor. She must have hit his jugular vein, because we were sprayed with his blood. A neighbour found us a few hours later just sitting there.'

'Why didn't you tell me any of this?' Lucy whispered. She thought she saw the first sign of a tear in the corner of his eye.

'That is the first time I have ever recounted that story in English. Hettie was too young to go to prison, so we were sent to my Aunt and Uncle who lived in Windsor. They were very rich and they tried their best to look after us but it was too late. The damage was done.'

Even though Lucy now knew that Marcus had murdered Tash, she couldn't help but feel sorry for what he had been through. If it was true.

'So, now I am what I am,' he said. 'If you expose young children to an unbearable amount of pain, fear, neglect and humiliation, the part of their brain that can love, feel and empathise just doesn't develop.'

He shrugged sadly as he reached into his pocket and pulled out a syringe.

Lucy's stomach lurched. 'Whatever you're about to do, don't do it Marcus.'

THE IMITATION OF DARKNESS

'I promised you a lovely day off, Lucy,' Marcus said, 'and I've been planning a little trip for some time now. So, you're coming with me.'

'Please don't do this,' Lucy pleaded, her voice full of fear.

Holding her arm still, he injected Lucy and took two steps back.

'Sweet dreams,' he said. 'I'll see you next lifetime.'

Everything went black.

CHAPTER 34

NOW ARMED WITH THE fact that Hadir Benali might have seen Marcus Jankel enter Tash's flat on the night of her murder, Ruth and Brooks climbed up the back staircase and headed for the CID office.

'If Benali is telling the truth, we need to pull in Marcus Jankel straight away,' Ruth said. She was beginning to panic that Lucy hadn't responded to the phone call and text she had made twenty minutes earlier. If she was with Jankel, and Benali was telling them the truth, then Lucy was in a great deal of danger.

'If Benali is telling us the truth, then we're in an almighty mess,' Brooks said picking up speed as they walked. 'But he's not a reliable witness. And he could have seen Marcus Jankel any other night when he was lurking about outside her home. In fact, if he had a vendetta against Jankel because of his relationship with Tash, telling us that he had seen him there on the night of the murder would make perfect sense.'

Ruth nodded but she still wasn't convinced. She'd had her doubts about Jankel from the very first time she had encountered him.

'Are we saying that Benali isn't guilty of Tash's murder?' Ruth asked.

'I don't know.' Brooks glanced sideways at her. 'If I'm honest, my instinct tells me he's not. I think he stalked her, took photos of her, stole from her bin, and sat outside her flat for hours on end. But I don't think he went in there and killed her, no.'

Jesus! So much for the drinks and celebrating in The Greyhound last night!

Brooks and Ruth went through the door into the CID office.

'Then who did? Marcus Jankel?' Ruth asked.

'Maybe, but he has an alibi for the time of the murder. Even if Polly Baker has a troubled past, it doesn't mean that she didn't see him that night.'

Ruth saw that Gaughran and Hassan were back at their desks.

'How did you two get on?' Brooks asked.

'Barbara York has done a runner to New York, Guv,' Gaughran said.

'I don't think that matters now, guys,' Brooks said. 'Benali has just confirmed that he saw an older woman go into the flat with Tash on the night of her murder, and leave in a mini-cab about twenty minutes later.'

Gaughran nodded. 'Okay, sounds like she's off the hook. Shame, because I had taken a serious dislike to that bitch.'

'What else has Benali had to say for himself, Guv?' Hassan asked.

'He claims he didn't do it.'

Gaughran grunted. 'Well, he would.'

'Yeah, but he also claims to have seen Marcus Jankel arrive at Tash's flat just after Barbara York left. He then said that Jankel left about ninety minutes later.'

'Jesus!' Gaughran said with a puff of his cheeks. 'Do we believe him, Guv?'

'I don't know,' Brooks said. 'He's managed to explain away most of the evidence against him. I've now got to have a very difficult conversation with the CPS and the Super and tell them we might have got the wrong man.'

Hassan frowned. 'Bloody hell. I thought we had this cracked.'

Ruth looked at Brooks. 'We need to get Jankel in right now.'

'Benali could have seen Jankel arriving at Tash's flat on various occasions before the night of the murder,' Brooks said, 'but I'm happy for us to get him in for interview again.'

Hassan stood up from his desk with a piece of paper in his hand. 'In that case Guv, this is relevant. I took a phone call about ten minutes ago from the Witness Protection Unit at Scotland Yard.'

'What did they say?'.

'You made an enquiry about a Polly Baker. That's the neighbour who saw Marcus Jankel the night of Tash's murder, isn't it?'

'Yeah, it is,' Brooks said. 'Anything come up?'

Hassan raised his brow in a show of surprise. 'You're not going to believe - but her real name is Hettie Jankel.'

'She's Marcus Jankel's sister?' Ruth spluttered.

Hassan shrugged. 'They didn't say any more than that.'

'Which is why she gave him the alibi,' Brooks said thinking out loud. 'Come on, we need to go and pick up Jankel.'

Ruth pulled a face as they headed for the door and said under her breath, 'We have a bit of an issue, Guv.'

THE IMITATION OF DARKNESS

As they came out into the corridor, Brooks stopped and looked at her. 'What is it?'

'I think Lucy is with Marcus Jankel today.'

Brooks' eyes widened. 'What the hell are you talking about, Ruth?'

'Lucy has been seeing Jankel.'

Brooks was stunned. 'What? You mean ...?'

Ruth winced. 'Yes. She seemed to think he was no longer a suspect in the case. I think she's with him now.'

'Jesus Christ!' Brooks thundered angrily as he shook his head. 'Have you called her?'

'She's not answering.'

'Fuck!' Brooks growled. 'I can't believe this!'

CHAPTER 35

AS SHE CAME TO, LUCY blinked but all she could see was darkness. Darting her eyes around rapidly, she still couldn't see anything. For a moment, she panicked that she was blind. Her head throbbed – it felt like someone had it in a vice. As she moved her hands, she realised that they were now tied behind her back.

Where the hell am I?

Shifting onto her side, she spotted a chink of light. She seemed to be inside a small enclosed space like a cupboard. It was freezing cold. As she strained to listen, she could hear traffic in the distance. She heard the sound of footsteps on a pavement, but then they faded away.

The wind picked up and she could smell the faint odour of petrol.

I'm in a car boot. I'm in Marcus' car boot.

Pulling at the cord around her wrists, she realised that all she was doing was making it tighter.

'HELP!' she yelled. 'HELP!'

Listening intently to see if anyone had heard her cries, she started to shout at the top of her voice, 'HELP! I'm in the car boot ...'

Suddenly, the boot opened and she was blinded by daylight.

Before she could react, Marcus leant in and shoved some kind of cloth into her mouth.

Jesus Christ! That tastes horrible.

He reached down to the pavement, lifted up two large petrol cans, and plonked them down next to her in the boot. He then turned and appeared with two more petrol cans which he positioned down by her feet.

What the hell is all the petrol for? Lucy thought, panicking. Her mind was slowly starting to clear. *Is he going to murder me and then burn the evidence?* The thought of that made her feel sick with fear. *How the hell am I going to get away?*

'Don't worry,' Marcus said with a smile. 'Slight change of plan. I promised you a trip out to the rural bliss of Royal Berkshire so that's where we're going to go. I want to show you the place that truly inspired me to create my dark scripts.'

No one knew where she was. No one was ever going to find her.

She began to sob as she tried to catch Marcus' eye, but he turned, reached up to the boot lid and slammed it shut.

She was plunged back into darkness.

BROOKS AND RUTH HAD the blues and two on full as they came tearing up St Marks Road, heading north through the backstreets of Notting Hill close to Ruston Mews. Ruth was waiting for a vehicle check for Marcus Jankel. If he decided to do a runner, with or without Lucy, they needed to know what car he would be driving.

'Control to Alpha Zero, over,' came the crackly voice of the CAD operator.

Ruth clicked her radio, 'Go ahead Control, over.'

Brooks hit the brakes to avoid a bus coming the other way through a very tight gap.

The CAD operator said, 'We have a cream 1966 Mercedes 190 SL registered to a Marcus Jankel of Ruston Mews, Notting Hill. Plate Mike, Juliet, one zero zero zero, over.'

'Received Control, over and out.' Ruth glanced over at Brooks. 'I don't suppose it's going to be hard to spot a cream 1960s Merc with an MJ 1000 plate.'

'No,' Brooks said as they reached the entrance to Ruston Mews.

Suddenly, Jankel's Mercedes came speeding out of the iron gates and turned right.

'Jesus!' Ruth said, her lips curled in a grimace.

'Right on cue.' Brooks hit the accelerator and began to follow. 'Let's stop this fucker before he does any more damage.'

Ruth peered through the windscreen but it was impossible to tell how many people were inside the Mercedes. She could feel the tension in her stomach. *What if Jankel has done something to Lucy in his house and is now making his escape?*

'Anyone in the passenger seat?' Brooks asked.

Ruth squinted but she couldn't see. Part of her prayed that Lucy was in the car so at least they'd know she was alive. 'I can't tell, Guv.'

She clicked the radio again and said urgently, 'Control from Alpha Zero, we need officers to enter the target property of 8 Ruston Mews, Notting Hill immediately. We are looking for a DC Lucy Henry or any evidence that she has been at the premises, over.'

'Alpha Zero from Control, received. I have a patrol car close to that location. Request clearance for a forced entry, over.'

Ruth looked at Brooks and he nodded anxiously to confirm the request. 'Do it. But if Jankel has done anything to her ...'

Ruth was concerned as she spoke into her radio. 'Control from Alpha Zero, request for forced entry is confirmed. We are currently in pursuit of target vehicle, Mike, Juliet, one zero zero zero, heading north on St Mark's Road towards the Westway. We have visual, over.'

'Received Alpha Zero. Stand by for information from target property, over.'

'Right, let's get this bastard, Guv.'

'It'll be my pleasure.' He put his foot down and they roared away.

They hurtled left onto the Westway, a major elevated dual carriageway that ran west out of London. The traffic was dense, as it always was.

Ruth felt herself pushed back in her seat as Brooks accelerated up to 60mph, weaving in and out of the traffic. Jankel's Mercedes might have been twenty years old, but it could still shift as it sped down the outside lane.

'Out of the way you idiot!' Brooks bellowed as he came screaming up behind a lorry which then indicated and pulled over.

'You would think the blue lights and siren might give him a clue to get out of the bloody way,' Ruth growled sarcastically.

She gripped the door handle as they screamed around a long bend. Jankel's Mercedes seemed to be getting further away as he darted recklessly in and out of the traffic heading west. She could feel the back tyres of their car skidding a little as they cornered another bend at high speed.

Ruth's radio crackled. 'Alpha Zero from Control. We have officers inside the target property, 8 Ruston Mews. There is no sign of DC Henry. Repeat, there is no sign of DC Henry, but officers have found a bag, coat and shoes there that they believe belong to her. There is also evidence that she might have been held there against her will, over.'

Thank God, Ruth thought. Part of her feared that officers were going to find Lucy's body at Jankel's home.

Where the hell is she then?

Ruth and Brooks looked at each other.

'He's got her in that car then, hasn't he?' Brooks said with a dark expression.

'That would be my guess, Guv,' she said as she clicked her radio. 'Alpha Zero to Control, message received. We now believe that DC Henry is on board the vehicle we are in pursuit of, Mike Juliet one zero zero zero, still heading west on the Westway, over.'

'Control to Alpha Zero, received. Will advise, over.'

'Lucy, what the bloody hell have you done?' Brooks said angrily under his breath.

They went thundering down the Westway as it became the A40. Jankel's Mercedes was now only about half a mile ahead, and Brooks was gaining. Ruth had no idea what they would do if they did catch him up.

'We can't hard stop Jankel's car if Lucy might be on board,' Brooks said thinking out loud.

Ruth nodded. 'No. All we can do at the moment is follow him.'

Brooks reached over and turned off the blues and twos. 'If she's in the car with him, we need to take this nice and steady.' He glanced over. 'See if we can get a chopper out.'

Ruth took her radio. 'Alpha Zero to Control, are you receiving, over?'

'Alpha Zero, go ahead, over.'

'Request for Air Support Unit from DCI Brooks. We still have visual on target vehicle heading west on the A40, over.'

'Alpha Zero from Control, received. Will advise, over.'

As they whizzed by the signs to Uxbridge and the M40, Brooks frowned. 'Where the hell is he going?

'No idea, Guv.' Ruth grabbed the map and opened it at a double page showing Greater London.

As she glanced up, she saw Jankel's Mercedes pull left and begin to veer off onto the M25, the major motorway that encircled the whole of London and its outer boroughs.

'Alpha Zero to Control, over.'

'Control to Alpha Zero, go ahead, over.'

'Target vehicle is taking the M25 southbound, over.'

'Control received, over.'

However, it seemed as if they had only just got going on the M25 when the Mercedes zipped across from the middle lane and sped off onto the M4.

'Bloody hell!' Breaking hard, Brooks managed to pull their car across as a lorry swerved to avoid them. 'Shit!' he growled as they tucked in behind the Mercedes. They were only about five hundred yards behind now and although the siren was off, the lights were still flashing across the grill of their navy BMW.

Ruth glanced at the map and then over to Brooks. 'He's going to Eton.'

'What?'

'My instinct is that for some reason he's heading for Eton College. It can't be more than five or six miles from here. Maybe he has some strange reason for taking Lucy there?'

'See if we can get local units alerted.'

'Alpha Zero to Control, target vehicle now on the M4 westbound and we believe heading for Eton College. Advise local units to be on the lookout, over.'

'Control to Alpha Zero, received. Will advise, over.'

As predicted, Jankel exited the M4 at the turning for Windsor and Eton.

'You were right,' Brooks said.

They screamed along the rural London road at 70mph, screeching around a corner through Datchet and past the railway station. They were going so fast, Ruth could hardly see the houses as the BMW flew past.

Up ahead, a small car pulled out of a side road in front of them. Brooks swung the BMW onto the opposite side of the road, missing it by a matter of inches.

'Jesus Christ!' he yelled.

Ruth held on for dear life as they careered around another bend.

The imposing sight of Eton College was in the distance. The turrets and towers, some of which dated back to the 13th century, were visible over the houses and shops of Eton High Street.

'This is it,' Ruth said, gesturing to a sign with an arrow that read *Eton College*.

She could see the 16th century gatehouse was closed off with dark, iron gates.

Jankel's Mercedes swerved right, smashing through the gates and disappearing out of sight.

Braking hard and skidding, Brooks veered right and followed.

Ahead of them was a large quadrant surrounded by cloisters.

The Mercedes was throwing up dirt as its tyres churned up the ground. It was making visibility for Ruth and Brooks difficult as they tried to follow.

Several students and staff appeared, looking to see what all the commotion was about.

In the far corner, Jankel's Mercedes sped through a very narrow stone archway as people scattered to get out of the way.

As Brooks followed, Ruth's eyes widened in alarm. There just didn't seem to be enough room to get through, but Brooks wasn't about to slow down. Ruth closed her eyes for a second as they roared through the arch, smashing off both wing mirrors in the process.

They thundered down what seemed to be an access road to the playing fields stretching out to their left.

The Mercedes was nowhere to be seen.

Shit!

'Where the hell are they?' Brooks said anxiously, slowing down and scanning the area for signs of the car.

Ruth saw a cloud of smoke lift into the sky from behind a row of storage units.

What the hell is that?

'Behind there!' she shouted, pointing to where the road split.

With the engine roaring, Brooks stamped on the accelerator.

As they skidded around the corner, they saw to their horror that Jankel's Mercedes had smashed into a tree close to a river bank. Black smoke was swirling into the air from the under the bonnet.

Oh my God! What if Lucy is in there?

'Bloody hell!' Brooks said as they drove closer and then stopped.

They jumped out and raced to the car.

Jankel had wound down the window of the driver's door which had been buckled by the impact of the crash. His face was covered in blood and he was grimacing. 'I appear to be stuck in here,' he said with a strange grin as he tried to free himself. 'Any chance you could give me a hand to get out?'

Ruth dashed around the car but there was no sign of Lucy inside. 'I can't see her, Guv.'

'Where is she, Jankel?' Brooks thundered.

'I think you should get me out first,' he replied.

Brooks reached in and grabbed him by the throat. 'Where's Lucy? And don't think I won't kill you right here.'

THE IMITATION OF DARKNESS

Jankel gasped for air. 'Yeah, you seem very angry.' He gestured to the boot. 'In there, if you want her. But I'd be careful, I think the car's about to blow.'

As Jankel continued to struggle and try to free himself, Brooks and Ruth raced to the boot and opened it.

Inside was a black body bag.

Jesus. What's he done to her?

Unzipping it, Ruth saw Lucy inside. Her eyes were closed.

Please God, let her be alive.

Ruth felt for a pulse on her neck.

Nothing.

She looked at Brooks and shook her head.

Come on, come on, you can't die on me!

Tilting Lucy's head to the side a little, Ruth pressed her fingers hard against her neck again, just below her ear.

She felt a faint rhythm.

'I've got a pulse,' Ruth gasped, but the air was thick with petrol fumes. There seemed to be a lake of petrol in the boot.

'Jesus! There's petrol everywhere!' Brooks yelled as they tried to lift Lucy from the boot.

Suddenly, the bonnet of the car burst into flames with a loud *WHOOSH!*

Ruth scooped her arms around Lucy's legs as Brooks took her top half. They lifted her out.

They were running out of time.

Ruth's heart was hammering. They were about to be engulfed in a ball of flames.

I don't want to die like this!

Staggering back with Lucy in their arms, Ruth and Brooks moved as quickly as they could.

They were still too close to the car.

Suddenly, they were thrown backwards as the fuel ignited and exploded.

VUMP!

A ball of orange and yellow flames mushroomed up into the sky, followed by thick black smoke as the car crackled.

Ruth felt herself lifted from the ground, then she landed hard on her back.

Jesus!

She tried to get her breath but realised that she was winded.

Sitting up on the grass, she sucked in air as best she could and saw that Brooks was checking on Lucy.

'Is she okay?' she gasped.

Brooks nodded. 'I think he's drugged her, but yes.'

Then Ruth had a thought. 'Jankel?'

Brooks looked at her as his face fell.

Getting up from where they had been thrown, Ruth gazed at the burning black shell of the car.

Marcus Jankel was dead.

CHAPTER 36
18 hours later
Monday 2nd February

RUTH WAS STANDING WITH her coffee in Peckham nick canteen when she became aware of a voice.

'That's fifty pence, dear.' It was the woman behind the till.

'Oh God, sorry,' Ruth said, handing over the fifty pence piece that was in her hand. 'Miles away.'

As she wandered off towards the doors, she focussed on the text she had received from Lucy an hour ago to say that she would be in hospital for a few more days – but she was going to be okay.

The events of yesterday were still playing in Ruth's head as she climbed the back stairs and then headed down the corridor towards the CID office. The atmosphere inside was palpably tense.

As she sat down at her desk, Brooks went to the centre of the room, rubbed his tired-looking face and said, 'Okay guys. I've spoken to Lucy and her doctors this morning, and the main thing is that she is safe and she's going to make a full recovery.'

There were relieved murmurs from around the room.

'She's still suffering the side effects of the Flunitrazepam, but I'm assured that there will be no lasting damage. As those of you who have managed to talk to me or Ruth this morning will know, we came very close to losing her.' Brooks took his coffee from the table and walked over to the scene boards. 'Although we've made many mistakes along the way, we do know now that Marcus Jankel murdered Tash. That means there is some justice for her and her family. I know most of you would have preferred to have seen Marcus Jankel stand trial for what he did, and so would I.'

Gaughran raised his chin defiantly. 'Off the record, Guv, I'm not going to lose any sleep at the thought of Marcus Jankel dying a horrible death in a burning car.'

There were mutterings around the room. His opinion seemed to be shared by other detectives.

Hassan nodded in agreement. 'I've just spoken to Forensics. They're struggling to find enough remains of him to do any kind of PM.'

'I understand it's been an emotive case,' Brooks continued, 'and you should all be proud of the work you've done. You've gone above and beyond what was asked of you.'

Ruth could see that Brooks seemed a little choked.

What's that about?

Brooks paused for a moment and then perched on the edge of a table. 'There's no easy way of saying this, but it's very likely that the investigation into Tash Weston's murder will be my last at this nick.'

What's he talking about? Ruth wondered.

There were some concerned whispering among the CID team.

'I have put in a transfer request to work as a DCI over at Guildford in Surrey ... and that request has been accepted,' he announced.

There was an air of disappointment in the room.

'Guildford, Guv? Are you sure?' Gaughran asked.

'It's a purely selfish decision Tim. If I want to progress up the career ladder, then I'll need experience of policing in all areas, not just the challenges of somewhere like Peckham.'

'I'm pretty sure that I speak for everyone here, Guv, when I say you've been a top gaffer and you're going to be sadly missed.'

There were nods of approval from around the room.

Brooks grinned. 'I can see how it's going to particularly affect you, Tim.'

'How's that?'

'Well, once the new DCI gets to know you, they'd have to be mental to recommend you for a promotion to DI.'

Ruth laughed along with the others.

'Thanks for the support, Guv,' Gaughran said with a wry smile.

ROLLING OVER IN HER hospital bed, Lucy was still feeling totally exhausted. She reached over slowly to get some lemon barley water from a plastic jug. She wondered why people in hospital seemed to live on lemon barley water and grapes.

As she gripped the cup, she felt a sharp pain in the tendons of her right forearm. It was where Marcus had injected her. For a second, her mind flashed back to the look on his face as he'd stood over her the day before. Laying back on a pile of pillows, she closed her eyes and wondered how on earth she was going to get her head around what had happened to her.

'Thought I'd check to see how you were,' a voice said.

She opened her eyes and saw Brooks standing in front of her holding a huge bunch of flowers.

'Hi Harry,' she said with a smile.

'How are you feeling?'

'Like I've been run over by a train,' she said as she tried to sit up. 'Sit down.'

He pulled an orange plastic chair to the side of the bed. 'I brought you these.'

'They're lovely,' she said. 'I'll get a nurse to pop them in some water.'

There were a few awkward seconds of silence.

They looked at each other uncertainly. 'I'm not going to ask what you were doing at Marcus Jankel's house,' he said. 'I don't want to know.'

'No,' Lucy said, feeling choked. 'I don't understand what I was thinking, Harry. I'm so sorry.'

'You were working an upsetting case while going through a difficult time with me. I'm guessing Marcus Jankel was as far removed from life in Peckham CID as you could get.' Brooks looked wounded. 'I suppose I understand that,' he added unconvincingly.

'Yeah, you forgot the bit where I missed any sign that he was a cold-blooded killer.'

Brooks gave her a wry smile. 'Yes, that bit wasn't so good.'

'Will I keep my job?' she asked. There was part of her that questioned whether she could ever go back into Peckham CID, or any CID office.

'I don't know,' he answered quietly. 'It's out of my hands, but I'll do what I can to smooth things out.'

'I don't want you to lie for me, Harry.'

'No,' Brooks said and gave her a meaningful look. 'By the time you come out of here, convalesce and sort all that out, I might not even be in Peckham.'

Lucy gazed at him with sadness in her eyes. 'They accepted the transfer to Surrey?'

He nodded.

'Congratulations, Harry. That's brilliant.'

'Is it?' he asked, raising an eyebrow.

'Of course it is!' Lucy said, but she just couldn't imagine going back to Peckham nick if Brooks wasn't going to be there.

'I've just been thinking about us,' he confessed. 'I came so close to losing you, Luce.'

She reached out and took his hand. 'I've been thinking about you too, Harry. But none of this changes anything does it?'

'I suppose not.'

She smiled at him for a few seconds. There was a lump in her throat. 'Right, so go and find a nurse and get some water for my flowers. And then you can go and get me a coffee and a Kit Kat.'

Brooks laughed as he got up. 'Yes, Ma'am.'

CHAPTER 37

DOWNING A BEER, GAUGHRAN walked out of the kitchen and into the lounge. The house was so familiar to him. He spotted his dad, Uncle Les and a few other retired coppers laughing on the other side of the room.

He glanced at the sideboard, and noticed that the photographs of him that had always been there were still in place. The day he graduated from Nottingham Polytechnic with a 2.2 in Economics and Sociology in 1990. He hated the photo if he was honest. He'd been on an all-night bender around Nottingham the night before, and had only had about three hours' sleep. His face was pasty, and his Rick Astley-style quiff had been greasy. The black mortarboard that his dad had insisted he hire for the photos didn't fit properly. However, Gaughran was secretly pleased to see it still sitting there.

'You know your dad told me that was the proudest day of his life,' said a voice.

Gaughran turned to see his Uncle Les, who was swigging from a can of Fosters.

'Really?' Gaughran said raising an eyebrow. 'He never told me that.'

'Well, he wouldn't, would he? Men of our generation don't say stuff like that directly to the people we're close to.'

Gaughran laughed. 'You just say it about them when they're not there?'

'Exactly,' Les said with an ironic grin. 'That's just how it works, sunshine.'

Out of the corner of his eye, Gaughran saw a figure loom into view – it was his dad.

'You gracing us with your presence tonight then, Tim?' Arthur said.

Gaughran couldn't work out if his dad was having a dig, but this wasn't the place to have a row.

'Happy birthday, Dad,' Gaughran said and looked directly at him.

'You two want another beer?' Les asked, clearly keen to leave the two of them alone for a moment.

'Yeah, ta, Les,' Arthur said handing him an empty bottle.

'Not Fosters though,' Gaughran said with a grin.

'What's wrong with Fosters?' Les asked, waving his can.

'It's Australian piss. I'll have a can of Stella if there's one going?'

As Les disappeared, Arthur nodded awkwardly. 'Good to see you, Tim.'

'It's been a while, hasn't it?' Gaughran said. He was going to let him know that he knew about his affair. 'I came up to the golf club the other night.'

'Did you? Les says you've been playing at GT over in Camberwell?'

'Yeah. I had a couple of lessons with the pro there,' Gaughran said, but he was being distracted from what he wanted to confront his dad with. 'So, I drove up and parked in the car park. Funny what you see when you're not expecting it, isn't it?'

Arthur frowned. 'Sorry, you've lost me.'

Gaughran glanced over at his mum who was surrounded by female relatives. They were all howling with laughter.

'Here you go, big boy,' Les said, shoving a can of Stella into his hand. 'You two alright then?'

'I dunno. Tim's being cryptic about something,' Arthur said. 'More importantly, isn't it time the three of us played a round of golf at the club?'

Les smiled. 'Yeah, I'd like that. I'm always happy taking money off Tim.'

'He's been having bloody lessons.'

'Lessons? In that case, we'll have to see if they've paid off. What d'you think, Tim, you up for that?'

Gaughran took a sip of his drink. 'Why not? It's about time I started taking my money back off you two wankers.'

They all laughed.

LUCY BLINKED AS SHE stirred in her bed. Someone was sitting by her – it was Ruth.

'Hey, why didn't you wake me up?' she croaked.

'I was letting you get some rest before I give you a right bollocking,' Ruth said with a grin.

'Yeah, not my finest hour,' she said pulling a face. 'You saved my life.'

'How are you feeling?'

'Like I went on a three-day bender in Magaluf,' Lucy joked.

'You'll be back in no time,' Ruth said with a smile.

'I don't know if I've even got a job to come back to,' Lucy said with a sigh.

'Don't be daft. It's only me and Brooks who know the whole story and neither of us are going to be throwing you under the bus.'

Lucy shifted her pillows and tried to sit up. She still had no strength.

'Do you want a hand?' Ruth asked getting up.

'No, no, it's fine,' Lucy said. 'I don't even know if I want to come back.'

'What?' Ruth snorted. 'Don't be daft. You can't leave me in Peckham CID on my own.'

Lucy reached over and took a sip of water. Her throat was dry and sore. 'You know that Brooks is leaving?'

'Yeah, he broke the news to the team this morning. I can't believe it, but I guess you two can't be working in the same place long term.'

A young nurse came in holding a vase in which there was a huge bunch of flowers. 'These are for you, Lucy. They've just arrived.'

'They're lovely.'

'I put them in water for you,' the nurse said as she left.

'Thanks,' Lucy said with a smile.

'They from Brooks?' Ruth asked.

'No, he brought flowers with him. Probably from Mum.'

'How long are you in here for?'

'Could be forty-eight hours, could be longer. Depends how long it takes to get all that Flunitrazepam out of my system.'

Ruth smiled. 'You're not going to be forgetting that word again in a hurry?'

'Definitely not.' Lucy laughed. 'You know that Polly Baker was Marcus' sister?'

'Yeah. Uniform went to pick her up a couple of hours ago and she's gone. Flatmate says she's taken everything with her and left without a word.'

'That's no surprise,' Lucy said. 'She must have seen the police swarming around Marcus' flat and got spooked.'

'Do you need me to bring you anything?' Ruth asked.

Lucy shook her head. 'Tell you what you could do. Pass me that copy of today's *Mirror* that's on that chair over there. I want to read the latest on the Clinton/Lewinsky affair when you've gone.'

Ruth got up, went over to the chair and brought the newspaper over to her. 'There you go.' She pointed to the flowers. 'There's a card in there. Do you want it?'

Lucy nodded and took the note from her. She opened it and read:

Hi Lucy
Hope you're making a speedy recovery.
By the way, it's half a sliced-up watermelon, toasted
pine nuts, crumbled goats' cheese, watercress and
rocket leaves, baby tomatoes and a mint dressing.
I'll be in touch.
Love MJ xx

The colour drained from Lucy's face. She looked up at Ruth.

'Are you okay?' Ruth asked. 'Who's it from?'

ENJOY THIS BOOK?
Why not pre-order the next in
the series?

'London, SE15' Book #4 in the
DC Ruth Hunter Murder Case series
https://www.amazon.co.uk/dp/B09B7Q4CWS
https://www.amazon.com/dp/B09B7Q4CWS

Your FREE book is waiting for you now

Get your FREE copy of the prequel to
the DI Ruth Hunter Series NOW
http://www.simonmccleave.com/vip-email-club
and join my VIP Email Club

Acknowledgements

I WILL ALWAYS BE INDEBTED to the people who have made this novel possible.

My mum, Pam, and my stronger half, Nicola, whose initial reaction, ideas and notes on my work I trust implicitly. And Dad, for his overwhelming enthusiasm.

Thanks also to Barry Asmus, former South London CID detective, for checking my work and explaining the complicated world of police procedure and investigation. Carole Kendal for her acerbic humour, copy editing and meticulous proofreading. My designer Stuart Bache for yet another incredible cover design. My superb agent, Millie Hoskins at United Agents, and Dave Gaughran and Nick Erick for invaluable support and advice.

Printed in Great Britain
by Amazon